SECOND SPRING

Max Egremont

SECOND SPRING

HAMISH HAMILTON · LONDON

HAMISH HAMILTON LTD
Published by the Penguin Group
Penguin Books Ltd, 27 Wrights Lane, London w8 5TZ, England
Penguin Books USA Inc., 375 Hudson Street, New York, New York 10014, USA
Penguin Books Australia Ltd, Ringwood, Victoria, Australia
Penguin Books Canada Ltd, 10 Alcorn Avenue, Toronto, Ontario, Canada M4V 3B2
Penguin Books (NZ) Ltd, 182–190 Wairau Road, Auckland 10, New Zealand

Penguin Books Ltd, Registered Offices: Harmondsworth, Middlesex, England

First published 1993
1 3 5 7 9 10 8 6 4 2

Typeset by Datix International Limited, Bungay, Suffolk
Filmset in 11/13½ Monophoto Sabon
Printed in England by Clays Ltd, St Ives plc

A CIP catalogue record for this book is available from the British Library

ISBN 0-241-13389-0

£36.815\ £14.99

For Hugh and Mirabel Cecil

Chapter One

Alex von Kierich is saying his piece.

'The Kloster is the most notable group of buildings in this small northern German town. They were founded in the thirteenth century by the daughter-in-law of the ruling prince, destroyed by fire a century later and then built again in their present form in various stages over the next two hundred years. In the sixteenth century a new foundation was created, for Protestant daughters of the nobility to live together as if in a convent, to pray and do works of charity. Today the tradition continues. Twelve widows and spinsters live in the Kloster although they are no longer daughters of the nobility. So the convent has become an almshouse for the elderly who can still look after themselves.'

Von Kierich, the guide who speaks these words to a group of English schoolchildren, is a tall, thin old man with a slight stoop and smooth grey hair. The children, who are visiting this place in Germany because it is twinned with their home town in Suffolk, seem quite interested because every now and then the old man makes a joke, perhaps about the smell from the nearby sugar beet factory or the behaviour of one of the early princes ('a naughty fellow') towards the women in the Kloster. Then his severe, taut face softens into a smile, the movement causing the wrinkled skin to hide his tight-slitted eyes almost entirely, raising the scars on his left cheek. He talks English carefully and well, and is courteous towards their escort, a teacher of languages called Sheila Bunkle.

I

The tour lasts an hour, part of it inside the dark buildings, the rest among the neat gardens, where late flowers sway in the slight wind and September sunlight. In the chapel, a boy plays the organ softly while the man talks about the great fifteenth-century altarpiece that depicts 'the sufferings of Christ'. When the tour is over and the children leave, Sheila Bunkle wonders if she should offer their guide a tip, then decides that he looks too grand in his green loden coat and polished dark brown shoes. She notices also, however, the crushed useless fourth and fifth fingers of his right hand, the deformed thumb with a nail sprouting strangely from scarred skin.

The old man waits at the great wooden doors while the coach turns to take the party off for an afternoon's scenic tour. He waves to the children, who smile and wave also from their seats behind tinted glass. Then he goes back into the Kloster and walks in long, quite rapid steps to the rooms at the end of the stone passage which are occupied by Frau Marietta Schneider who is a member of the community here. He knocks at the heavy front door, hears her voice and enters.

A small round woman of a similar age with cropped grey hair gets up from her chair. She points to the other end of the room where a door leads out into a garden with a fountain on its neat lawn from which water gushes gently into a pond half covered with the dark green leaves of water lilies. To one side of the door, on the grass, is a white-painted iron table. On the table rests a tray, two tall glasses and a jug of Frau Schneider's homemade fruit juice.

'Marietta,' he says.

'Alex,' she answers.

Only this summer, after several years of acquaintanceship, have they ceased to call each other Herr von Kierich and Frau Schneider. Previously he had shown no sign of wanting to change, and she, the widow of a Lutheran pastor, had been in awe of his name and reputation. Now they are friends. She likes to hear him talk about the past when he wishes and is pleased to store some of his things here in her apartment which is too big for a single old woman, much larger than the two small rooms where he lives in Herr Friesen's hotel on the Goethe Strasse at the centre of the town.

Today, after commenting briefly on the heat and the bad manners of the English group, he goes over to the lower shelf of Frau Schneider's bookcase where some thick photograph albums have been stacked flat. There are about ten of them, expensively bound in red, blue, or dark green leather with gold bands. The albums are his; quickly he pulls out a red one, the year stamped on its spine in gold, and carries it into the garden where Frau Schneider joins him at the white metal table.

She pours out the juice while he turns over the thick white pages of the album, showing her certain photographs and talking about them in his precise but vivid German. She sees that this is one of the books from Alex's days in Washington when he was director of the Survey, an international agency that exists to try to help the poorer countries or 'The Third World'. Even she remembers – and this was long before they had met – her slight feeling of pride at the appointment of a German to this international post. She had read the newspaper accounts of how he came from a landowning family in the east and of his involvement in the Stauffenberg plot to kill Hitler in July 1944 while serving in the foreign ministry under the Nazis; then of his quick rise in the new administration set up by the victorious allies and the diplomatic service of the Federal Republic.

Alex is lonely; she senses this. His career had had an unfortunate end. She knows the facts because he has told her. She is sure he is blameless. Now he refers to the business only occasionally and quickly becomes stern so she

3

dares not press him. Then they return to other subjects, perhaps her children or the weather or what he has been reading lately in English, French or German.

Frau Schneider is a simple woman at heart, or so she thinks, in spite of those years spent with her rather austere husband, Klaus. In the Kloster she has made great friends with another resident, Frau Hartmann, who is also about her age, the widow of one of the managers of the local brewery, a woman who loves gossip, tittle-tattle, the silly things of life. Frau Hartmann gets a women's magazine full of information about the European royal families, and together she and Frau Schneider drool over this, particularly enjoying the articles on the Queen of Sweden in whom they have a special interest because she was once a German working girl.

Frau Hartmann wants no more from life. She is frightened of Alex von Kierich and does not know how to deal with him. This makes Frau Schneider despise her, because he is a most distinguished man for whom Frau Hartmann should have enough sympathy to overcome her fear. She should support Alex against this new generation. Young people have no idea what it was like during the war, Frau Schneider thinks. They should not be so quick to judge or to condemn.

To Frau Schneider Alex is a little like Klaus, her dead husband, or at any rate a reminder of Klaus's absolute moral seriousness. Also like Klaus he frightens her at times, and with a shock she can find herself agreeing silently then with Frau Hartmann. Occasionally Alex will talk of the horror of those African trips he used to make, of the starvation and chaos, of the time he and his English assistant Edward West were captured by guerrillas and held under sentence of death. Alex had tried to help the millions of pathetic people and in the end almost no one had listened. He speaks angrily about this, as if resentful, and Frau

4

Schneider finds herself wondering which memory he hates most: the suffering or the disorder. He is so neat and sure of what is right. How chaos must displease him!

Then there is his occasionally disdainful manner. Alex von Kierich is an aristocrat, which does not show often but it is there when he speaks – as if to himself – perhaps about the ugliness, vulgar talk and coarseness of some German middle-class businessmen he had observed on a train or the horrible, common manners of the Nazis. Klaus Schneider could make his wife feel intellectually small; this man can diminish her in almost every way possible if he wishes, or so she thinks.

Yet he can laugh as well and likes to joke with her. He has never married: was this wise? She is a woman, so she must give him an opinion of marriage from her point of view, not of her own years with Klaus Schneider, which were happy of course, but in the abstract. The weather interests him, too. Will they have a Russian or an English summer: months of warm sun or a season of rain and cloud? In this part of Germany the two climates jostle for superiority, whereas in his old home in East Prussia the sun came always each year across the wide lakes and forest trees. He is like this, Frau Schneider thinks: a divided person, sometimes so bright, other times silent and formidable.

The albums seem so important to him now, although he has at last given up taking photographs with that old Agfa camera. How obsessed he must have been with photography! It was his way of defeating time, Frau Schneider has decided, yet this is something not even Alex can do. She has some of the albums here on that lower shelf in a bookcase full mostly of the devotional and theological works that had belonged to her late husband. Alex retains two or three in his room in the hotel, changing the volumes quite often for others from the set that she keeps for him. They are a record of his life, from the huge family home of his childhood and the flat country of fields, lakes and forests, to the student days in Germany and England, the Foreign Office in Berlin and the years of the war; then the period in Africa and Washington, his tours through the underdeveloped world as director of the Survey, the short time as a business consultant in Munich and retirement here alone in this small town, where it amuses him to act as one of the guides in the Kloster, which is open to tours all the year round.

Some of the photographs fascinate Frau Schneider. There is one of Hindenburg taken by Alex's mother on the steps of the great house where the Field Marshal had once been a guest; another of a student group at Göttingen, one of those duelling clubs, the origin of his still visible scars inflicted by a colleague's sword so dangerously near to his poor left eye. Frau Schneider's husband would have hated this: the frivolous student corps, so much drinking, the 'Landwehr' which Alex had described when the blood had flowed in 'great rivers' as the young men had tested each other's courage in those mad fencing matches. A strange start to a serious life!

Then come the Backs at Cambridge with punts in the foreground, old Berlin, pictures of the fires at night during an air raid, the ruins of Nuremberg after the war, the vast landscapes of Africa, floods and famine in Asia. Each one has a story which Alex will tell, content to repeat it for her again and again, probably adding one or two details that he had previously forgotten, until she feels that she knows much of his extraordinary life.

Sometimes he speaks of the tragedy of 1944, the failure of the plot to kill Hitler, his arrest and incredible good fortune in not being strung up like so many of the others on meat hooks in the Plötzensee Prison. That crushed part of his right hand shows the torture he had to endure during interrogation. Frau Schneider thinks that Alex may feel guilty that he survived. In death, he has told her, the conspirators became more glorious than they ever were in life.

Today in the garden, at the white table where they are both sitting, he opens the album without touching his glass. The English school group has reminded him of something: yes, here they are, look, taken during his time in Washington when he went to Charlottesville in Virginia one weekend with those English people and their children. Frau Schneider knows their names before he says them: Colonel Martin Riley (now a retired general) and his wife, and Mr and Mrs Edward West. The Colonel had been working in the British embassy and Edward West was one of Alex's assistants, perhaps rather like a private secretary or close confidential aide.

She has learnt about these people from Alex: the funny, rather eccentric English Colonel Riley and his sensible wife, Nancy, then Edward West with whom Alex had been captured that time in Africa, dear Edward, clever and faithful to the ideals of the Survey but a bit of a ladies' man who had made life difficult for his wife, Jane.

Alex von Kierich talks and laughs, one finger jabbing at the photographs. Here are the English children together in a group in front of Thomas Jefferson's house at Monticello, on a hill above Charlottesville: the little West boys, Nick and Charles, and the young Rileys, whose names he cannot now remember although he thinks the girl was called Mary. Were they nice children? Frau Schneider asks, sipping her drink in the sunlight. Oh yes, he answers, and with good manners, too: not so noisy as the group today. The Wests and the Rileys had been kind to him, a bachelor in Washington: the Wests in particular, and here is Jane, Edward's brown-haired wife, smiling at the camera, quite frail, caught by him alone on that same trip.

Frau Schneider smiles and says what she knows is expected of her: how pretty the young English woman was.

Alex inclines his head, seems remote for a moment, then agrees. Edward West had been most helpful at the Survey. Jane is dead now but he has Edward's address and he has written to the Englishman and to General Riley as well, to try to make contact again, at a time when so much is happening here. Frau Schneider brings her hands together and sits back in her chair. Oh yes, she says, that would be nice. What is there to worry about now? Alex, I am so glad. Alex looks across at the fountain and murmurs their names in English: 'Edward and Jane.'

September in the west of England is also calm, lusher than in northern Germany and with the light soft, as if more reluctant. Here there is a village, smaller than the German town, home now to several retired people: businessmen, bureaucrats or officers of the armed forces. On the edge of the village, screened by some fine trees, stands a late-sixteenth-century manor house, and it is on the terrace of this that a small group sits one warm Sunday evening.

'Alex von Kierich? Oh yes.'

Edward West says the words loudly to defeat any possible interruption. With Edward are Sir James Finch, the manor's owner, and his wife, Isabel; Martin Riley, a retired major-general, and his wife, Nancy, about the same age as Edward, sixty-two or -three: all neighbours in this village. Then the one outsider, Ben Talbot, an artist in his late forties, a guest of the Finches. Only one young person is there: Rose Finch, James's and Isabel's daughter, a serious dark-haired girl who watches for each nuance or sign of life.

Ben Talbot has asked about the Survey: Ben with his tangled hair, charm and simplicity, the perfect listener, so friendly. It is terrible now that Africa seems to go from bad to worse, from disaster to disaster, Ben says. Who was in charge of the Survey when Edward worked there? Had he or she been hopeful once?

8

Martin Riley tries to answer, talkative as usual, but Edward speaks loudly enough to stop his old friend. 'Alex von Kierich? Oh yes.'

'Von Kierich,' Ben says, repeating the name. 'I think I can remember. Wasn't there some kind of trouble?'

'He left the Survey,' Edward says.

'To return to Germany,' says Martin who is short and quite fat, eyes sharp behind tortoiseshell-rimmed spectacles, almost completely bald, not in the least military in appearance, more like a retired schoolmaster or old-fashioned grocer. Martin tries to change the subject. 'James, I hope you don't think there's anything personal in our opposition to this saw mill plan of yours.'

James Finch does not seem to have heard, but Rose, a girl of twenty-one, still at university, says, 'What sort of man was von Kierich?' and Edward, partly because of the wine and this beautiful place, talks suddenly about courage, torture, sacrifice, pain, solitary strength and a resurrection of the spirit: of the need some people have to suffer, as if to purge some great, abstract guilt. This seems odd to the others because he is usually rather a silent man.

Then no one speaks for a time until Martin says, 'Oh Edward,' and talks again about the saw mill, Isabel Finch answering him now with some asperity.

Rose looks down at the stones of the terrace, the moss black at their edges like broken bands of mourning. She remembers how Ben had kissed her that afternoon in the orchard and Edward had tried to kiss her once in his car after an evening at the theatre in Bath: Edward the old widower who worked for this German hero and is said to be a bit of a ladies' man. But the rest of the evening's talk is about local matters, which is what she expects in her parents' house.

The next day, Edward West sits in the garden of his house

in the village. On the whole he is glad that he spoke out last night.

On his knee lies a book about roses. He has not read much this afternoon, which is still warm for September. Since his retirement two years ago he has lived here, next to the church, the fifteenth-century tower of which looms in the distance.

It is twenty years since he bought the house. His wife Jane and he had felt they should have somewhere in England, and this village in the south-west, just under two hours from London by car, had seemed as good a place as any: quiet, out of the way. Beside the church are these two detached houses, the one nearest the graveyard his, the next owned by his friends the Rileys.

Edward wonders sometimes why he has stayed on alone. Occasionally he thinks he must leave, get away from these people. Then he finds the obstacles too great: the thought of packing up, the search for a new home, the question of where he will live. Washington, where he spent most of his working life with the Survey (when he was not travelling in Africa, India or the Far East) has too many reminders of the past. Also he likes this place, the countryside, the calm life. But the world still fascinates him even if he knows now that he will never solve most of its mysteries. He thinks and reads about them still, with the help of a pair of quite weak spectacles.

His house was once the village morgue, conveniently placed next to the graveyard of the church, and some of the older inhabitants remember when it was called the Old Morgue. In Edward's time the name has always been Church House. It is a mixture of dates, mostly nineteenth century, but amongst the dark low-ceilinged rooms and lattice windows are beams dating from 1400 or even earlier. The point of the place, however, is the garden at the back of about a quarter of an acre with two walls, one facing east, the other west, and a view of open fields stretching towards a small wood. At the front of the house is the quiet village street.

He has two apple trees, both Bramleys, in full fruit now in September with cookers which he gives away to his cleaning lady, Mrs Gifford, who comes to the house twice a week. Then there are the borders under the west- and east-facing walls. On the west, between him and the church, Edward has shrub roses: hybrid musks, the creamy white 'Penelope', 'Buff Beauty', the climber 'Mermaid' to remind him of the Mediterranean, then buddleia for the butterflies. Under the east wall are clumps of philadelphus, potentilla and viburnum. Mixed wisteria and jasmine, no longer in flower, grow up the red brick of the house. Edward pays Mrs Gifford's husband, recently retired from working for Sir James Finch at the manor, to help him occasionally with the garden. Perhaps this is really the reason that he has stayed on. He loves his roses.

Mrs Gifford keeps him in touch. She mentions often the 'hooligans' from the council estate who vandalize the telephone box by the village pub called the Bell and let Isabel Finch's horses out on to the road. She talks about the lack of jobs in the area, the boredom of the young, the sad loss when the beloved old clergyman the Reverend Robert Padstow (known in the village as 'Father Bobs') died, the inadequacies of the new vicar, the failings of the various local doctors, the plans for the new saw mill, of which she approves. She likes chatting but will not listen for long and never seems very interested in what Edward has to say.

Then there is Charles, one of his sons, who has a job in the City. The boy had been advised by Edward's elder son, Nick, who works in the United States in a bank in Boston, where he lives with his American wife and infant daughter. Charles telephones his father and comes sometimes to stay. Nick telephones occasionally.

Jane had been wonderful with the boys. Edward had been

an old father, more like a grandfather perhaps, and this is what he tells himself whenever he feels guilty about not having done more. He was almost forty when Nick, their first child, was born; Charles had followed two years later. Jane, fifteen years younger than he, had been much closer to them. Sometimes he finds it almost unbearably moving to remember the children and her together.

Edward looks over the low hedge at the open end of his garden and sees two people in the field, a large dog bounding ahead of them. For a moment he wonders if it may be yet another pair of newcomers; houses change hands so fast in this part of the world. Then he recognizes the Rileys, and walks quickly, almost running, to his boundary hedge.

'Martin!' he calls.

The Rileys, about to turn into the gate that leads into their own garden, stop and look round. Nancy shouts at the dog. 'Rick!'

Martin speaks to him. 'We went to the second wood where James Finch is doing some clearing. Have you been there recently? Of course it's sad to see the trees go but he's right to shift them. Their time had come. We met Rose in the top field, with her dog. She was asking about the new vicar.'

Comfortable village talk. 'You said you were happy with the Bishop's choice,' Edward says. Martin Riley is a church warden.

'Oh yes. A decent chap. He was ordained late, after some years working for an insurance company. Nice wife. Just what the village needs.'

'He must be an improvement on the last one,' Nancy says. She is at least a head taller than her husband and has an even louder voice.

Martin laughs. 'The rest of the village adored Robert Padstow.'

'And don't we know it! The blessed Father Bobs. Personally I found him wringing wet,' Nancy says. The dog has walked out into the field again. 'Rick!' she shouts. The creature, a pale golden retriever, returns. 'Of course I was sorry for the man after his wife's death, but he should have picked himself up and got on with it instead of moping about all over the place like a sick cow.' Again there is that lofty look, this time with arched eyebrows. She has a handsome head: narrow, with high cheekbones and a prominent nose. 'Padstow was never out of our house at one stage. I must have poured gallons of tea into that man. Then in the evening it was malt whisky. "My little weakness," he used to say.'

'Poor Robert was lonely.' Martin turns to Edward. 'You know that this question of the saw mill is coming to a head, don't you? They're going to build it. James Finch is renting that field to Dove who has the timber firm in Chilworth. Have you signed the petition of protest?'

'What petition?' He knows this will make the General angry. Martin is a disappointed man: frustrated as well. His career had prospered at first, then ran up against powerlessness, the humiliation of the tedious small tasks heaped upon him.

'The one against the saw mill of course! For God's sake, Edward. I drafted it with various other people in the village who are against the scheme. The Miss Horns who bought the old greengrocer's shop have been particularly helpful.'

The sun has gone behind the trees. Suddenly Edward feels the cold. He is still in his shirt sleeves. Martin wears an old hand-knitted jersey but Nancy stands bare-armed in her light summer dress. 'I want to see the plans first,' he says.

'They've just been published in the local paper. There's a public meeting on Thursday in the village hall to discuss them. James Finch and the man Dove are going to put their case.'

'I must have missed that particular issue.'

Martin's eyes are still keen, like those of a hunting animal. 'But you take it every week, Edward. I know you do. I see it in your house every week.'

'Taking it is not necessarily the same as reading it. What does James Finch say? I suppose he needs the money.'

Martin Riley's eyes are dazzlingly bright. 'James's motives, as always, seem admirable. He says that Dove will create more jobs for the young people of the village in the new saw mill.' Martin comes closer, so close that Edward can see the grey stubble beneath his lower lip where he has not shaved properly. 'But Dove is a hard man. He'll employ only those who are absolutely essential to his operations: no more. What do you think it's like to work for him, anyway?'

Nancy's voice comes between them. 'Martin!'

But Martin is in hot pursuit. 'Did you enjoy last night, Edward? Ben Talbot has charm, doesn't he? No wonder James and Isabel are so fond of him.'

'His work is too sweet.'

'Not enough strength, would you say?' asks Martin. 'You told him about Alex von Kierich. Now that's strong stuff.'

'It's the truth: just the truth.'

'Do you think so?'

Now Nancy comes in again. 'What are you doing tomorrow, Edward? Why not come to supper? We've asked Rose Finch and the two Miss Horns: just a village party.'

For a moment he becomes confused, suddenly a forgetful old man. 'How kind, Nancy, but I've got to go to London and may not be back on time. At least . . .' He pauses.

She butts in. 'Not another conference?' Last week Edward had gone to Toulouse for a gathering of economists to talk about the 'underdeveloped' nations. He does this sort of thing from time to time in retirement.

'No no. A day trip.' He has always told them almost everything, hoping to receive much in return. It has been the same for years, since they met in Washington, two young couples out from England, living in a strange country. 'Wait a minute. What is today? Monday, of course. I'm not going until Thursday. Damn! How idiotic. Yes, I'd love to come to-morrow.'

'Don't forget,' Nancy says. Then she calls to the dog. 'Rick!'

Martin smiles. 'Yes, Edward. Don't forget.'

Edward waves them goodbye. Turning to go back into his house, he thinks of the unspoken secrets of their friendship, the way Martin and he had never been able to talk rationally about Alex. Now there is a new rivalry, as each circles the other in long, slow strides, probing for the first sign of senility.

He is reading the book about roses in bed, the names a reminder of lush summer profusion. 'Madame Isaac Pereire', 'New Dawn', 'Albertine', 'Felicia', 'Moonlight', 'Cornelia'. Edward finds himself saying the words aloud, his deep voice strange against the silence of the house.

He thinks sometimes that he is drawn to the exotic because of the drabness of so much of his early life: the only son of a kind, unlucky man who had rented a few fields on the Kent–Sussex border, an asthmatic youth who had won scholarships to grammar school and the London School of Economics, been excused military service on account of his weak chest, then worked briefly in the Treasury before joining the Survey and leaving for abroad. Then the asthma had gone and Edward came up in the world by marrying an ambassador's daughter.

At first Jane had not wanted to live here. 'I wonder if it's right, Edward,' she had said when he received the contract for the house for which her money would pay. 'I mean if it's right for you. Martin and Nancy like the place and of course they want us to buy the house next door. I know you want a garden and of course that would be lovely.' Then she had become keen, most probably because of some romantic idea of herself in a long, flowing skirt and wide-brimmed straw hat dead-heading the flowers with a pair of trusty secateurs, lending a hand in the village, where she was loved for her culture and beauty. He had teased her about this. He remembers her laugh, a pure cascading sound. 'I love the village, Edward,' she had said.

Those roses. Their beautiful names. The Italian sunlight and that evening in Rome almost thirty years ago: it was a dinner given by one of his colleagues at the United Nations agency where Edward was on a three-year secondment from the Survey. 'I have asked the daughter of the British ambassador,' Vittorio Falconi had said.

Edward had just returned from India and Jane listened to his stories of suffering. That astonished face, tanned under the dark hair, the mouth slightly open as he explained what should be done: how young she was. 'As children we were in Africa for four years,' she said. 'When my father was *en poste* in Cairo.'

He told her that it was his job to try to persuade governments to give more money to these countries. He spoke of other trips to the Sahara and southern Turkey, where a dam was to be built. That evening those parted lips, the earnest interest, led him on. Edward had loved his work in those days – every minute of it, even the office politics. This was before Alex.

'You must meet my father,' Jane said at the end. 'May I ring you?'

Two days later she had telephoned: quite brave, he had thought, for a young girl. 'Please forgive me,' she said, 'but I was so intrigued by our conversation the other evening. I spoke to Vittorio and he said you would not mind. Will you come to dinner?' She mentioned some dates and he accepted the first of them. 'Oh good,' she said. 'I'm afraid we change in the evenings. Diplomatic protocol. I am sorry.'

So he had put on his dinner jacket and taken a taxi to that great, gaunt palace, then been shown up – passed from one white-coated butler to another – to the large room which seemed at first to be empty of people until a voice called from beside the fireplace and he saw a woman wearing a blue and gold dress, perhaps in her fifties, her face bright with a smile. He must be early. Surely there should be more guests. 'Jane will be here in a minute, Mr West,' the woman said. 'How inconsiderate of her to be late. I am her mother. And you work for the United Nations, I understand?'

That smile: a camouflage for feeling, a rich woman's protection. Jane's mother was an heiress, one of the inheritors of a great industrial fortune. Her hair shone grey, thick like her daughter's, cut to the same shoulder length. The butler asked if he would like a drink; then the clear, cold cocktail surprised him with its strength and he spoke to the ambassadress, trying to explain that he did not work for the United Nations but was on loan from the Survey.

'The Survey?' She frowned, as if insulted. 'What is that? I've never heard of it. Roger . . .' She looked towards the door. 'I don't know where Jane has gone. This is my husband, Mr West.' He bowed to the tall, fair-haired, thin ambassador who had just come in. 'Mr West is involved with something called the Survey.' She glanced at their guest. 'What does that mean?'

The huge room with the heavy furniture and cream and gold walls: a room without intimate life, a room for these rituals of courtesy, sycophancy or humiliation. Jane must have spent years in rooms like this, most of her childhood and youth. He remembers the elegance, the smiling woman, the man beside her, tall and benign, with a watchful power. That evening Sir Roger had been kind, slightly feline. 'The Survey?' he had murmured. 'Let me see. Of course, that outfit in Washington run by Alex von Kierich.' He looked straight into his wife's face where a gleam of anxiety showed frailty at last. 'It exists to promote the cause of what one might call the underdeveloped nations of the world. Is that right?' He smiled, aware of his slight provocation. 'To produce papers. Do you work closely with von Kierich?'

'Not yet. He arrived after I had been sent here.'

'I see.' Sir Roger raised his glass and drank most of the cocktail. 'I met Alex in London years ago, before the war, when he was up at Cambridge. We had some friends in common, although he's younger than I am of course. Then I lost touch. He went back to Germany. We've seen each other occasionally since 1945. A brave man, I should think, and an able one. I'm glad he's got this job.' He stared at the interloper. 'Tell me, how is the Survey funded?'

'The richer countries pay for us.' Edward tried a joke. 'From each according to his abilities, to each according to his needs.'

'Is agreement on the financing hard to achieve?' The ambassador lit a cigarette, keeping his eyes on West all the time.

'Sometimes the politicians take against us.'

Then he heard a commotion at the room's entrance and turned to see two young people, a girl and a boy, indistinct for a moment before he recognized Jane who was first, flustered but apparently delighted as if (he remembers thinking) she had won a great victory. 'I'm sorry to be so late.' She looked at him, her mouth open, panting after the rush. 'Did you introduce yourself, Edward? I told Mum and Dad all about you.' She clenched her small brown fists. 'How terrible of me. But it was the Roman traffic, wasn't it, Umberto? Umberto took me to a new gallery in the Via Condotti.' She smiled at her mother, then again full into his face. 'Have you been busy?'

'We were talking about the Survey,' her father said.

'The Survey?'

18

It was extraordinary, he thinks now, the way they had all taken up positions around her. 'Where I work.'

'Yes I know,' she answered. 'And you looked at that dam. Oh Edward. But India must be worse.'

'Than what?'

'Than Turkey.'

'It's hard to compare the two. The problems are very different. For instance in northern and central India the chief concern is the rains . . .'

She interrupted. 'I meant the people.'

'The people?'

'How do you mean, darling?' the ambassadress asked.

'Weren't you horrified?'

He was about to answer when her father spoke. 'Darling, I think Paolo has announced dinner. Shall we go in?' Sir Roger smiled. 'Bring your drink with you. Umberto, you know the way. We're in the small dining-room this evening.'

In the passage he walked behind her friend and ahead of the ambassador, who for reasons of protocol brought up the rear. Umberto must have known her for some time. Edward studied the ease of his walk, those flowing Italian movements where the limbs seem infinitely supple and elastic. She might find the boy wonderful, but Edward felt suddenly a surge of strength and obstinacy so great that he almost leapt with joy at that magic: her softening mouth as she listened or the childlike seriousness in her eyes. As they entered the smaller room and sat down at the round table (he was between Jane and her mother), he looked towards the long window behind Sir Roger and saw the roofs of Rome in the twilight. 'Weren't you horrified?' she asked again.

The others were watching. Her face seemed to shine. He threw the word back, making her wait. 'Horrified?'

'By what you saw.'

19

'Have you been to India?'

'No.' She shook her head. 'But Vittorio has shown me some of his photographs.' In her eyes there were tears, the light reflecting on a bright surface, but her cheeks stayed dry, a slight redness darkening the brown. 'The mothers and children. Last year it was terrible. The rains came late and were much shorter than usual. Such hopelessness.'

Such hopelessness. He had almost turned on her and said, That great horror and misery are terrible, but let me tell you about what I have known, just one story of a morass and how I climbed out of it and the way I found this career that takes me into a new world where suffering comes in thousands or millions of staring eyes. I find I can bear this and I write paper after paper on what ought to be done and sometimes people listen. But this evening we should surely start by looking over your father's shoulder at the view across Rome, then ask ourselves how we might at least make our corner of the world work well.

He had loved her. Those talks they had had, later in Washington and here in the village, particularly in Washington when he was working so hard, travelling the world with Alex von Kierich. 'What do you think of?' she might ask. 'On your own or with Alex, in the evenings and at night?' 'Of you and the children,' he had answered, and she had sometimes seemed near to tears: he hoped for his imagined loneliness, not her own isolation in the midst of a cruel world. Her words had come quickly. 'We must talk, please, darling. I can't bear it when you go away. Look how it leaves us, and you say, "You don't need me for the boys," but I worry that I can't give them enough, Edward. Tell me, do you think I should abandon my translation work? Then I would have more time.'

In Washington they had an Italian maid called Maria.

'Edward,' Jane had said, 'Maria was telling me the other day about her childhood in Naples. They were a family of twelve, living next to a slaughterhouse where the cattle and pigs and sheep were killed so the whole place smelt of offal and decaying flesh and the flies came in their hundreds and thousands to crawl all over the rotting meat. You know what those places are like. One used to see them in Rome sometimes, when one walked through the back streets. I remember once coming back to the embassy on the back of Umberto's bike. We were late and he had to take a short cut, through lanes and passages that are too narrow for cars.' She laughed. 'My darling, it was the second time you and I met, a summer night in Rome and we were on our way to a private view at a gallery off the Via Condotti before the dinner. I told Umberto to hurry. Suddenly we were in a different part of the city and there were these animals tied up and that terrible smell, not so bad I'm sure as it used to be in Naples when Maria was growing up but quite powerful enough. I thought, Behind all this beauty, the wonderful light of the Roman evening, there is still this blood and slaughter. So we rushed past and I was worrying because I thought of you waiting later for this unknown girl. Do you remember that, Edward?

'Tell me what your first impression of us was when we came into the room. I must have seemed such a child, which of course I was then: only just out of my teens, or perhaps a little bit older but not that much. Vittorio Falconi told me that he found you intimidating, with something of the English puritan about you: yes, those were his words. So it was quite brave of me to ring you at your office, wasn't it? What did you think when you heard my voice? Who is this little girl? I bet you did. Who is this girl who sits in the British embassy, bored and protected and spoilt? But you can't have been too shocked because you made it all so easy and said that you could come to see us on the first of the days I gave you.

'Then there was Umberto. I expect you imagined we were

21

lovers, or perhaps not, because things were much more proper then than they are now. He was a nice boy and he did want to go to bed with me, but I said no. You see I was still a bit frightened then, and it didn't seem quite right because I had to finish my course at the university. Umberto was just a student. We were in the same year and one of the younger professors used to ask me back to his apartment to help me with Dante and once I had to run out into the street! But Italians are good in that way. If you say no, they don't mind.'

She had laughed again and put her hand on her arm, stroking its bare, tanned skin. 'But what am I chattering about? Here, let me clear away the plates. Then I must write home. There won't be time tomorrow because I've got to go to a parents' afternoon at the school. Will you be taking the car to work? Darling, I know you like to drive Alex back in the evening so that you can get him on his own. Do you want to have Alex here again? He must get asked out a lot, I suppose, but probably mostly to official functions. I'm sure he'd enjoy a cosy evening. We could get Martin and Nancy.' Jane shook her head. 'Honestly, we mustn't worry about the children.' And she had talked once more of her own fabulous childhood in the tropics. 'How lucky I was in that paradise! Perhaps someday I'll write it all down in a book for Nick and Charles. Will you help me, Edward? We could do it together.' Such desperation.

Now he remembers an evening in the house Jane and he had in Washington, on the south side of Wisconsin Avenue. Martin and Nancy Riley were there and the talk was of some party that was to be held at the British embassy in a few days' time. Nancy wondered what she should wear and turned to Jane. 'You always look so wonderful on those evenings,' she said. Jane smiled and Martin suggested laughingly that they might be allowed a preview of the sensational outfit chosen by the beautiful Mrs West, wife of the distinguished economist. Nancy joined in. 'Oh yes please, Jane. Just us. Come on.' 'Jane . . .' Edward began, thinking she might be too shy, but Martin was not prepared to let it go. 'Come on, let's see,' and she had left them for five minutes to return in a long dress of dark red velvet cut high so that her dark hair swayed around the raised collar.

She paraded before them two or three times. 'Jane.' Both guests said her name in spontaneous admiration, Martin adding, 'You always steal the show.' Edward turned away from her beauty as if fearful, searching for words to hide his confusion: first, 'Very good'; then, 'Of course Jane is an ambassador's daughter, so perhaps she enters these functions with an unfair advantage.' She stopped, turned to look at him, angry and hurt. 'How?' The pomposity had covered his love. Then Martin made a joke about the Snow Queen and the moment passed.

The Snow Queen. The four of them – the Rileys and the Wests – had had nicknames for one another in those Washington days. Martin was the Boy (as in 'The boy stood on the burning deck'), Nancy the Beacon (because of her height and the way her face went red in the sun), Edward the Prof and Jane the Snow Queen. It would be wrong to think of them as inseparable because they had seen plenty of other people as well. Perhaps the fact that the children had been near in age had had something to do with the way the two families were often in and out of each other's houses. The Rileys had three sons and one daughter, the Wests two sons. Together the parents had discussed schools and compared notes about the best time of year to take their annual leave home. Martin had been attached to the British embassy. Then as now he was round and red in the face, a desk soldier with his expanding girth and fondness for wine and music. He plays the piano and has set up an elaborate stereo system in his house.

'They're such a happy couple: Martin and Nancy,' Jane

had said once when they were returning from one of the crowded beaches near Washington, Nick and Charles asleep in the back of the car, drugged by the heavy Potomac summer. 'I wonder sometimes what will happen to them. In the end, I mean. When they leave Washington and go home. What do you think, darling?'

Edward smiled, pleased with memories of the day. 'I expect they will manage in the way that most couples do,' he answered. 'Why? Do you foresee disaster?'

Jane spoke softly so as not to wake the boys. 'No,' she said. 'But one thinks of what they can expect: a posting to Germany or Hong Kong – or so Martin seems to think. Life in rented flats, houses or married quarters. For Nancy the drudgery of housekeeping and arranging the moves and settling the children into schools. For him a new office, new people. Then . . .'

She stopped. In her silence he saw a great darkness. 'What?'

'Then the children growing up and perhaps the doubts Martin might suddenly have about the army and the cost to their lives and how it will be too late by that time to change. I can't see Martin as a senior officer, can you? Can you see him in command of thousands of men?' She paused. 'Alex von Kierich agrees with me.'

He tried the calm method of deflation. 'It's not quite like that now, you know. Martin will not be asked to put on his armour and lead the cavalry towards the enemy's guns.'

She would not stop. 'Yes, I know that, Edward. But how will the military life suit them as they get older? I mean Nancy was telling me what it's like in Germany: the isolation of the camp or barracks, the cold, the boredom. That's why Washington came as such a wonderful surprise to her, because they've been able to mix with all sorts of people. Of course I know what she means because of the embassy days. My father always used to say that one had to make a determined effort not to sink back into the diplomatic world for one's friends. In Rome for instance . . .'

Jane and Edward had thought Martin funny at first: this quick, angry little soldier working on some joint defence programme between Britain and the United States. They would joke about their fear of Colonel Riley's finger on the nuclear button. Then as now Martin had talked too much, laughing, shouting other people down. Alex von Kierich, who met the Rileys at the Wests' house, called him 'eccentric', once 'a typical English eccentric'. Jane had brought them together, asking Alex to dinner with the Rileys in spite of Edward's doubts.

The first evening had gone well. Nancy started the conversation in such a friendly way, talking about the problems of their move to Washington from England. Alex complained of the lack of good music in the city and Martin had agreed. Soon both were discussing recordings of Schubert song cycles, then great performances of other works, Alex reaching back to the days of Furtwängler in pre-war Berlin, childhood memories of a Kreisler recital in Königsberg. After dinner Martin played on the upright piano in the drawing-room: some Bach, a short piece by Brahms, then *Das Lied im Grünen*, making a grotesque attempt to sing the German words. Alex laughed and joined in as well.

'Why has von Kierich never married?' Martin asked later. Edward answered that he did not know. This was before they were together in Africa, when the German had told him the truth. 'I enjoyed his company,' Martin said. 'Do you like him, Edward? No, that's not really the point, is it? To you he is an icon: an object of worship.' The General had not approved of Alex, or the Survey's utopian ideals.

One weekend the two families had driven down to Charlottesville, Jane suggesting that they should ask Alex to come as well, otherwise he would be alone in that dark bachelor's apartment on Q Street. An early start on a

clear, fresh spring day gave them time to walk with the
children through the Palladian buildings and long courtyards
of the university before visiting Jefferson's house at Monticello. Alex had taken photographs of the group, striding
about, often running, leaping with delight after their picnic
under the maples in the park, so happy, sweet with the
boys, a man outside himself at last. He teased Martin who
lectured them: that ponderous teasing. 'Do not forget about
his behaviour with the slaves, my dear Colonel,' he said.
'Maybe your Jefferson was not such a saint after all!'

So they had begun to see Alex von Kierich outside working hours: not too often, for Edward had been trained to
keep his distance from a superior. Usually he came alone,
the only guest, speaking sometimes of what had happened
in 1944 as if ticking off days and places on a list: the arrest
in his office, the first imprisonment at Ravensbrück, the
return to Berlin in chains and the Moabit Prison, then the
special cells at the Gestapo headquarters in Prinz Albrechtstrasse, the interrogation sessions, the long delay of his
trial.

'Were you tortured?' Jane asked.

Alex answered slowly. Not much, just some clumsy beat-
ings, the evidence there in the broken fingers, a thumb
squashed at its tip, the nail sprouting strangely from scarred
skin. He spoke of the destruction of the court-room during
an air raid, that flight south with Gestapo guards, the
miracle of his release by American troops. 'Then it ended at
last,' he had murmured. Never had he known such courage
as amongst those conspirators. What one of their widows
had written was surely true: that such lives are not in vain
and after death join those perpetual living examples of
human greatness.

Edward turns in his bed.

Nothing can match those first days in Rome. He would

arrive at the embassy to collect her, perhaps have a drink with her father and mother before she came down. 'Edward,' Jane's mother had said. 'I may call you Edward, may I? Edward, Jane is serious about this course at university. She wants to get her Italian good enough for translation work, as good as her French. She's only got one more year here. Then she'll go back to London. It's all gone so quickly! I expect she misses her old friends in England, don't you? Roger and I are so used to being birds of passage, flitting from one post to the next. One forgets how disorientating it can be.' Their opposition, the cunning of the campaign against him, had been a part of the great adventure: the romance.

In the end they had won, their victory coming out of Jane's death. Then on his visits to England he would stay with them in the house in Suffolk to which they had retired. Soon after the accident Sir Roger had walked with his son-in-law over the wide, flat fields. 'What was she doing in Munich?' he asked. 'Visiting von Kierich? I'd never have thought it of him, would you? Don't worry. You were away a lot, after all. One should try to forget.'

Sir Roger's calm was like a closed frontier. There were details to settle, he said. The boys had taken it badly. They must stay here now for most of the time. Edward could not have them as a widower in Washington. They would transfer to an English boarding school, something their grandfather had long wanted. There would be trips to the States of course, and to that village house he and Jane had bought together. 'We will help,' Sir Roger said.

How strong they had been, the old diplomat and his wife, looking after Nick and Charles through those years at school, fighting the past. Edward recalls a later conversation at the Suffolk farmhouse. First Sir Roger had mentioned the boys' progress: the half-term reports which Nick and Charles had brought home to their grandparents.

'Nick has come on a lot,' Sir Roger said. 'Look what the headmaster says here. A pity about Charles's French. But don't be too disappointed – or don't let your disappointment show. I might give him some extra coaching in the holidays. The boys have done well, considering they entered the school so late. Of course they miss their mother. The thing to do is to talk about it sometimes. Don't go on as if it never happened. I hear you've been to Germany on Survey business. Where was it? Bonn?'

'Yes.'

'Bad climate. Fogs. Mists. Very humid in summer, or so colleagues stationed there used to say. Did you have rain?'

'It was cold. Snow fell.'

'Snow! In Bonn?'

'Just a few flakes.'

'I should think it seldom lies there.'

'Probably not.'

Sir Roger smiled at him, prising the lid further open. 'Do you ever hear from von Kierich?'

'No.'

'Not since the accident?'

'Not since the accident.'

'I think that is better, Edward.' Sir Roger waited, then asked, 'Does he still keep in touch with the Survey?'

'He feels it might harm us if he did.'

'A generous act of self-denial. The poor man must want news of the organization he did so much to create. Perhaps the Italian speaks to him unofficially from time to time.'

'The Italian?' He felt, as so often with his father-in-law, like a witness under hostile cross-examination.

'Dr Falconi. Your present director. Von Kierich's successor. The chap you knew in Rome.' The words came fast, a sudden fusillade.

'He may.'

'Where is Alex now?'

'Living in a small town in northern Germany.'

'He had to leave Munich, didn't he?'

'He retired from his job there.'

Sir Roger sighed, a sound like wind on a barren plain. 'We always thought he'd been a bit of a hero: involved with Stauffenberg and the rest of them in the attempt to kill Hitler. And he was arrested, wasn't he? Tortured as well. One wonders if the world isn't a bit hard at times. How much longer has Falconi got at the Survey? It must be a terrible job.'

Sir Roger and his wife, Marjorie, had finished their task, he dying five years ago, she only last year in an old people's home in Windsor, much visited by her grandsons, sometimes by Edward, who would sneak in her favourite chocolates, the rich Belgian assortment specifically forbidden by the nurses. Might the sweets kill her? She had seemed indestructible, her frail body cast in iron. The money went to the boys, in trust. The old guard, Jane had called her parents: the best of a type.

The Survey changed. Vittorio Falconi retired. The next director was Bernt Kristiansen, a young, dour Dane. Under Kristiansen more emphasis was put on the collection of data, the publication of papers; much less on direct political approaches to the richer countries of the world. For Edward there were the affairs with Judith in Delhi, Barbara in New York. Then Judith married an Australian biologist from the World Health Organization ('Just for companionship's sake, Edward') and settled down in Geneva. Barbara went on a bit longer, then felt the lure of the south. Florida beckoned: a condominium shared with an old friend. He missed them. For years he had smiled secretly at the thought of a twin-headed monster: the Barbith or the Jubara.

There were other women of the same type: brisk, kindly, sure that to sleep together was no more than an extension of friendship. Always he had tried to follow Alex von

Kierich's code: the most important thing is that no one should be hurt. The Kristiansen regime had meant more conferences: in Europe, the Americas, Australia, the Far East. The same people came: experts, economists, bureaucrats, sometimes politicians.

For Edward they brought new adventures: a Turkish professor in Montreal, a Greek translator in Athens, that lively Dutch civil servant in Oslo. The conferences formed a series of jetties in his life on to which he would clamber for a few days before slipping back into the slow, soft stream. Once in Manila he found that the hall held at least a dozen women with whom he had slept since Jane's death. This shocked him.

Now he still goes to conferences but without the adventures. At Toulouse, from where he has just returned, there was Dr Marie Bourget from the university of Lille. In one of the discussion groups Alex's name had come up. Afterwards Marie asked about his former chief. 'What if the German was guilty?' she said. Guilty of what? 'I can't remember. It was in Russia, wasn't it? So long ago. We should forget, perhaps.' Then she asked, 'What is your life in England?' So he told her about his house, the village, the boys. Nothing else. He has two lives in retirement, Edward decides: one of feeling, one without.

Now he is tired. He takes off his spectacles, puts the rose book down and gets out of the double bed to go to the bathroom before he turns off his light. Often now he has to make this journey again, sometimes two or three times a night, but he accepts it as part of the onset of old age. He will think about Jane once more, perhaps also James Finch's daughter Rose and how she had looked this evening. Then he might imagine one or both of them for himself before he sleeps at last.

Chapter Two

In the manor house, Rose Finch is also awake in her bed. She still has her light on as if she is reading, but the book, *Under the Greenwood Tree*, lies on the eiderdown in front of her. She has three more weeks of holiday before she returns to the Scottish university where she is studying Italian and French.

She has had this room since childhood. Often her mother has suggested that she should move. 'It must be lonely up there, darling. Wouldn't you be happier on the first floor – and warmer, too?' Always her father would say, if he was there, 'Let Rose sleep where she wants, Isabel. You're fond of that room, aren't you, darling? And it's got all your clutter in it. You don't want to have to shift everything downstairs.'

Rose knows her father's fear, even terror, of change. She used to think it came from some memory he had of a golden time, perhaps when he and her mother were young together in this house with their small children. It was then that he had started to try to make something new out of the estate: a farming co-operative, the conversion of the large barn beside the wood into a summer school for artists, the restoration of the garden.

Rose was too young then to have seen what she thinks of as the full flood of his idealism. She has often imagined the meetings in the drawing-room: seven or eight people listening as he put forward a new scheme, wondering perhaps if he was either a genius or a madman, transfixed by that voice as it soared into some distant utopia. Her mother would have been there as well, behind the tea cups or looking up at him as he rose from his chair and began to pace up and down in front of the fireplace. She would put him right from time to time on some detail but never show any sign of substantial disagreement.

'Isabel, listen!' Even now these words preface another plan, another wish. But the difference is that they are the beginning and end of it: the sum of its possibility. Rose's mother, now quite deaf and forced to wear a hearing-aid, listens, perhaps occasionally glancing at a magazine or some papers to do with her beloved horses, or mending a torn sheet or elbow of a jersey that belongs to one of her grandchildren who come often to stay; then asks questions gently as if anxious to encourage him until eventually he argues himself into silence. 'No, it wouldn't work, the building's in too rotten a state,' or, 'It's financial lunacy of course,' or, 'There'd never be enough interest in this part of the world.'

Rose thinks her father takes refuge from an unkind present in these beautiful ideas. She wonders sometimes if there is not also a confusion about him that is almost sacred: that of someone lost in the modern world, a sort of holy idiot. Often he has stood for the county council as an Independent, always losing of course. For him to win would seem quite wrong, at odds with the way she thinks of him.

Rose laughs aloud. Her little dog, Trixie, a rough-haired Border terrier, stirs in the basket at the end of the bed and the wickerwork creaks through the silence. This room has been the background to almost the whole of her life, or her whole conscious life. When she went away for eight months to Florence to improve her Italian between school and university the room had been here, unchanged, awaiting her return with its faded pink paper, single bed with a dark mahogany bedstead, tall white bookcase full mostly of paperbacks, the two pictures, both landscapes, one early-nineteenth-century scene of a lake in mountainous country given to her by her parents. The single window faces south, on to a lawn of the garden.

In Florence Rose had stayed with a family called Alessandri in their apartment off the Via Belvedere and attended Italian classes and lectures on art. Here she had been so happy at first, quite intoxicated by her new independence, the adventure, the discovery of such beauty. Dr Alessandri, who was a doctor of medicine and worked at the nearby hospital, had seemed a part of all this with his smooth dark looks and slight air of mystery, so when his wife went to the coast with their two small children Rose had allowed him to become her lover. But this seemed somehow to make him more melancholic, less satisfied. Then the whole apartment became suffused with his gloomy presence, and Signora Alessandri had started to look oddly at Rose. She had been glad to leave.

Men are difficult, yet better than boys. At university Rose has a boyfriend called Simon Pumphrey. She quite likes Simon because he is sweet and clever, but she wishes their relationship had more to do with love. Then this summer Ben Talbot came to paint the murals in what they now call the Sun Room: someone she has known since childhood, an old friend of her parents.

Ben's kisses are so natural, as if conversation and companionship can slide into physical contact without any worry or barrier at all. Rose has gone away scarcely at all during this long vacation which became the summer of Ben. It had started with those long talks in the garden after his day's work, she describing her hopes and wishes, sometimes her time in Italy (yet never Dr Alessandri) or the books she enjoyed most in her studies: Leopardi in Italian, Verlaine and Baudelaire in French. She had chosen the university in Scotland, she said, because it was so far from home. Yet she does love this place. Ben agrees and calls the manor house and its wild garden a paradise on earth.

One evening by the sundial Ben had quoted some Baudelaire:

'Je suis comme le roi d'un pays pluvieux,
Riche, mais impuissant, jeune et pourtant très-vieux.'

'I think I'm falling in love with you,' he said. Then came the kisses, either in the evening in that yew-hedged circle or sometimes in the afternoon when Ben would play truant from his work to walk with her in the orchard or by the stream at the other end of the garden, well out of sight of the house and her father's study or the stables where Isabel Finch has her horses.

Ben would tell her about his life: why he has never married (he cannot bear the thought of settling down); his dependence on Kay Holden, the rich widow from New York who adores his work and is his chief patron; and how his present success allows him to be more independent of her although of course they will always be friends; the way he has been forced to produce the sort of decorative art that sells rather than the huge, fantastic abstract pictures with which he had hoped when young to make his name. Only with abstracts can he find real freedom.

'That's an old story,' he said. 'It doesn't matter. Look at this.' And he had shown her an article from a society magazine with photographs of Ben and Kay and his work in her place in the country, a farmhouse in Connecticut, near New York. 'I know what you're thinking, darling,' he had said. 'No, I'm not and never have been her lover.'

Rose likes being with Ben. She likes his comfortable, light, easy self: the smell of him after a day's work in the Sun Room, which had been the old nursery before her father had decided to redecorate it. Ben will talk about anything: Baudelaire, the landscape of the American West, the news from Eastern Europe, his love for his cat, Fred, who comes to his studio in London off the Fulham Road, or the contempt he feels for the stupidity of Kay Holden's two feather-brained King Charles spaniels. Once he had alarmed her slightly with a glimpse of anger, a complaint about the cruelty of youth. Young people want really to kill the old, he said: bury them, get their bodies out of sight.

Gradually the scenes in the new Sun Room covered the walls: the crossed rakes, the gently curving scythes, children at harvest time, shepherds in the fields, goose girls in picturesque rags, hayricks amongst green meadows. As the pictures grew, not only was the summer coming to an end but also the visible evidence of Rose's childhood; slowly the remnants of the old nursery disappeared under the bright colours of its new identity. At night she lay awake, waiting for Ben to make up for this destruction by leading her into a new adult self through her first real love affair, to banish Dr Alessandri and Simon Pumphrey, to transform her strange, rarefied family life. He never came. The kisses were still everything. She will see Ben this week in London, for he has asked her to have lunch with him alone.

Rose's mother must know. Probably Lady Finch is delaying her attack. She catches Rose alone sometimes, her tall, slim, grey-haired presence always elegant in late middle age, the deep voice lulling you into confidences and the belief that she cares. They might be in the drawing-room, perhaps seated on the big sofa, Isabel Finch with that look of slight strain she has had since her deafness, or in two of the large armchairs, the covers of which have faded in years of sunlight and washing to remove the hairs and stains of various household pets; another possible place is the new kitchen, a room made out of the old pantry off the hall some ten years ago after the last permanent domestic servant had left.

Isabel Finch can be fierce, cold, quick, irritable, expressing furious frustration at something or someone; Rose recoils from these outbursts, wanting to rush from the room. On other occasions, however, her mother adopts a confessional tone, her strong face less remote as she admits her worries to Rose alone in a way she does with none of the others. Often they talk about Rose's elder sister, Lucy, and brother, Hector. 'What do you think of Mike?' Isabel might say of Lucy's husband, or, 'Rose, does Hector do any work in London?'; her voice soft, almost wistful.

Ben Talbot has been discussed but only in a vague way. 'I love the Sun Room, don't you, darling?' her mother has said; then once, 'Ben should marry, don't you think? He needs domestication, someone to keep him clean. I believe he's a great Lothario.' No, of late Isabel has spoken more about Edward West, so much so that Rose wonders if her mother might be secretly fascinated by this man.

That would be understandable for Edward has done so much, or so it seems when he speaks of Africa or India or the Survey's office in Washington in that slightly hesitant yet persistent way, a revelation of stronger more desperate worlds. Rose has listened to him often, not daring to interrupt in case she might show a childish ignorance; this vague fear keeps her alert, grasping at each word, so different to how she is with Ben whose voice is soothing with its humorous, gentle regret. Ben's anger goes quickly, softening into the limpness of a fresh corpse. Edward's contempt would be fierce, silent and unforgiving.

Three or four days ago, at lunch in the kitchen, Edward's name had been raised again in that ostensibly artless way. 'What does Edward make of this Russian business?' Isabel Finch had asked. Neither her father nor Rose had answered until Lady Finch's eyes stared straight into her daughter's face. 'Do you know, darling? I mean he was a diplomat all those years and he must have had some contact with them.

What do his old friends think? Martin Riley, for instance? Do you know, darling?'

Her father, kindly as ever, had answered for her. Edward had not been a diplomat, he said, but an international civil servant, working to help the poorer nations. What a wonderful idea! Rose wondered if Sir James might be about to cry as he contemplated the Survey, that beautiful dream. Why, if he had been younger he might have pledged himself to a similar cause, for surely the Third World was the place now for the fortunate young. Of course the thing had gone wrong in the end, he said, human nature being what it is. He could not remember exactly what had happened.

'Why?' Isabel Finch asked, turning from her husband to Rose. 'Do you know, darling?' Rose said she did not; it felt wrong to discuss these matters in such a vague, disjointed way, to share what she knew of this lonely, rather awkward man. 'Edward is someone who has suffered, isn't he, with his wife's death and these other things?' her mother went on. 'I feel I know him, yet I don't know him, if you see what I mean. What do you think, James?' Then Isabel had looked suddenly at her watch. 'Good heavens,' she said. 'That stallion's coming this afternoon. Jack Taylor can't possibly manage on his own.' She smiled. 'I wish I could remember what happened to Edward. Martin or Nancy must have told me. Will you clear everything away? It'll have to be late supper tonight because of the Women's Institute at seven. I said they could come here. Don't wait for me if you're starving.'

Again the dog moves. Rose calls out, 'Trixie!' Her voice is quiet because she does not want to be heard, although there is no one near enough even if she shouts. Her parents' room is one floor down, on the other side of the house. Then she thinks, Oh God, I should not have said Trixie's name, because she may get out of her basket and jump on to the bed and start trying to lick my face or get under the blankets, and just at this moment I do not want that. Trixie does not stir again; there is no more creaking of the wicker-work, only the silence of the house at night. 'Do you believe in ghosts?' an old man in the village had asked her when she was a child. She had nodded her head, not sure what to say because she had not thought much about ghosts at that stage and now they are merely an idea that is outside her experience, like so much else. No sound in the night frightens her in this house.

It is strange how people in the village connect the manor house with ghosts: first the true villagers like the old man, and now even newcomers like the Rileys and Edward. Martin Riley, the General, brings the subject up sometimes when they meet, perhaps in the Rileys' place which was once the village poor house, next to Edward's house, where the morgue is supposed to have been, conveniently close to the graveyard of the church.

They are her best friends in the village, the Rileys and Edward. Rose goes to their houses and they have taken her to concerts and the theatre in Bath or Bristol. Now Martin Riley is angry with her father; Rose knows that too. She knows also that he will be too nice to mention it to her tomorrow evening over supper at the Old Poor House even though the question of the new saw mill will be on his mind. He is an obsessive man.

Edward West is another of those older men. He is quite quiet, apparently reserved, but often they speak about his work with the Survey, or rather Edward speaks and she listens. He has told her also how close they all were during their time together in Washington: Nancy and Martin and Jane and Edward. Their children had been more or less the same age; then Edward uses that phrase about Major-General Riley: 'a dark horse'. Yes, Martin is 'a bit of a dark horse'. 'Take his interest in music, for instance,' Edward might say. 'Did you know that he once thought of becoming

38

a concert pianist? But his father didn't like the idea. It was a military family, you see. So Martin was left in no doubt as to what was expected of him.'

Sometimes Martin plays the piano to them after supper or on dull winter afternoons when they have all had lunch together, perhaps at the manor or with the Rileys or Edward, and there is not much else to do. Almost always he starts with Bach; then Edward calls for Chopin or Schumann, and Nancy sighs because she is tone deaf. Once Edward and Rose, having met in the village by chance, had knocked on the Rileys' door so that Edward could ask for a copy of *The Times* of some days earlier (he said his had been thrown out by Mrs Gifford) in order to show her an article about the teaching of English in East Africa. 'I know they keep their old papers for precisely a month before throwing them out,' Edward had said. Then he whispered, 'Military precision, you see!' Several minutes had passed. Edward put his hand up on the brass knocker in the shape of a fish to have another try when suddenly the door had been opened by Martin Riley in shirt sleeves, a pair of old khaki trousers, slippers on his feet and sparse hair sticking up at the back and sides of his reddening skull.

'Alex!' he had said in a thick voice. Rose saw his eyes were blurred, almost dead as if he was coming round from a coma, and he looked quickly away from them towards the ground, but Edward seemed not to notice and asked firmly if he could borrow last Saturday's paper. Martin had smiled, his face suddenly alert. 'Edward,' he said louder, almost triumphantly, and went back into the house to return soon with what they wanted. 'Come in for a quick drink,' he asked and then she had heard, faint but now clear after the confusion, the sound of a record to which Martin must have been listening in this strange catatonic state: a soprano voice gliding above a rich orchestral background, most probably Puccini.

39

This disorientation, even chaos, of a man usually so brisk and efficient, now unable even to recognize his neighbour and old friend, that odd voice, as if he had been drinking or asleep: Rose wondered about the incident. Nancy had not been there; perhaps Martin needed her more than others could imagine. Martin Riley is quite old, but not that old: about the same age as Edward, just too young (as he has so often said) to have fought in the last war. Rose thought she must ask Edward if he had noticed anything strange, but then had said nothing because the moment had not arisen.

So the Rileys and Edward West are her friends. Occasionally at concerts or the theatre they make up a foursome; sometimes Edward rings up and asks her to come alone: most recently to *The Rivals* at the Theatre Royal, after which they had had dinner in a restaurant in Bath where he had spoken Italian to the waiters, inviting her to join in. Rose had listened to him, leaning forward to catch the words, for his deep voice was apt to trail off towards the end of sentences. That early-spring evening in Bath had been different, partly because they talked about Edward's family and her life at home instead of the usual memories of the Survey or his work in the poorer parts of the world.

'I can't remember if you've met my sons, Nick and Charles,' he said. 'Martin and Nancy's children you know, I think.'

Rose had nodded, remembering not all of the Rileys, because there are three sons and a daughter, but certainly one smallish man who works for a wine merchant in London, another, who is an accountant, and the girl, Mary, who married an estate agent and lives in Kent. Last year a travelling opera company had put on a performance of *Don Pasquale* in the drawing-room at the manor in aid of the church restoration fund. Some sixty neighbours had come, and the Rileys had brought Mary and her husband. Mary had advanced on Rose when the audience was having a glass of wine before the start of the performance 'to hear all the news', her attention only partly engaged whilst Rose had explained how hard they had all worked to clear the drawing-room and the way the opera company had momentarily fused the lights.

Determined to avoid Mary and the estate agent, Rose had sat next to Edward West at *Don Pasquale*, to which he had come alone. That night he had seemed vague, dropping his programme, searching for his spectacles, asking several times what charity the performance was in aid of, then lapsing into silence with a bemused smile as they waited for the opera to begin.

In Bath that other evening Edward was sharper at first, listening to Rose's answer about the Rileys' and his children, nodding as she says that she has never met Nick but, yes, Charles she does know, although she cannot explain why she finds the shy youth with a prominent Adam's apple duller than his father, even though Charles is so much nearer to her in age. Then they had talked of the play.

'I know the work well,' Edward said. 'When we lived in Washington, Martin, Nancy, Jane and I had a friend who used to have play-reading evenings when we would each take parts.' He laughed. 'It sounds silly, doesn't it? In fact we rather enjoyed ourselves. It took the Americans to get us inhibited English going.'

She heard him sigh. He is a fine-looking man, quite old now of course, with that gentle face which suddenly becomes sharp when he lifts his chin away from his neck. He is tall too, with a long body and a head of thick grey and dark brown hair. His hands and face are brown, from that time spent in hot countries. That evening in Bath she had asked, 'Did your children grow up in America?'

At first Edward seemed distracted, his eyes shifting away. 'Have you met my son, Charles?' he said, repeating himself, not answering her question. 'There is another: Nick, who lives in America with his wife and child.'

He turned again and called to the waiter, this time in English. 'Some more wine. Is it coming?' He frowned. 'They were slow the last time we came, do you remember, with Martin and Nancy?' Then he resumed. 'Charles is the younger by two years.' He looked again into the room, still agitated, until a waiter brought another bottle of wine. Edward spoke sharply to Rose. 'It's the same as before. That suit you all right? Have you met Charles? No, I've asked you that already. How old are you?'

'Twenty-two,' she answered, adding a year.

'When is your birthday?' She told him and he seemed to engage in some kind of private calculation, soundlessly moving his lips. 'Taurus,' he said at last. 'Am I right?' She nodded and saw that his hand, reaching for the new bottle, was shaking quite violently. 'Obstinate people, but loyal. I don't know you well enough. Probably nonsense, anyway. Now Charles is a Capricorn: not so different. You might get on well with each other, if one believes all that. Jane was interested in it: that's true, I know. Those Washington days were fun.' Edward took another gulp at his glass. 'But I've never understood people who hark back. No, that's not true. Of course I can see if they had a wonderful time, when they were children, for instance. Rose' – he said her name – 'I can just see you all in that beautiful house when you were younger; well, not see, because I seldom came there in those days, but imagine, yes I can imagine you all: Hector, the little boy, you and Lucy at nursery tea. Isn't it always nursery tea at the manor with Isabel and James there with the scones, the crumpets, a fruit cake and the huge brown earthenware teapot? Or perhaps the pot is silver.' She did not answer, so he asked, 'What does your brother do?'

'Hector works in an architect's office in Richmond. He hopes to qualify soon.' Hope is Hector's real speciality.

'Is he married?'

'Yes. To Emily. They have two children.' Surely he must

know this. Then she laughed and told him about Hector's idleness in London: slopping around his house in Clapham, getting on his wife's nerves, the flabby unshaven face at weekends.

'And your sister?'

'Married to Mike, a landscape gardener. They also live in London. Again Rose laughed and said Lucy was bored and spoke of moving to the country to grow vegetables, make yoghurt from the milk of goats or sheep. 'But who will pay for all this?'

The waiter interrupted him with two menu cards and Edward looked angrily up, then across at Rose again. 'Just coffee for me. What about you?' She nodded. 'Two coffees!' The man scurried off. 'I grew up in the country, just like you, Rose,' he went on. 'My father was a farmer, like yours. Isn't that what James says he does? A farmer? Is that right?'

'Farmer and ecologist,' she answered.

'Farmer and ecologist.' Edward looked down at the table and shook his head. 'Yes, I've spoken to James about his ideas.' He took another swig at his glass, then sat back from the table to allow the waiter to pour him a cup of coffee. 'Quite brave though, to go completely organic. I admire his courage. You have to take a long view in that sort of thing, I suppose. Oh, by the way, Martin is after him. Something to do with the saw mill and that field. The little Miss Horns are involved: the ones who bought the old greengrocer's shop. Warn your father. Martin can be awfully persistent. He seems to have taken it upon himself to be a sort of spokesman for the village. Tiresome, really. Poor Martin. He hasn't enough to do, that's the trouble. They retire us all too early now: just over sixty. Between you and me, Martin was hoping for something else: not in civilian life but in the army. Some cushy desk job in Whitehall to finish off his career. But it didn't come. Nancy told me that. Oh I know he has one or two interests in London that take him up there from time to time: that charity for army widows, for instance. Then he lends a hand with the Lifeboats. We were great friends in Washington, you know, the four of us. Really great friends.' Edward laughed. Rose thought she might be anyone as far as he was concerned: just a listener. 'We had these nicknames: the Beacon and the Boy, the Prof and the Snow Queen. Nancy was the Beacon because of her face which goes red in the sun and she never could be bothered to try to protect it with powder or cream or anything. The dear old Beacon! Then we called Martin the Boy because he was always so keen and eager: 'The Boy stood on the burning deck', you know. I suppose it was a bit of a joke about his appearance as well, because although he was a soldier he didn't look in the least like the usual idea of a hero. The Boy! I was the Prof. It seemed a good enough name for a professional economist. Then Jane.' Edward stopped, as if suddenly aware of her. 'The Snow Queen.' He laughed again. 'I can't remember. Have you met my son Charles? He seems to have settled down. Will you come back here when your time at college is over?'

'Oh no.' She waited.

'I never see Nick,' he said. 'They were both so good when their mother died.' And Rose remembers a photograph in her mother's album of a dark-haired woman in a long skirt or dress and a wide-brimmed straw hat, perhaps in the village or at lunch in the garden of the manor: delicate but beautiful.

She tried to draw him out further, intrigued now by his quietened voice: a sense of trembling on the edge of silence. It was his work that had given him strength, surely: that great shaded place of which he had spoken in a kind way, as if explaining somewhere abroad to a friend's child. She wanted to reach behind this, to the vivid truth. 'Do you miss your work?' she asked.

'At the Survey?' He spoke louder, as if he had emerged

from a holy place. 'Not really. I'm still slightly involved. I go to conferences, give advice, that sort of thing. It's all changed now. Very different. We didn't achieve much, or so it seems sometimes when one looks back. There were small triumphs, I suppose. We kept the pressure on, articulated the cause of the poor parts of the world. It was quite revolutionary, really, to go public in the way we did. A risk as well. But there seemed to be no other way to move the richer countries. Do you remember the campaign? No, you're too young.' Then the kind old man returned. 'What about you? What will you do after your studies are over?'

So she had tried again: a new approach to his admiration. 'I want to break away, set up on my own, travel, teach, use my knowledge for' – here she paused – 'the general good of the world!'

'Yes. You must do that, Rose. That is what you should do.'

Edward had drunk too much. But this made her more relaxed with him, so much so that when he asked her about her time in Italy before university she surprised herself by speaking of those months in the Via Belvedere, the Alessandri family and what had happened with the doctor. This was spontaneous, a childish outburst. Now she thinks she should regret it, yet the memory pleases her.

'Were you in love?' he asked.

'No,' she answered. 'I felt sorry for him.'

As they left the restaurant, Rose thought she should try to make him let her drive but he seemed in control as they went slowly home. Edward mentioned Robert Padstow, the vicar who had just retired. 'It's odd about Padstow. The people in the village adored him, didn't they? All that "Father Bobs" stuff. Everyone, that is, except for Nancy. Even Jane thought he was some sort of saint.' Then outside the door of the manor the old man had leant across from his side of the car, his hand holding her shoulder in an

45

attempt at a kiss. 'Rose.' Not yet, she thought, and had slipped easily from his grasp, out into the night.

She thinks now what she might say to Edward about Ben. It would be a question of justifying Ben's triviality, of turning it into a joke but defending him as well. 'Yes, I could see that you liked him, and he was so interested in what you said the other night about your work and the man who was so brave and good. Ben is a friend of my parents; well, you know that. He goes to America a lot now and does work for a rich widow from New York, although she spends most of her time in the country, in Connecticut. Have you ever been to Connecticut? This woman, Kay Holden, has an old farmhouse in a quiet part of the state, near a river. Ben explained to me how he is decorating the place: the colours and motifs, that sort of thing, and there was an article in a magazine about it with a photograph of him at the farmhouse with Kay and her two spaniel dogs. Ben doesn't like dogs, only cats, in particular a black cat called Fred which comes to his studio off the Fulham Road sometimes when he is working, and he says he thinks Fred brings him luck. That's Ben for you! Come to the Sun Room again and have another look at what he has done. It's good, of its kind. Mum laughs at Ben a bit. She can be quite cruel, my mother.'

The dog moves again. 'Trixie!' This time Rose whispers the name.

Chapter Three

Awake early, Edward West thinks: Alex von Kierich is an aristocrat and they are different because there is a self-certainty to them, an arrogance sometimes hidden yet very strong: like the Finches here in the manor, that bewitching, pale grey house with its mullion windows and two towers, the stone fountain on the circle of grass by the entrance, the yew hedges, that sundial, the overflowing border of species roses, the *moyesii* and *Rosa alba*, the way in summer it all seems to spill out and last for ever.

Today he will work in his garden, for the weather may hold. Then in the evening the Rileys again and Rose Finch, with whom he had been foolish that night in Bath when he was at his worst, self-pitying and garrulous, two of the symptoms of old age. Rose is a good girl: nice, quiet, not so shy as she seems. He likes the short brown hair, a firm body sure of itself: also the truth of her smile, the unaffected dark skirt and pink blouse she had worn to the theatre that evening when he had drunk too much and tried to kiss her. So he is still vulnerable to all this.

Then he thinks, Damn this place, it's so small and if she has talked everyone will know and laugh at me, and James and Isabel must be secretly appalled, perhaps disgusted. Just one moment when he had slipped and the poor girl had opened the car door and run. If she had stayed, they might have come here, to these dark beams and low ceilings, mostly bogus imitations of the style of her father's house. No, Rose would not want that.

47

Now he seems to hear Alex's voice. 'The whole country was crazy. You can't imagine, Edward, with your English idea of the world. Think of it, just try.'

Having worked late, they were driving to a Washington dinner party which was important because people from the government were going to be there. Edward drove, it was his car, and they passed slowly through a suburb, perhaps Alexandria, Chevy Chase, Arlington or Bethesda. Alex raised that pale hand, the fingers of which had been broken by the Gestapo. 'There was no trust. My father would tell me about the poverty after the First War: people searching for mushrooms or berries in the fields around our home. Women and children in rags, so thin. Like this!' His finger drew a line through the air.

Often in those days he had offered to drive Alex home, partly to listen to the German talk. The past came up occasionally: seldom his time in Hitler's prison, more often the great house in the eastern forests of the old Germany, the ruined place of his young manhood. After the war Alex had worked first in Hamburg, for the Allied Commission, before moving to the new capital of Bonn. In Hamburg there was a café where he would go because it reminded him of a haunt of his student days.

That evening, unusually, he had told a joke about work. 'Mr Sheth came to see me this afternoon, from the Indian embassy. Do you know him, Edward? They have some objections to one of our irrigation plans. What is the district called? I can't remember. In any case I called in Joseph Cage who made the original drawings and he looked at Sheth's ideas and said, "How are you going to push several thousand gallons of water uphill?" Sure enough, there it was on the map: the beginnings of what looks like a small mountain range. Not the Himalayas, but a sizeable gradient.'

Alex's strange, heaving laugh, like a man out of breath, his scarred, thin face raised as if on hinges towards his high forehead and smooth brown and grey hair. As the laugh died, he pulled at his ear. The attempts at informality had seemed oddly deliberate: the way he had used first names so freely, quite unlike the usual German practice, evidence perhaps of a wish to break with the past. Then in the car that question: 'You grew up in the English countryside, Edward?' A dive into intimacy. 'You seem surprised that I should know,' Alex had said. 'Blame Sir Roger, your father-in-law. He told me.' Another joke and that laugh. 'See, I have it all here in your dossier!' He had patted his leather briefcase.

'How was this childhood of yours?' Alex asked. 'I too was a country boy.' So different, though, to those few fields on the Kent border: the great kitchen copper, the black iron stove across one wall, his father lifting the coal scuttle, the rattle of the coke against tin; Edward, the only child, seated at the table before the walk to school: two miles, a short cut across the fields, then down a lane between banks of campion and Queen Anne's lace in summer, primroses and hawthorn blossom in spring.

The von Kierich family had been landowners in north-eastern Germany, descendants of the Teutonic knights, now dispossessed, their estates too far to the east for any hope of return. Alex would describe a great eighteenth-century house, his sisters, Fredericka and Josephine, in their print dresses and pigtails, playing piano duets on autumn evenings: a musical family with Alex's violin (long ago abandoned), the girls and their mother on the piano, their father's cello which he had found in a shop in Königsberg. Then came other rituals: the shooting parties, the pursuit of deer and elk and varieties of game. The forests and lakes of East Prussia were a paradise for sport. The German seemed quite dispassionate about the slaughter, as if it was inseparable from the rest of that magical past. Always the memories ended with the burning of the house by the Russians on their way to Berlin and the family's flight to the west.

'Have you been back?' the German had asked. 'I will never return. Good memories are too fragile to be put at risk.' Yes, Edward answered, he had gone back: only once since his parents' death, to show Jane. The farm had been sold by his father's landlord.

'She must have been young then,' Alex said. 'Twenty-three, twenty-four? I do not know her age so I am just guessing.' He laughed. 'A mere infant: younger than you, Edward, much younger. Let me guess.' He looked up at the roof of the car. 'You are fifteen years more than she? No, do not say. How dare I ask such a question? It must be the prospect of this dinner making me light-headed. Please do not answer.' Then the smile that softened his face. 'So she never met your parents.'

'My father couldn't make a living from the land,' Edward declared. 'It was beautiful, on the edge of the North Downs. I wanted her to see that: the beauty.' On their return from his old home they had made love in her parents' empty Chelsea flat. He did not mention this.

'Fascinating.' Alex's voice of compassion. Then as they approached the house of their host through the thin birch trees, he had asked, as Edward knew he would, 'Will Jane be there or are we without wives tonight?'

The Old Poor House and Church House, next to each other, near the church. In Washington, Jane spoke proudly of their English home.

'It's in a village in the West Country, a little overrun with outsiders now but still with the atmosphere of a village. There are two houses near the church, next to each other. Martin and Nancy Riley have one: the Old Poor House it's called, a red-brick Georgian building. Then there's us: smaller than the Rileys but older in parts, big enough to take Daddy's furniture which he's given us. They say it used to be the village morgue in the old days and some of the older people still call it that: the Old Morgue! It's not an easy house for tall people, and Edward and I seem to spend a lot of our time there trying to remember to duck, don't we, darling? Edward has bruises the size of eggs on his forehead when the time comes to go back to Washington. It's let sometimes, but we try to take the children there in the summer and this year I'm going over for longer, part of the time on my own so that I can get to know the place a bit better. I want to find out what I can expect when we finally leave Georgetown and go off into the sunset of our declining years. Charles will come with me, and Nick too of course: both of them.'

Then her death.

Edward reaches for his spectacles and the letter on the bedside table, separating some pages of loose paper from a small map and a postcard of a medieval chapel. He reads the familiar thin, neat writing again, smiling at that clumsiness of phrase.

Dear Edward,

How are you?

Some days I look at the photographs I have here of our time together when we were in Washington and doing such important work. They remind me of happy times, and this is also why I am writing as it would be tragic to lose oneself in bad memories and forget about so much that was good as well.

First I must say what I am doing now, which is of course not serious work but a little activity in this town where I have settled probably for the rest of my life. I have nice rooms in a hotel here, managed and owned by Otto Friesen, a cousin and friend. The von Kierich family is getting smaller! My sister Josephine lives in Salzburg as a widow, but my other sister, Fredericka, died although her husband, a doctor, still lives in Mainz. For something to do I take people around the Kloster here in our town, a historic place.

I have some friends here, not many it is true, but enough to give company when I need it. One of these friends, a lady who lives in the Kloster, the widow of a pastor, has said I should keep up with my old comrades and she knows you from your photograph, which I have shown her often. Frau Schneider is kind and we talk together, but do not worry, I will not break my vow to remain a solitary bachelor, not even now in old age! There is another woman, Frau Hartmann, also nice but a terrific chatterbox, great friends with Frau Schneider yet not so much with me. Their shared interest is the royal families of Europe, which they love to talk about, especially the Queen of Sweden, who is a German girl as you probably know. You would laugh at them, I think, as I do to myself. I tell you this to give an idea of my life.

What I wanted to say is that it makes me upset to think that we have each allowed ourselves to become so ignorant about what the other is doing. You have left the Survey now. I know that because Vittorio Falconi keeps in touch with me and I have heard of your move back to England and Vittorio gave me your address. You may curse him for this! My letter breaks a silence, I know, and when Jane died in Munich I would have done anything to help you over the pain, so for these last years I have respected our agreement not to keep in touch. Now surely enough time has passed for us to talk to each other again. We should not forget those years together.

Anyway I have broken the barrier and you can ignore me if you like. It used to worry me so much that you thought I had cheated you. I am still worried about it, but now I am older perhaps it should be possible to reach some sort of peace about these matters, and I am sure that Jane would have wanted you and I to be at peace together, for this was what she said to me during the difficult times in Washington and in Munich at the end. I do not think you have ever heard the whole story, or not from me, anyway: just a lot of rumours and so forth. We should put that behind us and be with each other again at least in spirit, for I am sure there is something in our consciousness which has never separated in the way that we two have physically and even intellectually drifted apart. Parts of the soul can become unconquerable in this world. Here we will have something precious always.

Edward, I am asking you to come here if you can. It is a strange part of the country for me, without a finite reality still, which as I grow older seems to exist only amongst those forests and lakes of my childhood. The land is flat, like the country near my old home, but tame and gentle, so neat, like a well-planned garden, and I miss those great skies. The townspeople are pleasant but they keep themselves back, so I talk mostly to Frau Schneider, the lady in the Kloster, sometimes with Frau Hartmann or Otto Friesen in the hotel as well when there is time. I cannot think of visiting England now because I am too old and the way to get to you is complicated. Yet I should like to see your house beside the church of which you and she used often to talk.

Edward, that is all. You can see the card of the Kloster, and it is rather beautiful, so that will be an interesting thing for you. The map shows where I am, with the town underlined in red. There are airports at Hamburg and in Hanover and a train station fifteen miles away where I could arrange a taxi because I have given up my driving licence now, or you could perhaps drive, which would give you a chance to take a closer look at the new Germany. The hotel is comfortable, peaceful also. We will be quite alone.

Forgive me, yet I feel it is right at this time before I go.

Yours,
Alex

Chapter Four

'These figures make no sense.'

Sir James Finch sits at breakfast in the new kitchen of the manor. Today he wears a checked shirt, open at the neck, and a pair of baggy brown corduroy trousers: a late-middle-aged man with a lean, eager face and pale blue eyes, clutching the quarterly results produced by the farm computer. With him is his daughter Rose.

Her father glances at his watch. She knows he has plenty of time. 'Look, Hector understands figures, doesn't he? Are he and Emily coming this weekend? Could we show these to him on Saturday or Sunday?' Sir James passes a hand through his sparse black and grey hair. 'Hector knows the way I want to run things here.' His lips soften into petulance. 'What do people think? It's the jobs I'm worried about, Rose; you know that, don't you? I must do my best for the village. It's the community I'm thinking of. There's nothing for young people. That's why these new men can come in and buy up all the houses. Not just men, but women too! Take those two spinsters who inhabit the old greengrocer's shop. Look what they've done to the place, turned it into a horrible fairyland, a gnomes' grotto of dingle dells and dwarf conifers. What are they called?'

'Horn.'

'I don't like them.'

'I think they know that.'

'Well, I don't want to seem difficult.' He frowns. 'Anyway, I like some of the new people. But they've bought their way in here and they think that gives them the right to tell us all what to do. They all want their little bit of England. Take Edward West, for example, a man who's spent his entire working life abroad, in America, India, Africa, other parts of the world. What does he do when he retires? He comes back to the English countryside, makes a garden, goes for walks. Has he got a dog?'

'No.'

'Most of them have dogs. The dogs chase the sheep and their owners get angry when you tell them to keep the animals under control, like General Riley with his golden retriever.' Now Martin is General Riley and Rose sees that her father is angry. Yet he is still happy to see the Rileys, even to have them in his house as he did the other evening: another sign of that tolerance which the world must not be allowed to defeat, or so she thinks. 'You say you're going to supper there tonight.' He shakes his head. 'All the conspirators.'

'The conspirators?'

'They're against me over the deal with Dove. They're doing their best to stop him building the saw mill in that field. But tell me this, darling: if there's no employment in the village for young people, how can one expect them to stay? Dove is going to create at least ten jobs.' Her father stops briefly. 'This could save us as well, you know. Remember those figures.' He points at the computer papers now lying on the kitchen table.

Rose looks at the source of his anxiety. 'But . . .'

'What?'

'It is rather near the village.' She feels ridiculous to be arguing when usually it is he who is so impractical. 'What will it look like?'

'The building? Oh, a simple one-storey affair. Dove is going to plant the field up with trees and shrubs so that you'll hardly see the place in a few years.' He frowns again, serious now, the petulance gone. 'Look, darling, when you're with the Rileys tonight try to reassure them. He keeps pestering me and I can't go on telling him that the scheme will have very little effect on the traffic because he quite obviously doesn't believe what I say. It's a bit much when someone as good as accuses one of being a liar! Anyway, the development is the other end of the village to where he lives.' Her father sighs, a loud rather theatrical sound. 'I hope there won't be too much unpleasantness at this public meeting in the hall on Thursday. Dove says it's necessary, to put our case to the village. You know I hate that sort of thing. Fascinating how people line up, isn't it, with that petition and so forth? Edward West is with the General, I presume. They're great friends, aren't they? The General doesn't seem particularly military, does he, until you cross him? That short, bald, overweight little man.' Sir James laughs, pleased with himself. 'He has quite a temper, or so I'm told.'

'I'm sure Martin has nothing personal against you.'

'You think so?' He is quiet for a moment. 'Well, I can't stand back any longer. If there's one thing I've learnt, it's the importance of change. Places develop down the years. They are added to, new settlements reach out from the centre, fresh history is made. Look at the field patterns here! You can see how the land has been worked since the Middle Ages, the centuries of feudalism, then on up to the present day. I see the village as a living entity, from the time of the first clearing in the primeval forest to our contemporary paradise for retired businessmen and civil servants. But there must be life! And to have life, you need work for the young so that they will stay. Darling, I know I'm right!' He laughs and hits the table gently with one hand. 'That's my thought for the day.'

She likes his enthusiasm. 'Will you say that at the meeting?'

'No. Dove will speak. He understands them better.'

'Understands who?'

'The people.' Then he asks, 'What does Edward West think? I know you see him from time to time. It's all right, darling, I'm not pressing you. Don't worry. But I wonder about him. He's rather a mysterious figure, isn't he? I remember his wife, Jane, from when they first came here – not that we knew them well in those days, because they lived mostly in Washington. A beautiful woman but not fond of country life, or so we thought. Then there was that tragedy. She was killed in a car crash. Did you know? In Germany, whilst Edward was working in Washington. Nancy Riley told Mum it wasn't the happiest of marriages but one never really knows, does one? Apparently he was rather a womanizer, quite discreet. Jane may have known. One can imagine it now, through his shyness. One feels women would be drawn to the mystery. Then he can suddenly talk, open up, so to speak. Like on Sunday evening when he spoke about the man he used to work for: that German.'

'But the General stopped him.'

'I know. Wasn't it odd? Martin was angry.' Sir James brings his thin arms together across his chest and seems briefly to hug himself, a gesture of excitement. 'Edward said this German had been the victim of a plot to get him out. Some story from the war had been dragged up. Edward was sure he was innocent. Then I remembered the reports in the papers at the time. The name rang a bell. Von Kierich.'

'What reports?'

'That the man had been involved in some wartime atrocity.' He shakes his head, his mouth arching down in distaste. 'What a ghastly business.' Sir James stands in a surprisingly quick movement, lifting the computer print-outs off the kitchen table. 'Darling, you should ask Edward about it.' He looks again at his watch. 'I must go.'

'Dad.' She stops. To ask more about Edward would be pointless, because her father will become muddled, blurt out half-remembered facts, then stop, suddenly ashamed to be spreading mere rumours. He hates gossip.

'Yes?' He looks down at her.

She stays in her chair. 'I'm going to London on Thursday to have lunch with Ben.'

'Ben Talbot? Are you really, darling?' Sir James stops by the door. 'Will you go to his studio? If you do, get him to show you some of those huge early abstracts of his: great canvases of browns and yellows and greens, such odd combinations of colours. That was Ben's style when I first met him. I never felt tempted by his early work. He's changed of course: much more conventional. I like Ben. He's such a civilized man.' And her father leaves before Rose can ask him anything else.

She walks into the Sun Room. How light it all is on this clear morning: the fantastic scenes of lads and lasses, picturesque carts, cornfields, apple trees laden with fruit, a pastoral bliss. So sweet as well.

Chapter Five

So bright is the glare from the evening sun when Edward enters the Rileys' drawing-room for supper that at first he cannot identify the five figures by the fireplace. Then he sees Martin in a cardigan, Nancy's red skirt, Rose wearing the same pink blouse and two elderly women in dark dresses, Clara and Avril Horn: small and plump, bowing slightly in shy deference, their grey hair pinned neatly back.

He likes the Rileys' home. Church House is much earlier in style, so different to the large, bright rooms and high windows here. Edward has a better garden, but Martin and Nancy seem quite happy with their circular beds of floribunda roses with names like Iceberg and the ancient mulberry tree from the fruit of which she makes sour jam. He sees that he has become a garden snob.

Then there is the girl: poor Rose. Sometimes he imagines a rescue, carrying her off from the manor to a new life outside time and memory, the only reality that of the two of them together. Age will not matter in this second spring, a return to that brightness of the first days in Rome: much more than an old man's lunge in the car, that mistimed kiss. At least he can still think of these things.

Martin is holding a bottle. 'Some of this, Edward?' he says. 'It's rather good.' The General knows about wine. 'We were talking about having one's portrait painted. Rose tells us that neither of her parents have ever been done. Is that right?'

Rose looks up from her glass but not towards Edward, who sits down on the sofa beside the Horn sisters. 'Yes.'

'Why not?' Martin asks. 'Surely it is customary in families like yours.'

Now she looks embarrassed. 'My sister Lucy and brother Hector and I were all painted as children, but never my parents. Perhaps they just couldn't bear to sit still for long enough!' She laughs.

'Who was the artist?' Nancy asks.

'Ben Talbot.' Then for the benefit of the Horn sisters. 'An old friend of my father's.' She falters only slightly, a brief glance at her hands before smiling back. Nancy leaves the room for the kitchen.

'Ben is a decorative artist,' Martin says. 'His work is quite charming, really delightful. But as a portraitist . . . well, I can't see him being quite ruthless enough. Not that portraits should be unpleasant. Oh no. But one needs a cold eye at times to capture the frailty of the sitter as well as his or her bravado and swagger.'

'Swagger!' Edward laughs.

The laughter brings Rose in again. 'I'm afraid we weren't very good sitters, except when Ben bribed us with sweets, which used to make my mother furious. The pictures are upstairs on the nursery landing: one of us in a group and then the individual portraits. I must have been about six at the time, Lucy eight, Hector ten.' Now she asks Edward a question. 'Haven't you seen them?'

'No, I don't think I have.'

'Have you, Clara?' asks Martin.

'No,' answers one of the Horn sisters, the taller of the two. Her voice is pleasant at first, then takes on a harder note. 'We've never been inside the manor, you see. Only to the garden when it is open to the public in aid of the church.' She looks at Rose. 'Of course I know the history of the house and of your family.'

'Never been into the manor!' Martin sounds so shocked that it is as if she has uttered an obscenity.

61

Now the other sister speaks: Avril. 'No. We have not been asked.'

Both women are looking at Rose, who says, obviously in some desperation, 'But surely you came to the opera last year, *Don Pasquale*, for the church again.' Then she adds, 'It was a charity performance. Anyone could buy tickets.'

'Only if they received an invitation.' Avril Horn's eyebrows rise.

Martin interrupts, playing the diplomat. 'Perhaps you will see that Clara and Avril are asked next time, Rose. They would be interested in the house.' He smiles at her and goes quickly on. 'I find it strange that James and Isabel have never been painted. They are a handsome couple, by no means the least of their line, and certainly not the last! Don't you agree, Avril?' Again Martin does not wait for an answer but returns to Rose. 'Your father is angry with me.'

'Why?'

'I have been pestering him about the proposed saw mill. You know we've got up this petition against it, don't you? Nothing personal, of course. Isn't that right, Avril? Do you agree with me, Clara?' He leaps up to pour some more wine into their glasses.

'Quite right, General.'

'Please, Clara! It must always be Martin. None of this General stuff.' Martin laughs loudly again.

'Quite right, Martin.'

The sisters smile now, those creased, round faces suddenly alive: Clara and Avril. Edward scarcely knows these women, although they must have lived in the village for seven or eight years. Fragments of what Martin and Nancy have said about the Horns return to him. Avril takes in typing, mostly manuscripts; Clara paints wild flowers. Avril has a degree in history from the University of London; Clara studied briefly at the Slade. The Horns help with flower-arranging in the church, editing the parish magazine, the organization

62

of the local horticultural society's show. They are assiduous in their calls on the sick, driving the elderly to Chilworth for hospital appointments if there is no other transport available. Free of husbands or children, they have so much time to do good. Yet they have been spurned by James and Isabel Finch. How strange. He wonders if he will ever understand the subtle snubs, the strong invisible forces, of this English life. 'Martin . . .' he begins.

Avril Horn cuts him off. 'May I ask you something, Rose? But perhaps I should not call you by your Christian name. May I ask you something, Miss Finch?'

Rose blushes. 'Please call me Rose, Miss Horn.'

'Well, how kind. And I am Avril. It is simply a question about this proposal for a new saw mill. As the General, or rather Martin, has said, we wish to avoid personal acrimony and unpleasantness as much as we can. But as I am not acquainted with Sir James or Lady Finch, except from a distance and by reputation of course, I feel I must not allow this meeting with you, a member of the Finch family, to pass without asking why your father wishes to bring this horrible new development to our beautiful corner of England.'

Rose looks at Avril Horn; the voice is oddly strained, the lips hard, the small hands tight together in her lap, the skin white over the bones. 'Is it really that horrible?' She glances at Martin, then at Edward, looking for help.

Martin is kind. 'Avril, we will have a chance to debate these things in the village hall on Thursday evening. Perhaps one should wait . . .'

Avril Horn shows that old sweet smile. 'I had hoped that Miss Finch might help us to understand her family's point of view.'

'Rose. Please.' The girl repeats her previous request, then manages a laugh, Edward joining her.

'Avril.' Clara Horn is warning her sister.

'Should I not speak about it? Very well.'

'The village needs the jobs,' Rose blurts out.

'At the expense of such terrible desecration?' Avril Horn asks. 'And how many jobs will there be? Five, perhaps six? The ruination of our countryside seems a high price to pay for six jobs of the most menial and degrading kind.'

'Why are they menial?' Now Rose is cross. 'What is so degrading about working with wood?'

'Do you not know of Mr Dove's reputation? Surely, Miss Finch, you have heard of the way he treats his men.'

'Please call me Rose!'

Both are breathing heavily when Nancy enters to say, 'It's ready,' a signal for the exchange to cease.

They stand up, abandoning their fortified positions, Martin clutching the bottle of wine like a weapon, to go through to the kitchen. In the centre is a long table on which rest two silver candlesticks holding three lit candles each, yet the light is dim, bright only over the squat red Aga against one wall. The room is too warm. Martin moves quickly to the head of the table. 'Rose, come on my right here,' he says. 'Here we are!' He flourishes the bottle again. 'A little of this?' Then he holds up his full glass in a joke imitation of a toast. 'Well, it's good to see you all. No quarrels please! Let us call a truce. Confusion to our enemies!'

Edward notices that wildness about Martin. The eyes reveal it: the way they seem strange, almost delirious, then return quickly to the disciplined calm one might expect from a retired major-general. He knows that odd mixture: the shouting temper, the soft playing of Chopin, the great runs of Bach, through which the tension seems to flow away, the steadiness of Nancy and their family life, so different to his own. Suddenly he feels worried for his old friend and says 'That's right' in a soothing voice.

'Down with them all!' Martin shouts, his glass still aloft.

'Down with them all.' Edward turns to Nancy who has sat down apparently without a care. Has she not noticed? 'I heard from my son Charles today,' he says. 'He rang from New York, where they've sent him on business.'

'Oh Edward.' She looks pleased.

'He comes home next week after flying up to Boston to see his brother Nick at the weekend.'

'Then they'll be together,' says Nancy. 'How marvellous.'

'How many children do you have, Mr West?' asks Clara Horn.

'Two boys.' He speaks quickly. 'Charles likes America and knows it well, so I'm glad they've given him a chance to go back there. You see, one can't really think of him as an Englishman, except by blood. Both Nick and he were educated in the United States until their mother died.'

'Oh I see,' says Avril Horn. 'So they both have foreign habits. Does that worry you, Mr West?'

'I don't know why you did that, Edward.' Martin interrupts, staring at his friend.

'Jane and I wanted to have the children near us.'

'It was von Kierich who persuaded you.'

Nancy tries to help. 'Martin, I'm sure Edward and Jane –'

'No!' He silences her. 'Edward knows what I mean. Jane was happy for Nick and Charles to come back with our boys, and the Survey would have helped towards the cost, or so she told me. Certainly her parents wanted it.'

'Her parents!' Edward exclaims. 'What did they know?'

'That's not the point. The point is that you could have sent Nick and Charles back. Jane told me. Do you remember, Nancy? She said it to us several times, once at the end of the summer holidays when we were packing up the boys. She said the Survey would have helped.'

'And you think they suffered as a result? Is that it?' Edward asks.

'You say Charles has no roots.'

'How I pity the rootless,' sighs Avril Horn. 'They are the true poor of our century. We are so lucky here.'

Edward is annoyed. 'Charles is not rootless. I didn't say that at all. I said that one should not think of him entirely as an Englishman because he lived abroad for most of his early life. Is there no other country in the world except England?'

'Of course there is. But you are English. Jane was English. Why should you not allow your sons to be the same? It is a denial of their parentage.'

'What do you mean, Martin?' asks Clara Horn, managing the General's first name with more confidence this time.

'What I say.'

Edward laughs. 'Jane was brought up abroad,' he says. 'Her father was a diplomat and they moved from place to place: France, Africa, the Middle East, Italy.'

'She was educated in England.'

'For a short time, yes. She also went to various English schools abroad: Paris, Tehran and Cairo, for instance. Why are you in such a xenophobic mood tonight?'

Now Martin's voice is quieter. 'I'm not. But our conversation brings back one aspect of that time. Nancy will bear me out. Remember how international you and Jane were then, how determined to break down the barriers between nations and peoples and languages and cultures. No, not to bring about uniformity. How furious Jane was when I accused her of that! She was like you, though. You both had this utopian concept of what you called "a more cooperative world". I wasn't surprised that you should think in this way, given the sort of work that you were engaged in for the Survey. All admirable, of course, Edward. I liked to talk to you about this, partly because at that stage I was so dissatisfied with what I was doing.' He has hardly touched his food. 'Yes, I envied you.' He turns to Rose. 'The Americans didn't really trust us. Charming people, of course.

66

We rarely saw the steel but when it came there was nothing you could do except snap to attention. And there was Edward preaching cooperation! Intoxicating stuff, especially if you'd just emerged from a good afternoon at the Pentagon. In the summer we had to play tennis with them as well, these brave boys of the New World, so if they hadn't got the message across to you in the office they bashed it into you on the court as well. Fifteen–love, thirty–love, forty–love: game, set and match! Ah what fun we had! And there was Edward preaching cooperation, not just between the two great nations of the English-speaking world as the Yanks used to say when they were being polite. No, not just between the two great nations of the English-speaking world, but everyone, the whole bloody lot!'

'Yes,' says Rose.

Martin Riley laughs. 'Edward and von Kierich. How should I explain Alex, Edward?'

'An international bureaucrat?' he suggests.

Martin shakes his head. 'No, not quite. It won't do, will it? Now Rose and Clara and Avril have a picture of a dull little man, grey, finicky, obsessed with ledgers and statistics and forms, skulking amongst filing-cabinets. No that won't quite do. Remember von Kierich's face: that reserve, the high eyebrows, the smooth, straight hair, the marked cheeks, those long, thin hands, the broken fingers. Think what he had seen, Edward. Was it this that gave him his force? Sometimes when he spoke I used to feel dumb, stupid! Bulldozed as well. Remember that, Edward?'

'I remember.'

'He must have been a brave man,' Rose says. She waits for more. Edward's hero is now the object of Martin's dislike, even hatred. Will she see virtue or wickedness?

'Was he a German?' asks Avril Horn.

'Oh yes.' Martin smiles. 'And a hero as well.'

Now Edward is angry. 'Look, Martin, you hardly knew Alex.'

67

'How well did you know him?'

'Is he still alive?' asks Rose. A child again, she dares not push too hard.

'Still alive?' Edward repeats her question as she slips back into his mind.

'You would know that, Edward,' Martin says. 'Is Alex von Kierich still alive? We were always told of his bad health: something to do with that time in prison. He must be old now, Edward – or perhaps not so old.' He starts to eat properly at last, quickly and greedily.

'Martin,' Nancy says. 'This is hardly the moment.'

Edward comes in now. 'Alex is still alive. He lives in a hotel in a small town in northern Germany. I had a letter from him recently.'

Martin's voice is almost a shriek. 'You still write to each other!'

'No. This came as a surprise. He wants me to visit him. I have decided to go.'

'When, Edward?' Nancy speaks as if he is a lunatic.

'On Friday.'

'To Germany?' she asks.

'Yes.'

Now Rose speaks from outside the circle of adult understanding. 'Will you go alone?' The words are crude, raw in the air, or so she feels.

'How else?' Then he thinks, To hell with this endless reticence. Suddenly the dream cracks open. 'Why don't you come with me?'

She blushes. 'Oh.' Then she sees: the man Alex is a grail, the end of a quest. Yes.

'Look, Edward.'

But Martin speaks too late because Nancy has already asked Rose when her term begins and the girl, anxious to escape, answers slowly but with great detail. Then, led by the Horn sisters, the whole party discusses the saintly last vicar, the Reverend Robert Padstow, Father Bobs, and the more modern style of his successor, the present incumbent, a man called Edge. So the evening drifts on, and at its end Edward says goodbye to Martin Riley, turning aside from his glare to kiss Nancy briefly on the cheek and Rose as well: the dry kisses of friendship.

Chapter Six

The next morning, Wednesday, Rose sits in silence, the dog Trixie at her feet, whilst her father talks to Mr Dove, a small thickset man with a round, smiling face who is to build and operate the new saw mill.

They are in the drawing-room of the manor, a dark-panelled oblong room with high white ceilings, and Sam Dove sits in an armchair clutching a glass of sherry in one of his huge red hands. Today he wears a tie and a grey suit, not the blue overalls in which he is usually to be seen.

'I hear they've started up a petition,' he says, his smile unctuous. 'Your family has done a lot for this village and got precious little gratitude in return, at least that's what I think, Sir James. Sometimes I'm ashamed to live here, make no mistake. How they can have voted that Peggy Upcher on to the council I don't know, and you standing against her. Colonel Heckstall I can understand. Now he was a gentleman. It was a fair contest between you and him and I was hard put to choose, but I voted for you, Sir James, even if you were standing as an Independent and I've been a Conservative all my life like my father before me. But Peggy Upcher! Peggy Wilson she used to be. I've known her family since I was a child and they lived at the top of Lawton Road. No good ever came out of a Wilson, we used to say.' Dove laughs, takes a sip of his sherry. He cannot quite conceal his distaste. 'But to get back to the vicar. He's certainly off to a good start with that money Lady Finch raised for the church, to help with the cost of modernizing the central-heating system. The Reverend Padstow was near to tears when he told me about it.'

Rose asks a question to stop Dove. She knows her father hates talking about money. 'Is the new vicar married?'

Dove looks at her, the smile condescending. 'Why yes, Rose, he is, or so Mrs Crick in the shop told me. His wife's been there already to speak about a weekly order. She says she wants to support the Cricks as much as possible and not drive into the Tesco like the rest of them.'

'What about the petition?' Rose asks.

'I know about the petition,' James Finch says, showing impatience at last.

'Well, Sir James, it's got up by the new people. The two Misses Horn who bought the old greengrocer's shop seem to be amongst the leaders, but I think it must be General Riley who's really behind it because he's very vociferous on the subject, as anyone will tell you who's heard him. Mrs Crick was saying that she mentioned the plans to him the other day and he gave her a lecture that held them all up in the shop for a good ten minutes. But it was the older Miss Horn who brought in the petition, all typed up on a big piece of paper. Mrs Crick said she couldn't have anything to do with it because someone in her position who relied on most of the village for custom couldn't be seen to take sides on a matter like this.'

'What does the petition say?' asks James Finch.

'Oh, it just says that all those who sign are against any further development in the village, in particular anything that would increase the number of heavy lorries coming in and out. I don't think the saw mill is mentioned by name, but you can see what it's all aimed at. Mrs Crick said the first sheet seemed to be covered with signatures already, and she spotted most of the names she expected to see like the Rileys and other new people.'

James Finch sighs. 'I asked Rose to be here because she often knows what goes on in the village better than I do. Frankly I'm too busy to keep in touch the way I should. She dined with the Rileys last night. Apparently the petition was mentioned but only in passing. The Horn sisters were there, both strongly against the saw mill. Where I think you may have made a mistake, Sam, is to have talked to the local paper.' He leans forward, his face tense. 'It's given them time to organize. If we'd stuck to the original idea of the meeting in the hall with you introducing the project to the village, there might have been none of this trouble. You could have stopped all these wild guesses about the increase in traffic.'

'Oh, Sir James, that's not quite true.' Dove laughs and then talks faster, as if in a panic. 'There will be a few extra lorry-loads coming in and out, and I'd be a liar if I didn't admit it. But when you weigh that up against the new jobs, it's nothing. You've always backed me up, Sir James. You said you were determined that the village should be a living community and not just a dormitory for rich outsiders. Those were your words. We all know you're not only doing this for the money and you preferred to deal with me because I come from a local family that's been in business here for several generations – well, since my old grandfather got out of farming just after the First War when he was one of your grandfather's tenants. It would have been your grandfather, wouldn't it? I'm going to say all that in the village hall on Thursday, Sir James, to show that you're doing what you and your family have always done: helping people here with little thought for yourselves. I'll start off with that, Sir James, after you've said your piece.'

'My piece?'

'Yes. You said you would introduce me to show that the idea has your support. I think that's very important, Sir James, if you'll forgive me saying so, for the village to know that a man of your standing is behind the scheme. After all, we don't want them to think it's just greedy old Sam Dove up to his usual tricks, do we?' Dove laughs and brings his great hands down sharply on the elbows of the armchair.

Then they hear Isabel Finch's voice. 'Still talking, darlings?' She enters the room in her old jeans, the long grey hair escaping in wisps from a loose knot at the back of her head: a woman of elderly grace. In one hand she has some letters, in the other a rose catalogue which she holds up. 'James, can I catch you for a moment? I want to put in an order.' Then she sees Dove who has got to his feet. 'Oh, Mr Dove, I am sorry.' She turns towards the door again. 'I'll come back later.'

'Isabel, listen!' James Finch shouts at her. 'Sam has been telling me about the petition.'

She hears a voice, stops, cannot quite make out whose it is and reaches up to her hearing-aid. 'You remember these catalogues, James. They send us one every year and Edward West was saying how good it is. I met him this morning outside the shop.' She smiles vaguely at Dove. 'The man who lives beside the church, next to the Rileys. You know the Rileys, Mr Dove: the General and his wife.'

'Isabel!' James Finch shouts again. 'The petition!'

Her hand drops to her side. 'Ah yes.' Again she smiles at Dove. 'Please sit down, Mr Dove. Here.' She sits on the sofa. 'Darling, I am sorry.'

'Did Edward West mention it this morning?' asks her husband, his voice quieter now.

'No.' Her mother turns to Rose, as Rose has suspected she would. 'Rose sees something of Edward, don't you, darling? Has he said anything to you?'

James Finch interrupts. 'They are trying to stop the new saw mill. It's a campaign led by Martin Riley and those Horn women.'

'The public meeting tomorrow might be rather stormy, Lady Finch, I'm afraid,' Dove says, raising his voice in deference to her well-known disability.

Isabel looks at Rose again. 'Darling, why not ask Edward what's going on?' Then she smiles at Dove. 'Nobody mentioned it last night at the Women's Institute when we heard Mrs Norton talk about her trip to the Holy Land. The Horn women weren't there, of course. Such evenings are not intellectual enough for their tastes!' The laugh is venomous. 'Jean Foxwell did say what a shame it was that the new vicar's wife hadn't come, particularly as the meeting had a religious flavour. Most unlike the Padstows who always took an interest. At the end of Mrs Norton's talk Mrs Crick came up to me and said how much Robert Padstow would have enjoyed it because he'd been to Jerusalem once.' Isabel Finch's face has assumed that courteous, rigid look. 'Don't you miss the Padstows, Mr Dove? He was such a good man.'

In desperation Dove takes another sip of sherry. 'The Reverend Padstow was an old-fashioned type,' he says.

'In the best sense,' says Isabel Finch. 'He was so brave after she died. They were very close, you know. He once told me that whilst it was sad they'd had no children, her health would never have stood the strain.' Here her mother glances at Rose. ' "But we have each other," he said and I nearly cried because this was when she was dying from that last illness. Poor man. Rose, darling, why not ask Edward West about the petition? He's very thick with the Rileys. Or ask Martin himself.' Rose thinks this is typical of her mother: the benign, vague chatter, then a flash of malice. Does she mean to embarrass her daughter? 'Surely it's not difficult to find out what's happening. If I'd known earlier, I would have mentioned it to Mrs Crick when I saw her this morning in the shop. She's my usual source of information about the village.' The invincible smile is still in place. 'Are you having lunch today, Rose?'

'Yes.'

'Well perhaps . . .' She stands and smooths her jeans down over her enviable hips. 'Don't let us disturb you, Mr Dove. James, you'll come through when you're finished, will you? Rose and I will get to work in the kitchen. Would you like to take pot luck with us, Mr Dove? It's only something cold, I'm afraid.'

Dove stands as well, bowing slightly to her. 'No, thank you, Lady Finch. I must be getting back.' He looks at his watch, then at James Finch who is also standing. 'If you'll excuse me, Sir James. I'll see you here tomorrow at seven o'clock before the meeting. If you need me in the meantime, I'll be in my office at Chilworth. The darkest hour before the dawn, eh? That's what they say.' He nods at Isabel. 'I must put my thinking cap on, Lady Finch. I've got to introduce our plans to the public tomorrow. Mustn't put my old foot in it, must I?'

'Introduce!' Isabel laughs, that same belittling sound. 'There's not much need to introduce the plans as they've been all over the local paper. How ever did they get in there, Mr Dove?'

Dove looks to Sir James for help, but Rose's father says nothing and he is on his own. 'Well, Lady Finch, I briefed one of their reporters myself, if you must know. He's a decent boy, responsible for the news from this village, so I thought it best to let him see exactly what we had in mind so as to stop the stupid rumours. He gave us a good hearing.'

'He certainly did!' Isabel Finch says.

'That's fair enough, Isabel,' her husband says. 'There's not much going on at the moment.'

'Do you think so?' She smiles again at Rose. 'Coming through?' So, followed by the little dog Trixie, they leave the two men and walk along the passage, into the dark-panelled dining-room, which is not used now except for the occasional rare party, across the stone-paved hall into another short passage that leads to the modern kitchen. On the way Isabel Finch looks over her shoulder and says to Rose, 'Did you know about this petition?' and Rose answers that she has heard of it, but that is all and they begin to lay up the kitchen table.

'There's bad feeling in the village, isn't there?' her mother says. She gets a lettuce out of the fridge and breaks it up before washing the pieces in the sink. Rose watches the sharp, strong movements of her hands. 'Fetch the ham, will you, Rose? It's downstairs in the larder. Mrs Marsden must have forgotten to bring it up.'

A woman comes to the manor house every morning from the village to make the beds and clean the rooms but her kitchen duties are unclear because Sir James and Lady Finch do not like binding arrangements. So Rose goes back to the short passage into the hall, to the right into what used to be the pantry and is now a storeroom for pairs of boots, stout walking shoes and thick jackets and overcoats hanging on pegs like strung-up corpses, and then down a short, narrow flight of stairs into the old stone-flagged kitchen. Light comes only from small, high windows set just below the ceiling; she is now in the basement of the house, once the servants' domain. Trixie, who has come with her, raises her head, sniffs the air, then follows her mistress into the cool larder, a huge, dark room. Here Rose finds a large ham under a dome-shaped mesh cover on a marble shelf. Rose lifts the cover off and carries the ham upstairs to find her mother searching through one of the drawers. Isabel Finch looks angrily at her.

'Where's the carving knife?' she says. 'Did you look in the larder? Oh no, I've got it.' She holds up the long knife as if threatening her daughter. 'When do you feed that dog? Are you sure you're giving it enough? When it lives with Mrs

Dawes at the farm whilst you're away, it looks much fatter. I've noticed that. Do you want to make the salad dressing? The oil and vinegar are over there.' Isabel Finch points to a shelf. 'No, I'll do it.' She looks at Rose as she stirs the mixture in a cup. 'What do you think of Mr Dove? He's done well for himself, hasn't he?' Isabel Finch starts to turn the salad slowly. 'You know James has never liked tomatoes. Odd, isn't it? Not even those little cherry ones. All my married life I've never been allowed to have tomatoes in the salad.' With a final, brisk movement she finishes. 'The vet's coming at half past two to look at that new mare. We'd better start. James won't be long.' Now she speaks of him as James to Rose, not Dad or Daddy, perhaps a sign that she no longer thinks of her as a child.

They each carve pieces off the ham, Isabel Finch first, and sit at the table on either side of the place at the head which is kept for Sir James. Rose shouts at Trixie, who is edging towards the door.

'You feed it scraps mostly, don't you?' her mother asks. 'The dog, I mean. It looks awfully thin. Don't take anything from the larder, will you? Mrs Marsden was saying yesterday that she couldn't find the remains of Sunday's leg of lamb. Did Trixie get it?'

'No.'

'Lucy rang this morning. She sounded very cheerful!' Her mother's words are a reproach. 'Mike has been asked to advise on a garden in Devon, so they want to come for the weekend on their way there.' Isabel Finch taps the catalogue which she has put by her place. 'I must ask him about Edward's rose people.' She laughs. 'It can be useful to have a garden designer as a son-in-law.' She pushes away her plate. As usual she has eaten sparely and fast. 'Mike and Lucy could have children now because he's beginning to get much more work. I wonder why they're waiting. I don't like to ask. Has Lucy said anything to you about it, darling?

How old is she now? Twenty-three?' She reaches for an apple from the bowl of fruit in the centre of the table and bites noisily into it. 'Jack's always late and if I'm not there the vet won't know which animal to look at. Wait for James, will you? He'll want to talk about what Dove has told him. Then you'd better put the ham back downstairs because it's cooler and there's no room in the fridge. Hector may ring to say if he and Emily are coming for the weekend as well. What does he do at work? I can never get him at his office.' She puts her hand up to her ear, about to turn off her hearing-aid.

'Mum.' Rose says the word and the hand stops level with her mother's brown, strangely unlined cheek.

'Yes?'

'Edward West's wife died in a car crash, didn't she?' Rose waits, imagining a woman's body taut after the terrifying sound before softening limply, blood pouring from the lifeless head which bleeds even after death (or so she has read); Edward at her side thrown forward also, turning to look for his beautiful wife through the spray of smashed glass; then the wind in a huge empty space, a survivor's solitude. 'It must have been terrible,' she hears herself whisper.

Isabel Finch looks steadily at her daughter. 'Yes, darling.'

'Did you know her?'

'Don't you remember Jane West? Perhaps you're too young.' Her mother drinks some water and wipes her mouth with a paper napkin. 'They weren't here so much in those days because Edward had that job in Washington. But we used to meet them sometimes with Martin and Nancy. You know Martin tried to commute from here when he was still in the army, working in the Ministry of Defence in London! That was before the high-speed trains. He was absolutely whacked by Friday. Eventually Nancy made him spend a couple of nights a week at the barracks or something.' Isabel Finch laughs. 'Don't forget about the ham.'

'What was Jane West like?' asks Rose.

'Dark. Good-looking. Rather affected, or so I thought. A nervous person. Edward seemed anxious to protect her. Her father was a diplomat, you know: the ambassador in Rome. Edward comes from a more humble background.' She raises her hand again, then lets it drop. 'Darling, do you see Edward often now?'

'Occasionally.'

'You go to the theatre together, don't you?'

'Yes.'

'Don't you find him rather uncommunicative? What do you talk about?'

Rose thinks what will sound best. 'The work he did in Africa and India and places like that.'

'I can't get much out of him.' Now Isabel Finch reaches up to her hearing-aid. 'The poor man must be lonely. Don't you agree? I suppose he has the house and garden to keep up. Nancy Riley tells me that he goes to conferences and meetings in London from time to time. But that can't be enough. He's still an active man. At least he doesn't get involved in village politics like Martin. I know James is upset by that. Try to comfort him during lunch, darling, will you? I must be on my way.' She pats the side of her ear and leans forward in her chair, as if about to stand up.

Rose speaks quickly. 'I'm going to London tomorrow.'

Her hearing-aid off now, Isabel Finch stays seated, a frown on her face. 'What did you say, darling?'

'I'm going to London tomorrow.' This time Rose shouts, shocked at the power of her voice.

Her mother has turned her aid back on and winces at the noise. 'Will you stay the night with Mike and Lucy? Let me know because of planning for meals and so on.'

'No. I'll get the train back.' Now she says it, a small statement of daring. But the words seem without resonance, suddenly limp and tame. 'I'm having lunch with Ben.'

Isabel Finch smiles faintly, as if acknowledging distant applause. 'How lovely.' She stands and in an almost flamboyant gesture turns off her hearing-aid before leaving the room.

Chapter Seven

Edward waits in his living-room for the rain to stop so that he can go into the garden again.

He was excited last night in a way he had not been for some time, suddenly asking that girl to come with him to Germany. The loss of restraint, the return of youth: it had happened twice now in the last week, as on Sunday after dinner on the terrace of the manor, facing the tall yew hedges across the lawn with James and Isabel's guests.

Now the itch returns, this time the memory of a Washington night: Jane and he in their bedroom. 'Will you ask Alex round again, Edward?' she said. 'Who could we have with him? Perhaps he would rather be alone: I mean with us but no other guests.' She laughed as if to herself. 'Will you ask him or shall I?'

She reached for the zip of her pale red dress. 'Edward, can you help?' As the silk parted, he kissed her soft skin, felt a sharp tightening of her shoulders. 'Do you want to see other women, Edward? I think I could understand. No, it would hurt me. Is that selfish? Oh darling.' That sigh, the shrug, a lowered dress, the way he might pull her down: then those recollected barriers, the turned shoulder, a long back, her fragile neck glimpsed through the thick brown hair, the wall of her sleep, those morning moves to escape his love. 'Edward.' She turned, letting the dress fall, her small breasts outlined under her slip. 'I can't now.' He brought her closer, moving his mouth to hers. She tried to comply, the resistance buried, the feat of will a reproach in itself.

Now he hears the telephone.

'Edward? It's Nancy here.' He waits. 'I'm sorry. Have I rung at a bad time?'

'No.'

'Look, I want to talk to you. Don't worry. I won't mention the saw mill. That's not my affair. Martin had to leave early this morning to catch the London train. He won't be back until late: some meeting at the home for retired officers. You're going away, aren't you?'

'Yes. Tomorrow.'

'Where?'

'To London. Don't you remember, Nancy? I told you.'

'Of course you did. Well, what about this evening?'

'Shall I come round?' he asks.

She waits before answering, then speaks awkwardly, like an unskilled liar. 'Look, I told the vicar I'd take my turn at doing the flowers in the church this week. Why don't we meet there in about an hour's time?'

Edward feels hurt. She does not want him in her house or not yet: a small gesture of disapproval, even dislike. Had he spoken too strongly last night? It is Alex again, the great divide, the cause of this loneliness in his heart. He laughs, a natural defence. 'In the church? That's a bit public, isn't it?'

'We could go for a walk outside.'

'Why do you want to see me, Nancy?'

'I can't talk about it over the telephone. Edward . . .' She stops. 'No, come to the church in about an hour. There's never anyone else there. Will you do that? You are good. Goodbye.'

Chapter Eight

The sun catches a brass memorial in the church, leaving the armorial hatchments of the Finch family dark against the pale walls where windows of Victorian stained glass depict boyish saints, a bearded Christ, heroic angels victorious over Satan's legions. Flowers decorate the nave: some vases of chrysanthemums, hybrid tea roses, sprigs of hazel, green foliage as a background.

At first Edward cannot find Nancy. Then he looks to the right, into a side chapel, and sees her bare plump arms through a lattice screen. She is putting some pink roses into a vase on a small altar. He walks up the aisle; she looks round. 'What do you think?'

'Are they from your garden?' he asks.

'Where else?'

'Do you still have a rota? People bring whatever they can, or so I seem to remember from when Jane was involved.' He speaks quickly at first, then she laughs and he slows down, relieved that she seems to bear no grudge or anger towards him at all.

'Oh yes. When it's their turn to do the flowers, they ransack their garden but not when it's anyone else's. There's a certain amount of competition, I'm afraid.'

He laughs as well. 'What about you?'

'Oh I don't mind. Nor did Jane. We tried to help each other.'

'So who competes?'

'The Miss Horns?' Nancy suggests. 'They used to be

desperate for praise from Robert Padstow. Imagine the absurdity of it!'

'And from the new vicar as well?'

'He probably hasn't had time to break any hearts yet.' She comes down the two steps from the small altar, smooths the front of her dress and stands beside him. Her face is bright in the sunless chapel. 'I'm sorry about last night.'

'Is that what you wanted to say to me?'

'A part of it.' She rubs hands together as if feeling the cold. 'No, Edward, I hate seeing Martin like that: so overbearing.'

'He was upset. I don't mind, Nancy.' He goes further, still slightly anxious. 'It was probably my fault. I don't mind at all.'

'I do.' Her voice tightens.

'I should be used to it by now!' He quickly recalls a harmless example of Martin's temper. 'Do you remember that time in America when Jane took the wrong turning off the highway to Virginia Beach and we had to go miles out of our way?' Nancy had been in tears that day.

'He never shouted at Jane, Edward. I had to bear the brunt that time because I was supposed to be reading the map. Don't you remember? A wife's duty, perhaps.' Nancy's voice is loud now in the emptiness of the church. 'No, Martin would never have shouted at Jane. He put her up there, right on a pedestal.' She points to a wooden crucifix on the wall. 'Jane could do no wrong.' This time her look is one of conspiratorial shrewdness. 'That's why he hates the thought of you seeing Alex von Kierich again.' She comes closer to him. 'Shall we talk outside?'

He thinks quickly. 'No, I'm sure we're safe here. Why not sit down?'

They are next to each other in the first of three rows of chairs, Nancy's flower basket on the stone floor beside her. 'You don't know how anxious he is to protect her, even after her death,' she says.

84

He turns away. 'They were friends, of course. We all were at that time: you and Jane, Martin and me.'

'And Alex?'

'Not like that, Nancy. I worked for him.'

'More like master and pupil? Or should I say disciple?'

'Martin didn't like him.'

She looks up at the altar. 'It was the vanity Martin couldn't stand. You didn't mind that, Edward, did you? I suppose it went with the fanaticism: the sense of there being no limits, if you see what I mean. The way Alex thought he could behave. Quite inhuman really, deciding to lead that monkish existence, dedicating himself to the general good of humanity to the exclusion of any personal life. Or almost any.' Her face goes even redder.

'Alex had friends,' he says.

'Who?'

'There were people in Germany. Other survivors of the resistance.'

'Did you meet them?'

'No. But he spoke sometimes of this sense of comradeship. They must have supported him when he had to leave Munich.'

'Do you know that?' Nancy asks. 'Do you know who they are?'

'Retired officers, civil servants, diplomats. Most of those involved were either executed or have died since. It was a long time ago. Not many escaped, you know. Over four thousand people were rounded up, interrogated, tortured and murdered. Some broke. Then they found lists of names. That's how Alex was incriminated.'

She brings a hand down on her knee. 'I know.'

'Don't you believe it?'

'It's been written about, hasn't it?' She laughs. 'Not that I've read any of the books. And you never met these former comrades?'

Suddenly he is angry. 'How could I have met them? I worked for him in Washington. We travelled together, but always on business. You know what a solitary person he was: the way he liked to divide his life into different parts, only occasionally bringing up the past in conversation or stories of what he had experienced. When he went home on leave, to his sisters or family, he saw his friends, or so I imagine.' He pauses, searching for more ammunition. 'Some of the survivors lived in Munich. That was why Alex went there when he left the Survey.'

'Would he have left the Survey if the rumours hadn't started to circulate?'

He lies. 'Probably.'

'Then he had to resign from his job in Munich.'

'He retired.'

'Retired!'

'Alex was quite old by then, Nancy. You must remember that.'

'Was he?' Nancy speaks fast now, her breath coming quickly. 'The point is that Martin knows something else.'

'Martin?'

'Yes.' She seems upset as she stares at the plain glass window above the altar. 'He won't tell me.'

'What has he said, Nancy?'

'My husband is tolerant on the whole, Edward.' Nancy laughs. 'He has these fits of temper, it is true, but then the incident is over. Often Martin will admit later that he was wrong. With Alex it is different, as if a curtain has fallen. That's why he can't bear the thought of you going to see the man again, to drag up the past. Martin is very loyal, Edward: loyal to his old friends. He doesn't want to see you hurt. Then of course there is the business with Jane.' Now she seems angry. 'What will your beloved Alex say about that?'

He lies again. 'I won't ask him.'

'Why go, then?'

'To see an old friend before he dies. You seem to forget what we went through together.'

'Don't go, Edward.'

He stands up. 'Is that all?'

'You're not listening to me.'

'I am.'

She holds out a hand. He takes it, remembering that her knees can be stiff now. They walk together down the aisle towards the door of the church and out into the brilliant day, pausing at the lych gate built as a memorial to those killed in the First World War. 'So tomorrow you will go to London,' Nancy says. 'Is it work?'

'Not really. Lunch with an old friend from the days in Rome. He worked briefly in Washington, then went back. Do you remember him?'

Nancy laughs. 'I might if you tell me what he's called.'

Another sign of a failing mind. Edward looks away from her, embarrassed. 'Bill. Bill Higginson.'

Now it is her turn to seem vague. 'I recall the name but not the face.'

'Bill didn't stay in Washington for long.'

She smiles briskly. 'You are right to go to London. One must keep busy. Martin believes that and says it often.'

So this is how the Rileys talk when they are alone together: the brainless patter of retirement, a twittering at dusk. Suddenly he wants to be rid of them, to run from this small, solid world; then the fierce wish dies with the hardness of the village pavement and her pitying farewell look.

Chapter Nine

Later, sitting alone, Edward remembers how Alex von Kierich had spoken of his childhood.

'What innocence there was then, Edward! Our village, for example, and the lands which surrounded it: the woods and fields, the forests with their larks and nightingales in summer, the people of that place. It was beautiful. The little festivals, gatherings at local inns, excuses for merry-making: those sounds!' Alex tapped his forehead. 'Once I heard them on an evening ride home from my cousin's house with my father in the October twilight, the air sharp, the trees dark along the path. Then came the noise from the village: an accordion, voices singing some song of the fields. My father joined in, just a few lines. When we returned, my mother and the girls were waiting, worried for we were late. My father kissed her, speaking of the other guests and how hard it had been to leave.'

Alex did not often summon up these memories: only occasionally, like that night over Africa.

'My father went often to Berlin. He would be driven to the station for the train, elegant in his dark greatcoat with the astrakhan collar in winter, a pale suit in summer. He had friends in official circles, people in the ministries or old men who had retired to pleasant villas in the suburbs, diplomats perhaps. His sympathies were cosmopolitan. He always said that if the estate had not come his way he would have liked to have been a diplomat, and I think maybe he had this vision of himself as ambassador perhaps in Rome or Paris or London, comfortable in the salons of Mayfair or the Faubourg Saint Germain.' Alex smiled, the scars tightening beneath his eyes. 'My father lacked courage. He was lazy. His position might have given him some influence.'

So he had unrolled his early life: the innocence and family love mixed with those ancient rites of aristocratic pleasure, like the shooting days when guests came from all over Germany to kill the game in the eastern woods and forests: 'A sportsman's paradise,' Alex said. Better perhaps were the evenings when he and his father or a cousin or neighbour waited for geese or duck in the twilight beside one of the nearby lakes, each alone at his stand. This killing too seemed an essential part of childhood, followed later by the tests of courage at university in a select student corps where they fenced with bare sabres until blood flowed 'in great rivers' or drank riotously to reach some fantastic idea of manliness. The scars on Alex's cheek came from this time, evidence that he had survived with honour.

Alex had wanted to be strong. Sometimes the military ideal seemed to possess him and he spoke metaphorically of bravery, resistance, the taking up of arms, the need for loyalty of course but independence too, as in the case of General von Yorck who had defied the orders of the King of Prussia and led his army against Napoleon. Yet during the war Alex had been kept out of the forces by his work in the Foreign Office and a slight weakness of the chest. Edward thought of his own childhood asthma, also gone. They had both always been civilians, observers of battle.

The glimpses of intimacy were confusing. It was hard to know if the German wanted expressions of sympathy, concern or just a silent audience, an excuse to listen to himself. Of course he was not alone. People visited him in Washington, women sometimes whom Edward saw at parties or

heard Alex refer to, Germans or Austrians, presumably
unattached, often travelling with one of his sisters: the tall,
fair Fredericka or the shorter, dark Josephine. For holidays
he returned to Europe, perhaps to the opera at Salzburg or a
trip to the Italian Alps, presumably at ease there with those
of his own kind. Once Alex had said that Germans do not
generally like foreigners; their history makes such relationships difficult, yet some view the winning of the trust of a
person who is not German as a triumph: a small victory
over the grim past. 'What conceit!' Alex had observed,
laughing. 'Really we are intolerable.'

There seemed often to be a sense of isolation, a disappointment perhaps that he could not achieve this particular
conquest. In the office he was remote, always correct,
invariably amiable. The bachelor apartment where he lived
appeared to reflect a barren personal life. It was in a grim
block on Q Street, the bare cream walls of the sitting-room
like a doctor's surgery, charmless and unloved; hard rented
furniture, uncomfortable chairs, a high bookcase filled with
German, French and English books, mostly poetry and the
classics, the photograph albums stacked flat on the lower
shelf. The only opulent feature was thick wall-to-wall carpet-
ing, the colour of plain chocolate: ugly and rich.

Alex scarcely ever asked anyone into this place, reluctantly
offering a quick drink sometimes as a reward for a lift
home. Then he might show Edward the albums, a substitute
perhaps for the company of that old, dead world. As they
turned the pages, seated next to each other on the bleak
sofa, the German kept up a quiet commentary, pointing first
to the early scenes – the long, grey classical house, his tall
bearded father, the strange formality of his mother's clothes,
Hindenburg emerging from church, he and his sisters seated
on their ponies – then passing to his student life, the time at
Cambridge, Berlin under the Nazis, the post-war years
hardly mentioned until his arrival in Washington and a new

job. There was a photograph of some of the conspirators of 1944, apparently carefree, laughing at their friend. Always Alex praised their courage, now known to the rest of the world. What a loss! So much had been destroyed, yet to regret this is futile, senseless, almost contemptible. Or so the German believed.

The days in Africa had shown so much, yet the mystery remains.

Edward remembers the aeroplane landing, the wheels on the runway, the burst of clapping from some passengers. 'We are on time,' Alex said. 'Nils will be waiting': Nils Thalberg, the Norwegian who represented the Survey in this part of the world.

In the small airport building, a queue formed at the barrier: two nuns in their white habits, some Africans, an Asian man and wife (she holding a sleeping baby against her bright sari), four or five Europeans. Thalberg, made conspicuous by his height and tanned fair head, had pushed through, waved past by an official. 'I telephoned the Ministry of the Interior,' he said. 'The regime is nervous because of the rebels. Now let us collect the cases. I have made a similar arrangement with the customs. The car is outside. The journey into town should be quicker than usual. This evening there are no road blocks. Come.'

In Thalberg's car, on the main highway, the Norwegian answered Alex's questions. The rebels had support in the north. The more populous south was still loyal to the president. The army seemed reliable. The big project in which the Survey was involved – an irrigation scheme two hundred miles from the capital – had been untouched by the troubles. He would drive them there the next day. 'Will you come in?' Alex said at the large, modern hotel.

The three of them had sat up late in the deserted bar, staring at charts and plans, comparing the figures.

Eventually Thalberg left; they put away the briefing papers. Through the open doors of the half-lit room Edward could see two Africans seated at the desk in the lobby, one tapping his hand in time to the faint piped music. There were no drinks available. He felt very tired. Then Alex asked about Jane: that strange, quick torrent of words.

'Does she mind you coming on these expeditions, Edward? Can you leave her and the children, knowing that she will be able to cope? You need not worry from the practical point of view; I am sure she is a most resourceful wife and mother. No, I mean will she miss you? Here is the conundrum. If Jane is unhappy whilst you are away, how can you know? Only if she makes each departure an agony, which I am sure she does not because she is aware of your professional duties. Perhaps she tells you when you return how much she has missed you. Her voice may even break as she says this. Does it upset her, Edward?' Alex raised one hand, the mutilated fingers bent into its palm. 'I have no such problems, either of missing or of being missed, as one might say. Is this an advantage, do you think? Perhaps such a condition is hard to imagine for someone like you. When did you marry?' Alex lowered his hand. 'Edward, think of your family. You have something to bind you close to this earth. Do you see what I mean? Jane's feelings, the boys, their excitement when their father comes home. What will you buy them here? The memento does not matter. They will be pleased with anything. I like your children, Edward. And Jane is beautiful, so lively. You are a lucky man.' Alex laughed. 'We should go to bed. Tomorrow Nils will give us a full day.'

In the morning Nils Thalberg drove them away from the hotel, Alex von Kierich in the front of the car, Edward behind with two briefcases full of papers. 'Such space!' Alex said as they sped towards a brilliant sun. 'One sees this nowhere but in Africa.' The talk flagged; the preparatory

92

work had been done. Soon they were in a huge, flat wilderness, Thalberg driving fast until the highway turned into a rough dirt road where the country closed in on them, becoming dense with vegetation, small trees, prickly bushes, the earth brown, sometimes grey through clouds of dust against a vast blue sky.

It was so quick. As the car came out of a long wide bend, Thalberg turned towards Alex, as if to speak, and Edward saw the oil drums and branches across the road ahead, the armed men, one raising a hand. 'Stop!' The car accelerated, Thalberg called out, 'Get down!' The first crack came when they hit one of the drums, then a second and a third and finally the shots, a short roar as the car swung right, pitched slightly, stopped at last, its engine dead, the only sound a man's cry.

He felt the pain in his forehead where it had hit the window: not yet unbearable, just a harsh ache. Thalberg's body covered the steering-wheel, a huge wound below one ear, the clear, tanned upper face almost unmarked by the thickening blood on his neck.

A voice said, 'Get out.'

Beside the road, they faced the men, black figures in faded khaki, some wearing caps or berets: the costume of a guerrilla army. One pushed Edward towards the front of the crushed car where Alex stood, his white shirt marked with Thalberg's blood. The leader was thin, the makeshift uniform loose on him, his eyes bright in a strong, sharp face. In one hand he had a pistol. 'Who are you?' Alex asked.

The thin man stepped forward. 'We are soldiers.'

Three men lifted Nils Thalberg out of the car. Alex bowed slightly. 'Let me see my friend.' The thin African gestured with his pistol and the German walked to where Thalberg lay on the grass. He knelt beside the body. 'You have killed him.' The leader came across, his pistol pointing downwards. The African spoke to his men, who began to lift Thalberg again. 'Wait!' Alex shouted. 'What are you doing?'

The pistol was raised. 'Come with us.'

Edward spoke at last. 'Who are you?'

Alex turned in surprise, as if he had forgotten him. 'I demand that you show us your authorization,' he said loudly. 'We are representatives of an international body, travelling in this country as guests of your government.'

'What government?' asked the African. He started to laugh. 'Will we drive in your car?' he asked, the voice gentler than Alex's. He pointed at the vehicle, the buckled wheels, the smashed windscreen and windows, the chassis holed by bullets. 'We have nothing else. You must walk. You and he.' The man pointed at Edward. 'Come.'

After a few hundred yards, the leader told the men to put Thalberg down. Already they were enclosed by the bush's dense scrub, on a path of sorts, almost invisible. Edward looked behind him at Alex to see that long face still apparently calm, and they walked on, leaving Thalberg behind on the hard cracked ground. Soon his head started to hurt so much that he knew he must stop even if they decided to leave him here, a few yards from Thalberg who was dead. Then he fell.

Chapter Ten

He woke in the cool of a hut.

'Edward?' Alex was beside him. 'They are outside. At least we have been left alone. Have some water.' He drank from the wooden cup. 'Is it your head that hurts?' The German's hand felt light on his forehead, oddly dry in the heat. 'You hit it when the car crashed. They carried you and I walked. We are approximately an hour from the road.'

'What about . . .?' The name had gone.

'Nils Thalberg?'

'Yes.'

'He is dead.' Alex said the word softly. 'They shot him. The body has been left near the road, not very far into the bush. Nils is our best hope now, Edward. A search party will be sent out when we do not arrive at the dam. The wreck of the car is still there, then the tracks into the bush. The path could be followed by anyone acquainted with this part of the country. Meanwhile I have had a talk with our kidnappers. The leader is quite articulate. An intelligent man, I should guess. He says his group is an offshoot of the rebels, attached to them yet independent. Tonight they will decide what to do. It may mean more walking, Edward. How do you feel?'

'Too weak. Leave me behind.'

'You must try.'

'Leave me.'

'Where, Edward?' Alex's voice was still low.

'Here. Anywhere.' He tried to laugh. 'I might be found by your search party.'

'Our captors will not want that. You will tell what has happened. At least Nils cannot talk because he is dead. No, we are hostages now.'

'When will they move us?'

'I don't know.' Alex stared at him, his hair erect like parched grass, the white, hairless, blue-veined skin of his chest visible through a torn blood-spattered shirt. 'You must try to walk when the time comes, Edward. They will help you because we are valuable to them. I have tried to convince their chief of that. You must not allow yourself to collapse. It is a question of will.'

Alex turned towards the entrance of the hut where a uniformed African had come in, a gun slung over his shoulder. The African gave two bowls to Alex who had stood up. 'Water?' The African pointed to the bucket on the bare ground. Alex nodded and the man took the bucket out of the hut to return soon with it full. Neither of the prisoners spoke until the guard had gone.

Then Alex said, 'You must eat some of it, Edward.'

He sat up, formed a thick ball in his fingers from the maize porridge. Almost immediately he felt a sharp nausea and had just enough strength to turn away to the dirt floor beyond his blanket before lying back with that same sense of lightness, almost disembodied. Then Alex's voice again. 'They want me now. Lie here. Try to rest until I return.' So he had slept, waking at dusk to find the German beside him.

'Did you see them?'

'Yes, Edward.'

'I feel better.' He raised himself on one elbow. 'Is it dark outside?'

'Almost.'

'What did he say?'

Alex laughed. 'It doesn't matter.'

'Why not?'

'It doesn't matter about your sickness. You can stay here.

We are all staying here. There will be no ordeal of a walk through the bush.'

'Is that all?'

'All of what?'

'That he said.'

'Oh Edward.' Alex smiled and shook his head. 'You should be pleased. There are no more worries. Look, the night is here. Can you see the sky?'

'No.'

Edward tried to stand, raising the top part of his body. Alex restrained him with his arm. 'Don't move now. It is not good for you. Here, some water.' He passed the full cup. 'Take more. I was wrong. Of course you should stand. Do you want to go to the toilet? The guard will come as well, but he waits some distance away. Let us go out together. I can help you: like this.' He held out a thin arm, torn white strips of shirt hanging from his shoulder. Edward got up slowly, frightened that he might pull Alex over, trying to take all his weight on himself yet in need of support until he stood in the hut.

Alex's thin, scarred face was close. 'Here.' At the entrance, as they came out, two guards moved quickly against the background of the huts and a night sky crowded with stars. They were in some kind of small settlement, an outpost in the bush. 'Now, Edward, go forward a little so that you are on your own. Can you manage? Come back to me here when you have finished. Take your time.'

Back in the hut it seemed darker than before. Edward lay down again, still weak, von Kierich sitting beside him, his face a grey outline. 'Do you think they are looking already?'

Alex laughed. 'In the dark?'

'They must know.'

'Oh yes. Nils is our best hope. The trail should be obvious from his body. There will be a row.' Alex's voice was low, discreet. 'We were given no protection. After all, we are like diplomats, you know, and should have been treated in the same way.'

'It's a bit late to insist upon protocol.'

'Is it?' He felt tired, almost slept until roused by that same soft voice. 'What about this, Edward? Tomorrow morning when the sun gets up you and I may be shot.'

'What?'

'It is a possibility.'

'Did they tell you?'

'No. The man asked me about the Survey. He was interested. But the moment they decide we are in their way and no longer useful, they may kill us.' Edward felt a hand on his shoulder as Alex's outline moved. 'Please, Edward. We have all night. Shall we talk a little? What are you thinking about? Yourself? Your family? Jane and the children?'

'Yes.'

'At least you have them.'

'Alex, why didn't you marry?'

Then he heard that dry laugh. 'It was not right.'

'Why?'

'I made a vow, Edward, after what I had seen. Do you want to know? Why not? Then you can say what you like to me. Perhaps this is better than the presence of a priest.' Now the laugh was louder. 'How you would hate to have a priest here, Edward! No, it must be hard for you. For instance, I am consoled by the fact that tomorrow, if we die, I will face my God and he will judge me in the way He thinks fit, with mercy, knowing all that has happened inside and outside of myself; whereas for you there is no idea of the soul or immortality or eternity, simply oblivion joined now with a fear of what is to come, a fear which makes no sense. Why should we be frightened of nothingness, the end of our conscience, our understanding, all that civilization has taught us to cherish? Why? What do you think, Edward?'

'I don't know.'

'Come, you can tell me now. But I will not press you. Why should I torment a friend at this moment? That would be unfair and ridiculous, futile as well. Listen, should we make a run for it in the dark? Try to sneak out past the sentries? If they shoot it will not matter because tomorrow the end might come in any case. Is that a good idea? No. You are too weak after the accident. Better stay here and hope that we will survive. We should stand our ground. You know, I learnt that at an early age in my student days in Göttingen when I was in one of those clubs. Duels were still fought then although they had been forbidden by law. I have the scars. At Göttingen I stood my ground, but not so well later.'

'That is over.'

'Is it?'

'Yes.'

'Perhaps not for me.' The German sighed, then seemed to have a new burst of energy. 'Let me take you back to when I was working in our Foreign Office in Berlin, during the war: those long brown passages of the Wilhelmstrasse, worse than where we are today in Washington and always with not enough light because of the wartime economies. We were an odd team, most of us young ones in my section against the regime but patriotic Germans all the same: this you should remember. We worked hard, of course, often in bad conditions. Later there were air raids most days and nights, a sense too that the first triumphs were a false guide and we were gradually to be forced back on to the horror and cruelty of what had been done. Then I felt I was living some kind of fable, not part of the real world but an example to humanity of what man can be if the restraints of humanist or Christian civilization are removed. In this, Edward, some things happened to me which I want to explain. Will you listen? It is quite simple.'

'Simple?' He echoed the word, a meek whisper.

'Yes. What do you know about me? How much? Let me tell you my first memory. This may give you some idea of what I was. I have this picture in my mind of a huge old man in a grey uniform, wearing one of those spiked helmets that the military had in those days, a huge man not walking so much as shuffling out of the door of the church at home, escorted by the much smaller figure of my mother in a long, dark dress, carrying a parasol, her head covered by one of those great, absurd hats which were the fashion. It was Hindenburg, the Field Marshal, on leave after his victory over the Russians: one of my heroes, there as our guest. The day was bright, as so often in the east. The great man waved to the crowd who had gathered in the village street as he and my mother walked to the car that would take us back to the house. Yet here is a joke!' Alex let out a hoot of laughter, loud through the night.

'Listen, Edward, the memory is impossible. The visit of Hindenburg took place in 1915, the year I was ill in hospital for much of the time with that lung trouble which was the curse of my childhood. So I was not there. How could I possibly recall anything about it, not even the vaguest picture of the people by the church gate, certainly not the shape of my mother's hat? No, it is in my head because of a photograph, one large photograph that used to stand on top of the grand piano in the drawing-room at home. Now I have it in one of my albums. Do you remember? I must have stared so many hours at that photograph, almost as many as I listened to the account of the Field Marshal's stay from my parents: everything he had said, almost every movement. He came only for one night, brought by a neighbour who was a close friend. I know all this. I can see him clearly yet I could not have seen him. Hindenburg was so much a part of my childhood, so much in the talk at home. He was a hero for us: for me an inherited hero because I never saw him in spite of his presence in my imagination as a concept of honour, strength, an abiding integrity.' The laugh came, followed by an outburst of coughing, a doubling-up of the thin figure in the dark, until Alex straightened and resumed the story in the same soft voice. 'Now, Edward, let us move on. Hindenburg, this icon of my childhood, is gone, dead, his tomb erected near Tannenberg, and I am in Berlin, in the Wilhelmstrasse, when the next great excitement comes, the next personal earthquake.

'Many of us joined the army before the war. By doing that you could avoid becoming a member of the Nazi party, which was more or less compulsory if you were involved in any other kind of service to the State. But because of my health problems it was decided that I should try for the Foreign Office. My languages and talents such as they were seemed to be suited to the work. It was also what my father wanted me to do as an attempt perhaps to make amends for the impossibility of fulfilling his own diplomatic ambitions! Then my friends said, Yes, this will be a good idea, to have one of us in the Foreign Office to see what is going on and help hasten the end of this foolery. Although they had become soldiers in the way of our caste, it was by no means certain that a war would come. In a way I was glad to be a bureaucrat. The army was quite full of itself then because it had so much more money and arms: not like under Weimar when all its glory seemed to lie somewhere with Hindenburg in the past.' Alex's breathing slowed and the tone became softer. 'No, Edward, these Africans will not kill us. I do not believe it.'

'Were you frightened during the war?'

'Yes. But I was not alone. We shared our knowledge of the resistance to Hitler: I and my friends. This was what bound us together. I was very young. My part in it was not of great significance, but I was there and this makes me feel proud. The hatred had gone deep into me. Here we must go back further to a trip I made for my masters in the Wilhelm-strasse, well, not my true masters, Ribbentrop and his cronies, but others who were also against the regime and wished to find out what was really happening in the conquered territories in the east and if the rumours were true. They sent me because they believed someone so young would be quite inconspicuous. The idea was for the Foreign Office to liaise with the SS, but of course the SS had no intention of allowing us to see even a fraction of the atrocities. It was my task to try to get under the curtain. I would write an official report but should save much of what I saw and heard for a private briefing of my more rebellious friends. Will you listen carefully to this?

'Edward, I had a contact, or so I hoped: an old friend from my student days. He was called Philip. Poor Philip had always been of an extreme disposition, a good hater if you like, but someone of character and pride as well. It was this pride which betrayed him because he came to believe that only through the Nazis could the old Germany be restored. If Hitler was against the aristocrats, Philip thought, he must be made to see sense. More of them should join his movement to show that they were not all so decadent or idle or defeatist after all. My way to Philip was through the Jews, or so I hoped, for he was now a member of the SS. It was as a convert and member of the party that I approached Philip, saying that I agreed with him and his new order. We met at the Adlon Hotel, a survivor of better times. The day was cold and grey, in the early spring, I am sure because my trip to the east took place when the weather was warmer and the snow had become pools of slush and mud at the start of the summer heat. I am sorry, Edward, I must talk more slowly in order to get it right. It is important. So on that spring morning, cold and grey, remember, I entered the Adlon. Louis, the manager, greeted me in the hall; my parents were old customers of the hotel. There was the excitement of conspiracy, of working against evil, a sense of virtue, even strength. I felt so brave.' The voice was loud, almost a shout; then fell back again.

'Yes, I felt brave as I said good morning to Louis. He asked after my father. I saw Philip, dressed in his dark uniform, stand up to shake my hand. He explained that he was on leave but had stayed in Berlin, not having enough time to go back to his family home in Silesia. Philip was so friendly, full of that banter that I remembered from college days, a cover then for hard pride. He had that absolute division between social behaviour and more serious matters, so that often there seemed to be nothing about which he could not laugh or that you might not include in the charming conversation of teases and jokes. Suddenly a chance comment or reference might sink deeper. Then he revealed a sternness, an anger, a strength of will. But this morning Philip showed such courtesy. As if embarrassed for me, he made no reference to what I had described to him in my letter as my "Pauline" conversion. That was for me to broach. Instead we spoke first about his family and mine who knew each other. He made a joke about our old arguments over which was better: East Prussia or his own homeland. Then I asked him if he had been surprised to hear from me, and he said in a way yes, for I had seemed immune to the present day when we had both been students, not really wanting to see that in history great changes come at certain times, demanding brave and extraordinary responses, and this was the message of Adolf Hitler. Philip was pleased because (and here he was particularly insistent) the more people of our kind became involved in the movement, the more easily some of its more unfortunate tendencies could be changed. The leader must understand that families such as our own should be a source of strength and pride for Germany. We are not decadent, you and I, said Philip.

'Then he smiled, once more relaxed because we were gentlemen together, two people whose families had played their part in the building of an older Prussia, with which this new system might surely be reconciled. Were we not also at this time pressing eastward, on the same civilizing mission as the Teutonic knights, against the backward Bolshevik slavs? He asked me if I had been hunting lately, if the deer and game were still good at our family home, that sportsman's paradise. Before the war, Philip had stayed often with us: always calm then and laughing as well with the perpetual banter, yet amazed when he saw the size of the beasts in the forest, so much greater and more numerous than where he came from. The heads of those he had killed, even when they were quite small, he had wished always to take home and have mounted to remind him of these visits.

'"A paradise," ' Philip had called my family's property, not just for its beauty but also because of the great, dark woods where one could kill as if there was an endless supply of these huge beasts. Their antlers lined the hall of our old house, each dated as a record of our hunting down the years. How skilful the marksmen of our family and friends had been! It was not only deer that we hunted but the wild fowl and the geese on the lakes. Autumn brought the hare shoots when the whole estate, all the men from the farms and the forestry and the village and most of the women too, would come out to drive the hares towards the guns. Philip and our guests from the more westerly parts of Germany used to say that they had seen nothing to compare with this way of life. In the more remote districts of the east the seasons still ruled the small towns and villages. The roads were often blocked or impassable for much of the winter months. Almost always we had snow from December until March.

'So Philip began with his question about the hunting, nodding his head when I replied that although much of our sport had been stopped by the war, the possibilities and the richness of game were still there. He reminded me that he had come once to our harvest celebrations when the whole community came together for an evening of happiness. He had danced then with both of my sisters, one after the other: such pretty young girls with their braids and first long dresses, laughing as the village band played in the late summer night. I must miss all this, he said. He missed his home and the old ways which had been a part of his childhood and youth. They had seemed some of the few certainties during the difficult years into which he and I had been born.

'Philip smoked. I remember that. There was an elegance, a grace to his movements. I can see him now twist his long, thin body quickly to one side, reach into a pocket of his black tunic, pull out a silver case which he passed across to me. I took a cigarette. Philip offered me a light from a small gold lighter. He smiled at my surprise to see once again those oval-shaped Turkish cigarettes which had vanished during the war. "Oh yes," he said, as he too lit up, blowing out a line of rich blue smoke, "I took steps to ensure my supplies." He laughed, reaching his arms out slightly. "One should not bow down before the enemy by allowing him to inconvenience one's life too much. If you want some, I can oblige. One's position allows one a certain latitude. And why not?" He may have seen a look of shock on my face.

'The food arrived. As usual the dining-room seemed full, for the Adlon was one of the few agreeable places left in which to lunch or dine. We spoke of old friends from our student days who had fallen in the war. I mentioned one sent to the worst of the fighting on the eastern front because his father had been arrested on the suspicion of being against the regime. Of course the boy had been killed. No one knew of the father's whereabouts or fate. He had disappeared into a network of interrogation rooms, holding camps, prisons and punishment centres. Philip looked away from me. I thought, Now he is ashamed, lost for an answer as to why this old friend of ours and his upright family should suddenly have been pushed into a hell created by these people he so much admires. I was wrong. He had seen a colleague, an older man in SS uniform, who was passing our table with a woman, perhaps his wife.

'Philip stood and saluted. The other man returned his salute, a brief, rough movement, then smiled before introducing his companion, who shook Philip's hand. I stood as well. The newcomer was told my name and where I worked. "A diplomat?" the man asked. He stared at me, unyielding, amused. I saw on his uniform, as on Philip's, the skull and crossed bones, the death's head symbol; also the insignia and braid of high command. He was large, bronzed, with a wide mouth, his short hair grey on the edges of his scalp. Philip said that I wished to see something of the eastern territories: Poland, the Ukraine, Byelorussia. "You are interested?" the man asked. "Why?" I answered that I had heard of the work that was being done there. "Ah yes." The man turned to Philip. "I leave it in your hands." Then back to me. "You are stuck in Berlin?" Yes, I said. I asked if he suffered the same fate. The answer came slowly, in a gruff, drawling tone. "I? No. I travel. Trieste, Belgrade, Brussels, Oslo, Warsaw, Prague, Lvov, Minsk, Sebastopol: a long journey." Then the General looked at his companion. "And of course Paris."

'They left. We sat down. Philip, for a moment confused, repeated the man's name. "The General sees what is wrong," he said. "The vulgarity, the petty-bourgeois standards: those dreadful parties at the Chancellery, the lack of taste, the coarseness. Göring's entertainments, his crude attempts to be a sportsman." Philip shook his head. "Like you, I regret the loss of each old comrade. But that is war. These political disputes should never have been allowed to disturb our friendship. This is what matters most to us: the ideals with which you and I grew up. Courage, a sense of chivalry: an absolute determination to stamp on the tawdry, the mean, those people who have no loyalty to a cause that is outside themselves."

'Philip spoke of how he had planned our journey. "When I heard from you, I was determined to get the greatest amount of freedom possible so that we might see the truth. So I spoke to the General who I felt would understand. You do not know his family? They have land in Pomerania, east of Stettin; a cousin lives there now. The General has given me the necessary permissions. I had to assure him of your absolute dedication to our ideals. He knew of our meeting today and came here I am sure not by accident but to see you for himself. What interests him in us both is that he too is working from the inside, a believer of course but attempting to make them see reason about the patriotism of our kind."

'Philip was to be my guide. I reported the lunch to our circle. It was decided that I should develop this friendship as much as possible and go on this trip with him, taking care at all times to remember what I saw, also to establish myself as a true believer.'

Chapter Eleven

Alex's face was as still as marble in the dark, soundless hut. Then he spoke again, quietly, methodically slow.

'So I went on the journey with Philip. We were together always, he in his uniform and I in my civilian clothes: the soldier and the bureaucrat. We discussed often the old days, remembering perhaps a stag glimpsed amongst the trees, the name of an old forester, the way Philip planned to try new threshing methods in his fields after the war.

'Poor Philip. He was not strong enough. As we left Berlin in the car that was to take us to the airport, I watched him carefully, fascinated. I was still not convinced of his evil. He chaffed me about some girl with whom I had once been friendly, then said he had no time now for such things. Yet he felt the need sometimes not for love but a person with whom he could relax, unbuckle his belt so to speak, tell the truth in that language which he and I used to each other: words which did not have to be qualified or explained because we knew exactly what they meant. These were difficult times. One could justify the violence, the force needed to move the world forward from communism and anarchist disorder. It was important for us here in Germany to give a modern response, with true German courage. "I believe this," Philip said. On the aeroplane, as we flew east across the Brandenburg plain in the clear spring air, I felt his desperation, that loneliness. "I was so pleased to hear from you," he said, "and now this trip." He pointed to the window. "Look, we are turning southwards," he said;

perhaps he hoped we might fly over his family home. Then he and I glanced at the few other passengers on the flight; some soldiers on their way back to the war.

'We landed on a strip near a small town in the central Ukraine, I cannot remember its name. Philip and I were the only people to disembark before the aeroplane flew on with its cargo of those few humans and the large piles of medical supplies needed for the advance eastwards. At the end of the runway, beside a collection of huts, a car waited for us. An officer from the army supply section who had some duties on the airfield had arranged with the driver to hitch a lift. His pleasure at finding a ride to his quarters turned to apology, even shock, when he saw that he would be accompanying a member of the SS and someone dressed in civilian clothes, most probably from the party or even the Gestapo.

'It was warmer than Berlin. The roads were rutted and muddy with pools of water where late snow had thawed, warm enough for the canopy of the car to be down. I remember the town: some small wooden houses, fading paintwork, an onion-domed church that had been allowed to decay by its Bolshevik masters, a few people in the streets, mostly soldiers. We were driven to the former offices of the local administration, a block in the centre. Here two members of the SS stood guard outside the entrance. Both saluted us, one opened the front door.

'They had laid on a bit of a show. A junior officer was in charge temporarily, or so he said. The others were all at a staff meeting some fifty miles away. This boy, no more than a boy, took us to a large bright room on the ground floor arranged as if for a lecture with chairs in rows in front of an easel. On the easel was a map marked with arrows, strips and dots. "Please," he said. We sat in two of the chairs in the front row whilst he stood by the map with a wooden pointer and began to talk slowly in the thick accent of the Rhineland. There was coffee, good coffee, served by an orderly.

'At first I believed the boy must be going to give us the details of the military campaign and the great advance eastwards. Surely this was the clue to the arrows. Then I saw they were pointing in the direction of the west, to ground which I knew from the incessant propaganda had been captured weeks earlier. I glanced at Philip's face, which showed no surprise or excitement. Now we were locked together in complicity. For the lieutenant was speaking of the movement and eventual extermination of whole categories of people: political undesirables, those associated closely with communist rule, and of course the Jews. I had not been ignorant of this, Edward, I must tell you. We knew it was a part of the Nazi programme. There were rumours. But how well the lieutenant explained this! He must have risen through his zeal. The thickness of the accent showed that he came from poor, probably country stock. When his back was turned, as he pointed to the map, Philip smiled at me. I smiled back: a silent, shared joke at the voice, something that took us deeper together, our background, the same boyhood pleasures, then the truth of this horror as well.

'It was explained that some of the victims went westward by train. For this there needed to be convenient railheads, where they could be assembled without the need to be driven too far in convoys of lorries. Petrol was precious out here because there were so many vehicles connected with the war. Our great victories had brought problems of their own! Philip and I laughed. This semblance of a joke enabled us to let out our amusement at the Rhineland voice. The lieutenant smiled in response: the shy smile of youth, a little embarrassed perhaps. How pleased he must have been that this staff meeting had given him his chance, or so I thought to myself. But this boy had already seen more terrible and strange things than I will see in the whole of my life, even including these grand tours you and I go on, Edward, to the suffering peoples of the world. His smile, I think now, came from a private delight at what was in store for us: pleasure that these two innocent strangers would see the truth as opposed to cold reports, the unreal rumours, the lies of propaganda. Most probably he despised our innocence: that comfortable illusion.'

Alex stopped, as if to sort out the tangle of his quickening words. When he continued, the pace soon quickened again, now beyond his control.

'The lieutenant had talked of petrol, of the difficulties with transport. He put great emphasis on this, sometimes repeating himself. There was a huge swathe of territory to cover. Railheads were often hard to reach. The distances were vast. Fuel for the lorries was too valuable to be used in this particular operation, however great its importance. So we had these groups, highly mobile of course, who came in behind the advance, spread out along almost the whole length of the front to places where large numbers of victims were assembled. The method was quick. They were lined up. One man with a machine gun was enough, possibly two if the line was long and there was another weapon to hand. An officer was there to supervise. At the end the bodies were covered with earth. Was that clear? Now the lieutenant had his instructions. We were to be shown as much as possible. A car should be waiting outside. It was a short journey, along a bad road, into a wooded region only a few miles away. We must hurry. He had been told that we were to be flown out in an aeroplane from the landing strip in the early evening.

'So we left the town on the bad road, braking sharply in front of pot-holes, the driver steering round them when he could, the lieutenant sitting in the front, Philip and I next to each other on the back seat of the open car. The sun shone. Wide fields were on either side of us, a huge sky on top in this empty land. From the distance came the thud of artillery fire. We knew the push forward had been stopped by hard fighting. Even our leaders had admitted that. On the horizon was the beginning of more wooded country, trees in a dark line, and as I looked Philip pointed ahead, grimaced, shook his head, for what purpose I do not know. The road became worse, then better. We entered the wood quite fast. The lieutenant spoke sharply to the driver. Now there were men walking on the verge, between the trees and the road. A column came towards us at a crossroads: men and women in poor, ragged clothing, a line escorted by some of our soldiers, mostly with their rifles still slung over the shoulder, only a few holding a gun at the ready. "The operation is almost over," the lieutenant said above the noise of the engine and the slight wind. "These are the last groups. It has been decided to move to another site nearer to the front because the programme has been carried out faster than expected. We have covered most of the territory." He spoke again to the driver. We turned off the main thoroughfare on to what seemed like a rough track suitable only for carts. But the road was better than I had expected, the impression of roughness given more by grass growing up through ground that had obviously been levelled. We passed another column.

'Philip shouted from the back seat to our guide, asking how these people had been brought here. "Some have been marched a short distance," the lieutenant answered. "Others were unloaded from lorries which you cannot see because they arrive at a point some way from here so that they can get away quickly to collect the next load. Also we did not want to risk the heavier vehicles becoming bogged down on these wet tracks. I am sure you will see this is right. After only a short rain the interior of the wood can become almost impassable in spite of the work of our engineers." He spoke like that, Edward: rather primly, correctly, great care in the choice of words, always in the Rhineland accent.

Perhaps many of the answers or explanations had been learnt by heart. He may have done this before.

'The car pulled in to the side just ahead of the column, on to a stretch of cleared ground. We stopped. The lieutenant turned. "We get out here," he said and leapt from the car, then to the back door, which, conscious of rank, he opened on Philip's side so that the superior officer could be first. I followed. As we stood by the car, before I had time to take in my surroundings, the boy looked down at my thin shoes and spoke to Philip. "The ground is wet, especially in the clearing. I wonder if, for your comrade" — yes, that was the word he used — "there are other boots." He turned to the driver, asked a question. I said that I would be all right. It did not really matter for a short time, or so I thought.

'Now I saw the column. They were behind us, their footsteps slapping on the wet ground the only sound as the first few people in the line approached. I turned. So did Philip. I could not see the lieutenant because he had already started to move on, although he must have stopped when he realized that both his guests were still standing in the same place by the car. We watched these people. There must have been about a hundred of them, a mixture of course of men and women, children as well, several women carrying children, other children almost running to keep up with what to them was a fast pace. The sound of those feet in the mud was irregular, like people beating upon wet clothes, for naturally they could not keep in step. So I looked into some of those faces which had turned towards us, curiosity still bright even at this last moment in their lives.

'I saw first a middle-aged man with a black beard, some streaks of grey too, probably in his mid-forties, thin yet the face sharp: no dulled eyes of defeat here nor in the woman at his side, although she seemed more distressed no doubt because of the two boys with her, one about eleven I should say, the other eight; they could not have been more than that. Both boys were quite tall, like their father (if the black-bearded man was their father), but not bent, which he was slightly: a schoolmaster or some such person, I thought, used to a life of the mind rather than the manual work for which his physique would have been no good. The man was leaning down for a moment to speak to the woman, only a short sentence, perhaps two or three words: about the children, I think, because she pulled the boys even closer to her. The younger held her hand and the older took the hand of his brother. It was to the older one's head that she reached out with her other hand, as if to ruffle his hair. He looked up at her, a dark-headed youngster, and smiled, which seemed so odd to me. I knew in my mind what was going to happen to these people. It was terrible. One could imagine the sort of people they had been in their lives – the types, if you understand what I mean, Edward. Because in that short time, as they came near, I saw the schoolmaster, the men who must have been mere labourers, the faces of sensitivity, a coarse look here perhaps, someone who was impractical, fat women aged by child-bearing and the dull routine of domestic life, pretty younger women, no longer girls but in what should have been life's time of greatest fulfilment; then the girls, the children and the older people. These were the ones who slowed the column down: the elderly and the children.

'I knew I must look, take in as much as I could, for this seemed to me to be what my life had been shaped for up to this moment: the trail that had led to this remote place, beginning with my birth and those strangely protected years of childhood and growing up, the sense of living in a world hedged off as you might say, then the luxury of vague but not too pronounced opposition to the regime, the little plot I had joined. Now the reunion with Philip and the journey here had introduced me at last to the shock of the positive truth. Can you see, Edward?

'Those eyes. The eyes of this thin man, his beard and hair flecked with grey because he was bare-headed like most of the men in the column although some women had their hair tied up in scarves, usually white or grey. The woman stared too, and the children. I knew I had to mark this family, if it was a family. These individuals would make me understand the horror. I wanted to say to Philip, Look at that group at the head of the column, think what they believe as they see us. They must see your uniform and my position alongside you and the lieutenant. They must think that we are all together in this infamy, devils sent to see that not one single one of the prisoners survives. Then I saw he had turned to ask the lieutenant a question. "Where do the guards come from?" The boy answered that there were of course some Germans, from his own group, "but we have no shortage of volunteers from the occupied territories. They are useful in case of language problems with the prisoners, although it is mostly just a question of giving a few orders. Let us walk on."

'The family had moved ahead but we were soon level with them again. The lieutenant called one of the guards over, another young man, a German I should say by what I could hear of his voice, which was not much because they spoke quickly before the man returned to his position. "My colleague will be waiting at the lorry. You can see it," the boy said. I had not noticed. There ahead at what looked to be some sort of crossroads in the wood, at any rate a place where trees had been cut back on both sides, were two large lorries, and I remember wondering in the midst of this horror why our guide had not allowed the driver to take us right up to this place so that we need not have walked quite so far through the wet grass on the tracks. I glanced back at the column where the man and woman stared ahead towards the clearing. Only the younger of the two children still looked at me: large eyes like an infant in those first picture books of my childhood, at that time not so long ago.

'Some people in uniform stood at the crossroads. The lieutenant called out to a soldier who was walking near him and this man shouted the order to halt. At first the captives did not seem to have heard the command, then after a few seconds the sound of the footsteps slowed gradually. The people in front stopped first so that it seemed for a moment as if the whole length of the column would slide up together like an enormous telescope, those at the back pushing the ones ahead of them towards the standing figures at the end where my family had halted, all – the man, the woman and two children – staring ahead at the lorries and the new uniformed people. One of the group at the crossroads, whom I could see now, was an officer perhaps slightly older than Philip. There was another officer, a lieutenant surely, a similar-looking boy to our fair-haired guide from the Rhineland. We saluted. The older officer, the man in command, shook hands with Philip and then with me: a man of average height, a fat face, stocky body, narrow eyes slightly close together, teeth brilliantly white, a flash of gold from the back of his mouth when he smiled.

'"You are most welcome," he said. "We received the message from the General. I take it that you will be reporting personally to him on your return?" Philip bowed. The other smiled, as if acknowledging a *fait accompli*. We were formidable intruders. He nodded to our lieutenant who called out once more to one of the escorting soldiers. The column began to move, this time down a track to the right of the crossroads. The fat officer invited us to accompany him; so we left the lorries, this small group of us, Philip, I and the officer in charge, a little ahead of our lieutenant, who fell in with the rest. I heard a laugh from behind as something was said about this God-forsaken part of the world. The officer spoke again. I could not trace his accent at first; then I began to hear echoes of Westphalia perhaps, a region I did not know well although my family had come from there many centuries ago before our trek eastwards. Yet he seemed to be not so dour as one would expect a Westphalian to be, for his conversation was of a slightly humorous turn. "When can we expect a visit from the General in person?" he asked. "Soon perhaps?" He laughed, his mouth slightly open. Again I saw the flash of a gold tooth. "No, he is wise to remain in Berlin. This work is better to read about in the reports that we send back." Then, perhaps remembering our high connections or our quite high-sounding names, although as a good Nazi he should have had no admiration for this, he added, "Of course we have no doubt as to its great importance."

'So he explained how the prisoners had been transported, often repeating what we had already been told by the lieutenant. Philip asked several questions. I wondered if he was talking to avoid time for imagination or shock. "We have made a clearing here," the officer said. After about five minutes' walk, during which time we and the column had marched around a long wide corner in the track so that the crossroads and the lorries were out of sight, we reached a large, open space, almost a small field in the centre of this dark wood. Here the trees were so close together that I felt sealed off from the rest of the world.

'More people waited, all in uniform. To the left, stretching away, a huge trench had been dug, the pile of earth on its other side between the trench and the trees of the rest of the wood. By this time my thin walking shoes were soaked, but I walked one or two paces into the longer grass, away from the track along which we had come. There was another shout for the column to halt. Philip said, "Stay here, Alex." The officer pointed in the direction of the trench. I noticed two men sitting behind a machine gun that had been set in a fixed position so that it had a wide line of fire along the length of the great mass grave.

'The column began to move again. I knew I must look at

my family, the first people in the line. Perhaps they would be fortunate enough to die quickly, for surely the gun would swing over to them at the beginning before the killers twisted it through the whole row of victims. The man stared ahead, into the dense thicket of trees, then briefly up at the clear sky where there were no clouds on this sharp early-spring day. I could not see his face. I hoped that none of them would turn towards us, and this was unlikely because, although I had been stopped from moving away, the officer and Philip and I were not close to the prisoners any longer. In the walk from the crossroads our group had shifted further from the column to a smoother part of the track where the grass was shorter and not so wet. Do not turn, I thought. Yet I wanted to see how they would be at this moment before death. Would a dull acceptance come over them? Would that sense of animation, of life, last until the end? Would human intelligence, even love, vanish at the last moment of their lives? Then she looked at me.'

Alex stopped, breathless for a moment. There were footsteps, a voice outside answered by another voice. Then the sounds faded into the African night. The German spoke again.

'She is still there, Edward. When I sleep it comes back often: the wood, the dark trees, the wet roads, that fat Westphalian officer, the lieutenant from the Rhineland so keen to please, Philip himself already beaten by what he had joined. It is all there. That look – how strange! – not of violence or any part of this wickedness: just a glance, no more, a stare perhaps, because it lasted long enough for me to be almost hypnotized. A stare of compassion. I was going to say pity, but that is not quite right because it brings to mind an arrogance or pride which was not there. This compassion is something I will never forget because it made me feel suddenly that there was nothing else to do but to get to my knees and pray. Of course I stood still. Like a good officer or servant I stood. The column was spread out into a line in front of the great trench, the guards pushing men and women into the correct position and the children as well so that all the backs, and there must have been about a hundred of them, were within range of the machine gun's fire.

'The children tried to cling to their mothers, or some did. They were pushed away by the guards but allowed to hold her hand or each other's hands if their backs were facing in the right direction. My children, my family, were quiet and orderly, just what we wanted them to be, the two boys on either side of their mother, the oldest not even holding her hand but anxious to show strength, then the father next to his oldest son, also straight, all their backs now to the machine gun, all in dark clothes: the man's black jacket, the boy's shorts, the woman's grey skirt and scarf, dark there against the deeper darkness of the wood into which they were looking for their last sight of this life. They did not turn round again, my family: not at all. I could see them only from the back.

'The officer gave the order. The sound of the machine gun drowned his voice almost immediately, a long rattling shriek through the clearing, yet no longer than was strictly necessary because it would be foolish to waste ammunition. The bodies fell forward into the trench, or almost all of them. Clearly the system of slaughter had been devised so that the guards would not need to heave many corpses into the grave. Sometimes the work of burial was done at gunpoint by the next line of victims before their own execution. How clever we were about it all! But this time they were not all dead.

'Most of the bodies had fallen forward, it was true, with the exception of three or four: two corpses down the far end and, much nearer, the one from whom I had not been able to take my eyes, or only for a brief moment to watch the astonishing collapse of the row of prisoners, one after the other pitched down as the bullets ripped into their backs. The two boys had fallen forward with their father, but their mother lay on the edge of the pit still, I was sure, moving or at least trying to move, for I could see from that distance no sign of blood.

'I tell you, Edward, that if I had had a gun at that moment I would have killed that woman to save her from evil, so that she would never see the world or us again. But instead I watched the Westphalian officer walk forward, accompanied by our lieutenant, still anxious no doubt to impress us. They both drew their pistols. In six shots they finished off the victims. The woman was saved. Or killed to be saved. Edward!'

Chapter Twelve

'Edward.'

'You killed no one,' he murmured.

'How are you feeling?' Alex asked. 'Can you walk? A weakness? Is that it?'

'Do you want to tell me the rest, Alex?'

'There is not much more.'

'You saw the massacre.'

'Yes. But listen: that was all. There are no more horror stories. Is that what you want? Horror stories? There are no more horror stories from that trip. We drove off with the lieutenant and caught the aeroplane out. We went to a conference somewhere: a small town about a hundred miles or so to the north, I forget the name. Philip had to see these people. I remained in the guest house, not yet trusted enough to be allowed to hear all that was going on.'

Alex paused. 'I know what you are thinking, Edward: how did they speak to each other about what they had just seen, these two great friends? Surely they cannot have been silent. Well, look, remember. In a sense we were friends, Philip and I, and we had been friends for years, since university and even earlier. But between us was this great secret: that I was against him and all he stood for. I had lied, of course, pretending to have become a Nazi. So for me the massacre reinforced what I already believed. For him the feeling must have been far more complex. Was this the mission of civilization he wished to take eastwards? It seemed a travesty of our history, of what we had learnt as boys about those first conquering crusades of chivalry and the brave knights who had set out for the dark Slav lands. On the aeroplane he said, "It is a terrible thing." I did not answer. Again he said, "It is a terrible thing." He asked, "Are you still a believer?" Again I said nothing. Then he was silent. We did not speak about it any more, except for him to say, "You have survived. You have not whimpered or wept. That is good."' Alex laughed. 'Philip was killed. What else could one expect? That was his destiny. He had not the necessary fanaticism or stupidity. Poor Philip. He had doubts. He never told me but I saw it in all the talk about the past, the old days: those memories. The people for whom he was working must have sensed this, too. Soon afterwards he was sent to the eastern front, then killed in fighting near Sebastopol. I wrote to his family. His mother answered, mentioning their pride that he had fallen in battle, fighting for his country. She made no reference to politics.

'We were all under fire then, Edward: even the civilians. I remember a November day when I walked through Berlin after one of the worst of the raids, past the burnt-out memorial church, through the Nettelbackstrasse to the Lützow Platz and on to the Tiergarten. This was the end, or so I thought. Slowly the news came through of the destruction: the Golden Gallery in the Charlottenburg Palace; the old west side of Berlin where I had once felt able to escape into a historic, more noble world; those landmarks of pleasure, the Habel Restaurant, the Kaiserhof, the Bristol and Eden hotels; some of the ministries, the French and British embassies. But not the new Chancellery, oh no, the English and American pilots missed that. Not the propaganda headquarters of Goebbels or Rosenberg's crazy Ministry for Eastern Affairs; they remained. At the Adlon Hotel, battered but still standing, we would meet each other sometimes, finding our way through the evening darkness and the raids, the explosions of the bombs night after night. There was no uninterrupted sleep at that time. Perhaps this is why it all has a curious half-awake feel to it now, the exhaustion coming back to me. I would not have believed it possible to be so tired.'

The German sighed. 'It's curious, isn't it? I can talk about almost everything now, although for years I did not like to, except to those who knew: for instance, what happened in 1944 when we were all rounded up after the Stauffenberg bombing.' Alex laughed. 'Jane was interested in the July plot, I think. You know some women are always looking for heroes. Tell me, Edward, do you love her? You are her hero. See the way that she looks at you. Once when we were talking, Jane and I, at one of those Washington parties, I said I would have to take you off on another trip soon, either to Africa or the Far East. Did she mind? I asked. "Oh yes," she answered, "but your work can change things. This is what I want Edward to do. You will take care of him, won't you?"'

Quickly he pushed the challenge away. 'Where did you and the conspirators meet?'

Alex let it lie, returning to himself. 'In Berlin. Our houses were watched, towards the end. Occasionally we would visit friends in the country.' He sighed again, then laughed, as if to banish the melancholy. 'It was extraordinary: so hard during the raids, yet the dislocation and chaos of the bombing also permitted almost anything. There was this great tension, also my memory of what I had seen, the guilt of this, the idea sometimes that it might be better for me simply to stand outside, perhaps on the Unter den Linden, by the Pariser Platz or the Potsdamer Strasse or the Leipziger Platz, not go to the shelters when the sirens went but seek the bombs, offer myself as a sacrifice to atone for what had been done in our name. Instead I chose to live for this – no, not this but for work that might help rebuild the destruction.'

'I can tell you about it: the end of that world. Later in Berlin, when the war was over, I walked to the house where one of my dear friends had lived: Hans-Dieter who was involved also in the plot. A bomb had sliced the place open, through the room where he used to receive guests. I saw the smashed cream-painted woodwork, the cracked mirror over the blue and white marble chimneypiece, the bare, damp floorboards. I saw also the rooms of the apartment beneath, the residence of a certain Herr Hofmann about whom Hans-Dieter and I had often joked, imagining him to be all sorts of things from a monster to a saint. Our knowledge of Herr Hofmann had been restricted to occasional sightings of an elderly gentleman with his wife and their dachshund setting off for a walk. Sometimes on still summer evenings when there were no raids and the windows were open, we had heard one of them playing the piano, a soft piece perhaps by Schubert or Brahms, something anyway that one thought of as a lullaby. Standing in the ruins of the city, I thought of one time in particular, a time I return to even now, both awake and in my dreams.

'It was perhaps a year before the end. I had left the office that afternoon much earlier than usual. The next day was to be the start of a period of leave for me. My superior had suggested I go off in the middle of the afternoon as I had just finished work on a draft for him and there was not really much else I could hope to complete that day. I must tell you this, Edward. Then I will be quiet.

'So I walked down the Wilhelmstrasse towards Hans-Dieter's apartment. I knew the journey well, but on that day I had originally intended to go to where I lived, which was in the same direction but further out. The bus that I climbed on to was full even at that unusual time. When it reached the stop by the Lützow Platz, from which the place was an easy short walk, I got off, for some strange external force seemed to have worked on my mind. There was sun that afternoon. I turned into the short street and pressed the bell, expecting nothing or just an answer that everyone was out from the short, fat, bad-tempered woman caretaker who lived in some rooms at the back of the building on the ground floor. But the old woman came to the door and said I should go up because she recognized me as a caller who had come often during the past year since I had got to know Hans-Dieter. He was not in but I could wait for him inside. She had a key. Better take the stairs because the frequent electricity cuts caused by the raids made the lift unsafe. Even the old caretaker took the stairs now. She in her condition: imagine!

'I went up to the second floor, to those large brown wooden doors of the apartment, elegant in the heavy nineteenth-century way of so much of Berlin, and let myself in, sitting down in the cold, empty room from which the owners of the place – friends of Hans-Dieter's family – had taken almost everything to another house where they lived. At last there was quiet, peace of a kind here in this strange no man's land, for the place had no personality: not that of Hans-Dieter, who was a good man but only really camping there temporarily, or its owners' or anyone's. I thought of Dr Schulz, the stern, absurd Nazi who kept watch over us in my department at the Wilhelmstrasse, of how we worked at upsetting the British Empire; of poor Philip, so neat and tidy that when we were younger there used to be jokes about the way his hands might one day vanish from having been rubbed and scrubbed and washed so often; then of course back to my childhood and home where the Russians would soon reach, or so I believed because I knew we were defeated already and that it would be all lost for ever, and out of this defeat must come all the terrible truth about those years of madness. I sat like this, Edward, alone. It must have been a long time as the darkness came and I seemed unable to move to turn on the lights whilst the sky changed outside.

'Then the bombs started again, as they did most nights during that time. Again I did not move in spite of the sirens and alarms and explosions and flickering of flames and fire, the hell that was created each night in the city. And do you know what I learnt later, that as I had been sitting there in his chair, Hans-Dieter was travelling south in a train on some diplomatic errand and the train was hit outside Munich, waiting for the line to be cleared, and he too was killed? When I was in gaol later in the Prinz Albrechtstrasse, after the failure of the plot, I thought again death might be better than the attentions of the Gestapo. It is still here!' Alex hit his chest, a sharp, angry movement. 'Remember those men in the pit, the women and the children. That I have seen. Then the end of all I had known: a life gone, my own beautiful world. Like that!

'But the rest was bad, too. When it was all over and the camp in which I had been held was liberated by the Americans, I made a vow. I must atone for all this: for what I had seen and failed to stop and survived when so many much better and braver people had died. I vowed to devote myself to the unfortunate: first in my own country through joining the administration of our ruined nation, then this work with the underdeveloped world. It was like entering a religious order, Edward, yet more difficult in a way because I could not retire into a monastery where everyone around me had taken the same vows. I had to live in the world outside, subject to that world's pressures and temptations. To remain alone, not to marry: these were conscious decisions, an expiation of guilt, or an attempt at this. I have found friendships in Germany, Edward, romantic friendships, affairs also, I must confess, because I am not strong enough for complete celibacy or solitude. I will not talk about them now. In a way they have been important, but not important in the ultimate sense: more the kind of relationships where both sides stand back a little, keep a part of themselves secret and uninvolved. Does that sound cold? Perhaps it is. But I keep to another promise. I have been always determined that no one else should be hurt, that there must be no more victims, including myself.

'For time has not moved fast enough. I still wake at night to think of those years. I wonder if it would have been easier if I had found someone to be there beside me, to give truth to the old saying that suffering is not all sadness. Really this sacrifice I made, this personal solitude, has killed a part of me. That is what happens. After years of frustration, even torment, the impulse is stifled by other demands of hard work, the effort of control. It withers into the ground. All that is left is a husk of a man, an automaton. So the sacrifice was worthless, utterly worthless: a piece of vanity which made not the slightest difference to anything or anyone else, except to me. And I gradually lost that human quality: the power to give and to love. So I too have become a victim.'

The German stopped. Three men stood in the doorway of the hut, the bright sky of day behind them. Their leader spoke, looking at Alex and Edward West who stood up.

'We are leaving you here.'

Chapter Thirteen

Rose sees him on the station platform: Edward West in a dark blue suit, carrying an umbrella and a folded newspaper. 'Good morning,' he says. 'Going to London?'

'Yes. And you?'

The train arrives, doors open, a few passengers get out. Those who have been waiting on the platform in the slight chill of an early-autumn morning board the carriages quickly. 'Shall we sit together?' Edward asks. So the train starts, almost toppling him over with its slight jerk, and they sit down next to each other with an old woman opposite them who does not look up from her magazine. The carriage is quite empty. 'Is your trip for business or pleasure?'

Rose thinks of Ben, probably now painting in his studio, standing back perhaps to smile at some particularly skilful effect. He starts work early when he is on his own in London. 'Oh, pleasure.' She wears a loose black jacket, a white T-shirt, a black and white checked skirt, and dark tights. She has a book on her knee. 'And yours?'

'I'm having lunch with an old colleague who is over from Rome.' Edward smiles. 'We meet whenever he's here.'

As he seems keen to talk, she pushes gently at the boundary of their friendship. 'Some one who worked with you at the UN?'

'That's right. He stayed on, whereas I went to Washington.'

'To the Survey?' She tries to coax him forward. 'You told us the other evening . . .'

'Did I? How dull for you.'

'No, no. Then you spoke about the man you worked for: the German.'

'Von Kierich?' His face draws in, like a shut door.

'He had to leave.'

'Yes.' Edward glares at her, a sudden fierce blow from which Rose must fall back, clutching her paperback book as if for protection. She recalls his strange invitation at the Rileys' to come to Germany, a leap so apparently out of character for this quiet, remote man. Then his words come easily, the strain gone. 'This must be a difficult time on the farm. Is your father pleased with the harvest?'

She surrenders to the change of subject. 'My father has diversified,' she says.

'What do you think, Rose?'

'Sometimes he consults too much, at other times too little. Then he has these theories. And it's all so expensive. He needs more money, Edward. That's what's behind the deal with Dove about the saw mill.'

'Is Hector interested?'

'Not really.'

'Will you be at the meeting in the village hall tonight?' He glances at the old woman opposite who is still intent on her magazine.

'Yes.' Rose also looks at the old woman but does not recognize her so feels she can say almost anything. 'Have you signed the petition?'

'Certainly not.' He laughs. 'I don't like being bullied. That's what Martin is trying to do.'

'What about Nancy?'

'She's much more sensible.'

'You've known them for years, haven't you?' She wonders if he will repeat the invitation. It is as if anything might come from him: a hint of infinite possibility. The thought brings the blood to her cheeks.

'Years.'

129

The train comes to a halt at the first of its two stops on the way to London. The old woman opposite stands up, puts her magazine into a carrier bag decorated with flowers and walks away down the carriage towards the door. 'What does Charles think?' Rose asks quickly, remembering the name of that shy, dull son.

'About what?'

'The saw mill.'

He smiles again. 'Charles hasn't the time to think about that sort of thing.'

'Does he enjoy his work?' she goes on, not giving Edward time to answer. 'I'm not sure what it is. Something to do with investment. Is that it?'

'That's right.' Edward has settled back into his seat. 'On the whole he seems happy.' He looks out of the window again, then back. 'Did your mother order those roses from that new catalogue? Perhaps you don't know.'

'Yes. She did.'

Then Edward is silent. Rose is on the point of opening her book when he says, 'Jane would have been surprised.'

'Why? Was she a keen gardener?'

'No. About Charles. She always thought he was the artistic one. She wanted Nick to go into the Foreign Office, like her father.'

'And Charles?'

'Publishing, perhaps. Something to do with the arts. He never went to university, you know.'

Rose looks at him, forcing her eyes to be steady. 'Edward, how did she die?'

'In a car crash. I told you, didn't I?'

'Where?'

'Munich. She was on holiday.'

'Were you badly hurt?'

'I wasn't with her.' His eyes look downwards. 'She was alone.'

'In the car?'

'And in Munich. Well, not quite. She was visiting a friend. When I heard, I flew out, of course.'

'I am sorry, Edward.'

The train stops again. An elderly man and a younger woman, perhaps his daughter, take the seats opposite them and the carriage soon fills up. Edward unfolds his copy of *The Times* and Rose opens her book, that same *Under the Greenwood Tree*. When they reach Paddington, the two of them part at the entrance to the Underground station for he will take a taxi to his club. 'Enjoy yourself,' he says to her before walking away.

Bill Higginson, the friend from Rome, is late.

Edward West waits in the club's hall. People are arriving for lunch, pushing through the front door to this comfortable retreat from the world outside, a huge neo-classical building with high ceilings and dim recesses. Over the years the type of member has stayed more or less the same: lawyers, journalists, a few publishers, diplomats, actors and people from the theatre. There is only a slight air of snobbery, more of an exclusive conviviality. Sometimes it seems as if everyone is surrounded by laughing companions except oneself. But the waiting-list is long and applications need to be well supported.

Edward comes alone occasionally to the large round communal table in the centre of the dining-room, where he makes polite conversation to his neighbour, perhaps a judge with a booming voice or a shy publisher, whilst around them rises the great swell of English male camaraderie. These visits can be rather an ordeal. Yet he continues year after year to pay the large subscription because he likes to watch what goes on; it is, he tells himself, of anthropological interest, like the study of animals in some condition halfway between captivity and the wild. Jane's father had made him a member soon after his marriage. The club is a remnant of Sir Roger's world.

Once during lunch at the centre table Edward had drunk too much, partly from nerves, and found himself lurching into a garrulous questioning of his neighbour (on this occasion a retired barrister), then a soliloquy on his own condition: also retired but with much to look back on, many memories like those years in Rome and Washington and journeys further afield, even days of fear in Africa where Thalberg's body had pitched forward in the ambushed car. Other heads had turned in the club dining-room. His voice must have become loud, but he did not mind for he found himself reaching even further back to his time at university, to how he had been excused National Service because of his childhood asthma, why the job at the Survey had seemed a good way out of Whitehall. 'But the security of the Civil Service had suited me. My parents were simple people. To them a trip into Tunbridge Wells was a major event. But they weren't in my life for long. I find it hard to see that they influenced me at all, although some pattern must be set in those early years. Don't you agree?'

He wonders now if he had made himself clear on that day, jumbling up references to how hard 'we' had found looking for a place to live in Washington with the drama of the African captivity and the trips into the Indian desert or the flooded regions of East Bengal. He had tried to explain that Jane had never come with him on these journeys. 'She grew up abroad,' he had said, 'the child of a diplomat.' He had mentioned Sir Roger's name. 'You may have heard of him. She's dead now. I live in the country on my own.' Then came a silence before the other man's few words of pity and regret.

Jane had mocked the club, in spite of her father's membership. 'I don't know how you can bear to go there. Who on earth do you see?' she had said. He would mention some of the senior people at the Foreign Office; then there were the lawyers and the men of the theatre: quite a variety. 'Lawyers are often pedants, and actors have very little to say for themselves,' she said, probably repeating one of Sir Roger's opinions. 'They cannot avoid playing a part.' She mentioned a theatrical knight who had stayed once at the embassy in Rome. 'It was quite absurd. At the dinner Daddy gave for him he assumed the role of the English gentleman, complete with velvet smoking jacket and talk about how much he liked a glass of port. Then the next day, when an Italian director who was making a film of *Macbeth* came to lunch, Sir Charles felt it safe at last to talk about his real subject, which is the way to declaim Shakespeare. A typical actor!'

Suddenly Edward thinks of Jane on the bed in their Washington house, her tears, the desperate attempts to understand: that memory of her sad young helpless self, a strange dream of the dead. This is what he has become: a prisoner of fantasy, for nothing can happen now except the offering of a crazy invitation to a young girl like Rose, who he is sure was secretly laughing at him on the train. Such sorrow, such shame. Then he sees Bill Higginson, his guest: a slight, small, stooped figure in a grey pinstripe suit. If she were to come in now behind Bill, perhaps clasp his arm, they would kiss to celebrate this surprise meeting, the joy of her company, what Alex had once called 'Jane's glow of beauty', the reason he had come often to their house in Georgetown to laugh and see the Wests in those days of the Prof, the Beacon, the Boy and the Snow Queen.

Bill turns. 'Edward!'

He has also retired but looks older than Edward or Martin Riley, more bald and wrinkled, although the difference in age can only be that of a year or so, a very short time. But there is serenity in his round, soft, slightly tanned face, the grey, pleasant eyes. Bill was always a contented man, with Helen, his cheerful wife. Not brilliant, a steady worker on the administrative side, planning budgets and so on, slightly inferior to the economists or theoreticians like Edward. They shake hands, Bill's grip steady, and go up the broad staircase to the bar in a large room on the first floor crowded with men only, because women guests are restricted to other parts of the club. Edward orders a glass of sherry for himself and a Martini for his old friend.

They take their drinks over to a small table beside one of the tall, narrow windows. Bill pats him on the arm. 'I got in yesterday from Rome two hours late.' He sips at the cocktail. 'These European flights are often delayed. Do you find that?'

Edward laughs. 'Last week I went to a conference in Toulouse,' he says. 'We waited for an hour on the tarmac at Heathrow.' He thinks, Two old men complaining about the modern world.

'Toulouse!' Bill's voice jumps in surprise. 'What took you there?'

'I gave a paper looking at Africa over the last thirty years. The transition from colonialism to self-government. How this has affected agricultural development.'

'I'm sure you were tactful.' Bill laughs.

He is pleased to hear that friendly sound again. 'How is Helen?'

'Very well. Very, very well.' Bill stares into the mass of people at the bar. 'She does some translation work for Italian publishers. It's rather fun; profitable too.' Jane had once tried her hand at this. Bill would be too tactful to say that he remembers. 'What about your boys? Is Nick still in Boston?'

'Yes.' Edward tells him about his sons. 'They work hard now. And your children?' He waits, thinking that it is right to canter through these preliminary courtesies as Bill speaks of a doctor son in Bristol and a daughter in Milan married to an Italian called Carlo who works in the chemical industry. Then they remember Rome together and the pleasures of living there: the light at evening, those long views of the great domed city. At last Edward stands. 'Let's go and eat. I want to tell you what happened at Toulouse.'

The dining-room is full, the voices of the members loud even in this deep place where the distant, dark ceiling has been blackened by years of smoke from coal fires and members' cigarettes and cigars. Their table is in one of the quieter corners, beside a window that looks on to the street where people walk hurriedly by, seldom turning to stare through the glass. They order and he asks the waiter to bring the wine as soon as possible. His guest's Martini glass is still half full, evidence of calm.

'Was your paper received well?' Bill asks, his voice low, slightly amused.

'I think so.'

'Don't you find it's quite difficult now?' Bill says. 'The position has changed so much. In our day, there was a definite sense of obligation, the old idea of doling out wisdom from on high, so to speak. We knew better: that seemed to be the message. Am I being unfair? Of course some of us had it more than others. I'm not thinking particularly of you, Edward. Now doubt is much more fashionable, or so it seems to me. Not that I'm ever invited to these congresses.' Bill laughs. 'You must be pleased that your reputation has stood up so well. If only –'

'What?'

'If only we were all remembered in a similar way.'

Rather startled, Edward looks for a sign of malice. Bill had never been malicious in the past. The pale eyes are still gentle, quite firm. 'Oh no.'

'So what happened with the paper?'

'There were a few questions.' He is conscious of a stiffness: that lecturing tone. He looks down at the table, then up again. 'Alex von Kierich's name was mentioned.'

'That's not surprising.'

'This was different. Obviously Alex's part in the history of the Survey is important, in spite of what Kristiansen may say about new brooms and fresh starts and all those other clichés!' Edward's anger at the overbearing Dane breaks through, then subsides. 'I was expecting the usual stuff about administrative methods and so forth. But in the discussion after my paper one of the French delegates, a woman, asked if Alex had given any indication of his feelings for the people we were trying to help. At first I wasn't sure if I'd understood her properly. Matters of that kind are so much more suited to informal conversation than the actual proceedings of the conference when they have to be included in the published report. So I asked her to repeat what she had said, which she did. Then I answered that he had seemed as committed as all of us to the humanitarian aims of the Survey. That was how I had understood his feelings at the time.'

'You said that?' asks Bill, his eyes humorous, flickering like mercury.

'Why not?'

Bill lifts one hand. 'No particular reason.'

'Alex has written to me.' Edward says, stabbing into what might be mockery with a sharp, quick lunge. 'I'm going to see him.'

Bill sips at his wine. 'Are you really?'

Edward feels angry now. This is complacency, not contentment. The apartment in Rome, the close family, a loving wife, a wish for no more: complacency or spiritual death. 'You never liked him, did you?'

'It wasn't a question of dislike.' The smile has gone at last. 'Alex was why I left the Survey, Edward. You must remember that. I stood a year of it in Washington. The vanity, the personalizing of what we were trying to do, as if our chief purpose was to cleanse his soul. He pushed us of

136

course. This was right, or so I thought at first. The Survey should be a crusade, certainly for the younger members of staff, and von Kierich's idea was to make it into precisely that: a question not only of feeding the poor but making the world more decent and tidy as well. But it was a cold crusade: ice rather than fire. Imperialism of a kind, I suppose: a benevolent imperialism, but just as sure of itself as the empire builders had ever been. Conquest as a cure for personal shame. That was Alex's motive.'

'It worked. The Survey prospered under him.'

'Not at the end it didn't.' Bill's slight smile returns: a look of strength. 'Or had you forgotten?'

'Surely you don't –'

'Believe those rumours about him? No I don't. But he shouldn't have taken the job. The Survey's purpose was a moral one: deeply moral, not just facts and administration. He had to be above reproach. The stories had enough force to make him leave. Then he gave up the job in Munich. Von Kierich is a man on the run, Edward. How well did you and Jane know him?'

The mention of Jane. 'We saw Alex often in Washington.'

'What did she think?' Perhaps the smile widens; Edward searches, a swift, sharp look. Bill had known her years ago in Rome, when they were all young together with Vittorio and the others: the days of his embassy visits. 'But Jane admired him. I remember. She told me long after I'd left the Survey that she looked after von Kierich whilst you were in hospital, when the two of you got back from Africa.' Now the pale eyes retreat, as if Bill sees suddenly the extent of his trespass. 'The time you were both captured.' His voice loses that easy flow and rises into a new, thin tightness, almost shrill. 'Poor Jane.' He blushes, looks away.

'Why?'

'I miss her, Edward. So does Helen.' The ease returns,

and the sympathy. It was strange, that flash of embarrass-ment, yet not so strange if Bill knows more about Alex's power, either by rumour or fact: the power to lure a woman to her death. Bill twists away like a swift, sly fish back to the German. 'Your questioner in Toulouse had a point. I wish Alex had shown more emotion, more care for those people we were trying to help.' He shifts in his seat, raises one hand to push the points home. 'It was all so reasoned and sensible, his planning for their welfare. But cold, or not cold but never outside himself: still the Prussian looking to rearrange the world according to his own ideals of efficiency and fairness. A new conquest, Edward, a new imperialism. The patrician approach. That was what I saw.'

Edward rallies. 'He was no sentimentalist. Of course not.'

'Except towards himself. I detected a strong vein of self-pity.'

He ignores this. 'What good would sentimentality have done?'

'None at all. But those of us who worked with him might have felt we were dealing with a human being.' Bill raises his hand again in a gesture of mock surrender. 'I'm sorry. I dare say you're right.' That easy capitulation: the lazy way out. 'At least he was tough. And the Survey needs defending now. Perhaps that's another question for Alex. How did he manage to get more money for us year after year? Even Vittorio couldn't do that. And look at it now under Kris-tiansen. All he does is to produce papers which nobody reads.'

'Bernt Kristiansen is a dull man,' Edward says.

'Not like Alex.' They both look out of the window into the crowded street. 'Now tell me more about Toulouse,' Bill says. 'Were the Americans there in force?'

Chapter Fourteen

It is a warm clear day and Rose Finch walks from the Piccadilly Underground station to the London Library in St James's Square. Now she has time to search slyly for a possible clue to those outbursts of the last few days, the sudden excitement on the terrace and in the General's kitchen. On the train, Edward had retired again into that kind, vague courtesy. She needs more.

Gentleness is such a feature of her life, she decides. She thinks of her father, remembering how Ben Talbot had once described him. 'A sweet man, Rose: so anxious to help, so kind to those like me who were struggling a bit to survive. He was one of the first people to buy my work. How grateful I was!' Rose knows that her father has come already to despise the prettiness of the Sun Room: its bouquets of flowers and crossed rakes, quaint hoes and scythes with their bright, curved blades, the boys and girls playing amongst the hayricks. 'Quite sweet, though,' is what he says, 'Rex Whistler pastiche.' Ultimately he will always be kind with Ben or anyone else. Will no one be strong? She crosses Lower Regent Street, almost oblivious to the noise and rush of the traffic.

In the London Library she puts her bag down in the alcove by the door, taking out her small pocket diary, a pad of paper and a pencil, and walks through the hall, where several people wait at the counter. One of the librarians looks up at her. Conscious of his attention, she smiles briefly at him before descending into the basement where the back numbers of *The Times* are stored.

The room is empty. She looks in her diary where she has written some possible dates and takes down the index for those years from the metal shelves. The name is there: von Kierich, followed by several entries. With difficulty she carries one tall, heavy volume to the table in the centre of the room. The pages are stiff, slightly brown, the type a clear deep black and the text seems already to have the authority of age, telling of old crises, dead leaders, forgotten issues. A rail strike is threatened in Britain. In France there is doubt about the survival of a government. In London a pundit predicts 'alarming' increases in the level of traffic within the next ten years. After turning a few pages Rose sees the name of the Survey.

The report mentions rumours that various governments have threatened to withdraw their support from the Survey, a body set up to investigate what should be done to help the poorer nations of the world, unless its German director, Dr Alexander von Kierich, resigns. Questions were to be asked in the House of Commons. Was it a plot led by the United States and its allies to get rid of someone who often had harsh words for the way the rich countries ignored the needs of what Dr von Kierich called 'the South'?

The next issue takes the story further. Dr von Kierich had resigned. His successor was to be Dr Vittorio Falconi, an Italian economist who had worked for some years with the United Nations in Rome. The Survey's international supervisory board had made the announcement the previous day in the form of a press release signed by their chairman, a former American Secretary of State. It had come as a surprise. Dr von Kierich's contract had another three years to run and the staff had understood that he would be there until he retired. The press release said that he was to return to Germany. An anonymous member of the Survey's staff was quoted as saying how 'shocked' he or she was at the news.

In the following day's *Times* there is another report, this time in a more prominent position, with a photograph of a tall man in a dark suit leaving an office building. His head is down, the long, expressionless face partly hidden. Behind him is a younger man carrying a briefcase who looks straight at the camera. Rose thinks, That face! The menace is frightening, the fury of affronted loyalty; she recognizes Edward West, the 'bag carrier' as he had once described himself, several paces behind his threatened master.

The article mentions strange gaps in the history of von Kierich's war which may be behind his departure. The report says that friends of von Kierich and members of the Survey's staff believed these new suspicions were a plot in themselves: lies concocted by enemies to get rid of him. His part in the 1944 conspiracy against Hitler was well known, as was his opposition to the Nazis when he had worked at the German Foreign Office. *The Times* mentions again that questions were to be asked in the United States Congress and the House of Commons.

Rose turns more pages. The paper for the next day has nothing. On the day after there is a head-and-shoulders photograph of von Kierich: stiff features, a thin face marked on the left cheek just below the eye, a long chin, a high forehead from which silver hair is brushed smoothly back, straight, firm lips. The report says that the American State Department has denied that there is a plot. Dr von Kierich is resigning on private grounds, not in response to pressure. It should be understood that this is a matter between Dr von Kierich and the board of the Survey, which is an independent international body.

The clichés amuse her: the language of public denial. Then she reads a statement from von Kierich himself. It is true, he declares, that he has decided to leave the Survey. The idea has been in his mind for a long time and he has not talked about it because he knew people would only try

141

to persuade him to stay. After all – and here he makes a joke – it is so much easier not to have a change, not to have to look for a successor. He is, von Kierich goes on, still with humour, in some ways a weak man. Appeals to his sense of responsibility will always be hard to resist. It is better to go now, to the surprise of everyone. He will return to Germany, do consultancy work and write. It will not really be retirement. He will still work hard.

Von Kierich's name is in the next day's parliamentary report. In the House of Commons a minister from the Foreign Office was asked about the resignation of this distinguished international civil servant. Would the minister deny that there was any political pressure put upon von Kierich to leave? Would he also confirm that the British government will continue to support the Survey in the valuable work that it is doing in spite of attempts by other nations to interfere with its independence? The minister answered briefly, referring to Dr von Kierich's own statement. Another Member of Parliament had joined in the exchange to deplore the Opposition's habit of searching for conspiracies where none exist.

On subsequent days, *The Times* reports further rumours from Washington. Then the question of von Kierich's involvement in wartime atrocities in eastern Europe is raised openly for the first time. An international Jewish group has announced that its researchers will look into the case. They will interview Dr von Kierich and seek evidence in Germany and Israel. Long, inconclusive articles have appeared in the *New York Times* and the *Washington Post*. Below a piece on the Common Market, *The Times* has a short editorial of its own, declaring that judgement should be suspended in the von Kierich affair until the Jewish group has finished its work.

Heeding its own words, *The Times* abandons the story for several weeks, apart from a few lines to say that the Jewish investigators had visited Bonn and were on their way to Israel to check documents and speak to survivors of the Holocaust. They wished to complete their work as quickly as possible. Meanwhile Dr Falconi had declared what an honour it was to succeed such a great public servant. He felt humbled by the huge task ahead of him.

Rose takes another volume down from the shelf. The next reference comes in a more prominent column on the foreign news page. It says that the Jewish investigators have declared that there is no evidence of Dr Alexander von Kierich's involvement in war crimes. Apart from 'guilt by association' (of which many Germans could be accused), they have found nothing. Von Kierich is then quoted as saying that he feels exonerated. He will still leave the Survey at the end of September. He is sure that Doctor Falconi will make an excellent successor to him as its director.

There is another question in Parliament, answered by a reference to the Jewish investigators, and a short statement to say that Dr von Kierich has gone to live and work in Munich, then silence for the rest of the year. Rose looks through the next year's index. She finds nothing, so she goes on to the year after and there is his name again with several entries beside it: the beginning of the serious trouble.

The report says that the German magazine *Der Spiegel*, always on the trail of former Nazis, has compiled a dossier on Dr Alexander von Kierich, the former director of the Survey. Dr von Kierich's departure from Washington had coincided with rumours of his earlier involvement in war-time atrocities in eastern Europe but these had been denied. Investigations at that time had cleared him. Von Kierich, the descendant of an aristocratic family from East Prussia, had taken up a position as a consultant to an international trading company based in Munich. Now *Der Spiegel* has published the results of its researches, the most damaging of which was a report written and signed by Dr von Kierich on his return from a visit to the Russian front.

In 1942 von Kierich had apparently travelled by air to a remote district of the Ukraine with an officer of the SS. *Der Spiegel* had a photograph of his signature on the report of the trip. The place described had been the scene of a series of notorious massacres at that time. The report named the local commander and gave details of the forces stationed there. It mentioned the slaughter itself only indirectly in a paragraph at the end which said that operations seemed to be proceeding satisfactorily; then came von Kierich's signature. Once more *The Times* had a photograph of the thin-faced man, the lips tight, caught in the street by a photographer, the smooth hair unruffled even on such a difficult day.

There is worse to come. Often it is personal recollection that shows the true horror of such events. A Ukrainian emigré in Chicago, recently arrested for war crimes on evidence from the Simon Wiesenthal Centre, had been a member of one of the units involved in the massacres. During interrogation the Ukrainian had collapsed and admitted that his hatred of the Soviet system had led him to join the German army after Hitler's invasion of Russia.

Then came the accusation. The Ukrainian said it was wrong to victimize soldiers who had merely obeyed orders, often under threat of execution. There were much greater murderers still at large, some in positions of power. He told how a year ago he had seen on television a man who had visited their unit, watched the execution of a group of prisoners and then gone up to one of the bodies which might possibly have been still alive and fired a bullet into its head from a pistol seized from the officer in command. This man was now listened to by governments throughout the world; then the Ukrainian had said von Kierich's name.

The story continued over several issues of *The Times*. The Ukrainian said that he particularly remembered the incident because von Kierich had not been wearing a uniform but a dark suit with no mackintosh or overcoat as the day was quite warm. The man's face seemed almost unchanged on television, the Ukrainian said, although the hair had of course turned grey. How surprised the Ukrainian had been by this murderer in civilian clothes.

Von Kierich had answered the accusation. The report had been written by him, he said. He had been sent to the eastern front by his superiors in the Foreign Office, who had wished to find out the truth behind rumours. Of course it had been necessary to have authorization for the journey from the Nazi authorities; this was arranged by the SS officer who had accompanied him, an old acquaintance from childhood. Von Kierich's mission was to separate truth from lies. That was why he had gone, to return in disgust and horror.

Von Kierich said that his record of opposition to Hitler was well known; these lies could not destroy it. He had been imprisoned and tortured by the Nazis, saved only by the Allies' liberation of his country. He had never shot at or killed anyone, having spent the entire war as a civil servant in the Wilhelmstrasse. The Ukrainian had invented the murder to try to exonerate himself. Von Kierich had seen some terrible things; this he had never denied. But these accusations had been dealt with two years ago at the time of his departure from the Survey. He had been cleared. He cannot help wondering now if there is more to the 'resurrection' of the case than this solitary man in Chicago. *The Times* then reports that *Der Spiegel* had repeated the idea that certain forces in the West, particularly in the United States, might still want to destroy Dr von Kierich who had persisted with his campaign for better treatment of the Third World.

Apparently no one else had come forward to add to the Ukrainian's testimony. Rose imagines that the affair might end there. Then she reads in a later issue of *The Times* that Dr Alexander von Kierich has left his job in Munich, insisting that his resignation is not an admission of guilt. Recent protests and a vicious campaign against him had made work impossible. At first he had been determined to resist this new fascism. Now he could see that the dispute was affecting his colleagues. Last week there had been an attempt to burn down the building where he had his office, foiled only by an early discovery of the fire by a Turkish cleaner. He believed it was better for him to go.

That is all. *The Times* makes no more mention of the case: not where Dr von Kierich had gone nor the result of the prosecution of the Ukrainian. Rose shuts the volume, then lifts it and the others up on to the shelves, also replacing the index. She is thankful that no one has come in all the time she has been here. Even a complete stranger would have made her fear that her search might be discovered and somehow reported to Edward West. She wishes to keep her secret. The hall of the London Library is also empty when she leaves.

In a sunlit St James's Square she hails a taxi and settles on to the back seat as she is driven out from the centre of London towards Chelsea and Fulham, the scene of Ben Talbot's casual bohemian life. The fact that she is late does not worry her; Ben has a contempt for time, rarely arriving anywhere punctually himself. Slowly she tries at least partly to empty her mind of what she has just read.

The studio is in a long, low block built for artists in the early years of the century. She pushes the bell, then remembers that he has said it does not always work so also knocks hard at the door. Almost immediately he is there, Ben in his working clothes: a blue denim shirt, open at the neck, loose khaki trousers, moccasins on his sockless feet. He smiles at her in that oddly bashful way, the slightly curling brown hair chaotic above his round, comfortable face. They are more or less the same height: quite tall for a woman, average for a man.

'Rose. I was worried . . .' They kiss, Ben lingering a little, holding her shoulders so she thinks he may become amorous straight away. 'Was the traffic bad?'

'No. I went to the London Library.'

'Really?' He laughs, then looks serious. 'Why?'

'To look up something.'

'In connection with your work?'

'No, I'll tell you. It's interesting.' They both laugh and she is not sure why.

'Oh darling.' He has said the first loving word. 'Anyway, come in. I thought it would be nicer to have lunch here, so I got some food from the delicatessen around the corner. Nothing terribly exciting, I'm afraid.'

She enters the small space which serves as a hall, then walks up some narrow wooden stairs to the first floor and the enormous white studio where a large window frames a now cloudy sky. Against one wall is a long sofa covered in pale green material. A round table and four wooden chairs are in front of a small window on the left. In an alcove is the bed, its end just visible from where she is standing; in another alcove, opposite her, a black velvet curtain has been drawn to reveal the small stove, fridge and sink of his kitchen. On the wall opposite the sofa, on either side of the smaller window, hang two large abstract pictures: bright, wild colours of yellow, red and blue, quite different to what Ben paints now.

She glances at his work in progress: a large canvas on an easel in the centre of the room facing the other way so she cannot see it, a small table beside the easel for his palette and a glass jar holding several brushes. Next to the jar are tubes of paint, smaller empty unwashed jars and a heap of stained rags. Under the large window other canvases of different sizes rest against the wall with their backs to her. Three or four worn rugs cover parts of the floor's bare boards. A controlled chaos, Rose thinks.

'Is Fred the cat here today?' she asks.

'No. Not yet.'

They stand beside each other. 'And where's Mrs Holden?'

'Kay? Oh, she's in Connecticut.' He smiles at her. 'I go back a week tomorrow. Kay can't travel much because of the dogs. She doesn't like to be away from them for more than a day or two.' He puts a hand briefly on her arm. 'What about a drink? There's some white wine in the fridge. Let me fetch it.' He goes quickly to the kitchen alcove and returns with two full glasses. 'Sit down. Rose . . .' They sit, each at one corner of the sofa, an expanse of faded green a demilitarized zone between them. 'Did I tell you? I have a commission from the Rufford family.'

'The who?'

'The Ruffords. I'm sure James must know them. They live in Yorkshire.'

'Why should he know the Ruffords?'

'Oh, you know, same sort of background: country gents, that kind of thing. I've got the picture here to work on before I go up to Yorkshire for a last visit on Monday. Have a look.'

Ben walks ahead of her to the other side of the easel. On it is the large canvas of a family group in a big room, presumably a library because there are bookcases sunk into the walls, the brown bindings of the books at one end speckled by beams of sunlight amid the dark tones of the rest. A man in a tweed jacket stands by the fireplace. Next to him sits a woman in an armchair, a black dog at her feet. To the left of the dog stand a younger man and woman, he in a blue jersey and she in a long, green skirt. In the foreground, on the floor, apparently preoccupied with a toy of some sort, is a small boy in shorts.

At first Rose does not speak. Then she says, 'What are you going to call it?'

'Nothing. Pictures like that don't have names. It's not

148

quite finished. Look.' He points to a sketched area above the bookcase. 'Three generations of one family. What do you think?'

She considers the scene: its mixture of precision and vagueness, all overlaid with that familiar elegance. 'Well, as I've never met the people . . .'

'No. As a composition.'

'It seems fine: as a composition.'

'I like the Ruffords.'

'Really? Why?'

'They're nice people, particularly the old man.'

'How old is he?'

'Nearly seventy? I don't know.' Ben shrugs his shoulders.

'How old is Kay, Ben?'

'Fifty. Or so she says.' He laughs and comes closer to her.

'Why don't you marry her?'

He steps back. 'Rose, what is this?'

'I'm interested, Ben.' She hears her words quicken, the voice hard.

'I've already told you, surely. I'm happy as I am. We are friends. But I have my work.' He laughs. 'I need to earn a living.'

'I thought she was rich.'

'That's not right: to live off her.' Ben steps further away as she turns to face him. 'Look, Rose, we're not lovers. I told you. There's nothing predatory about Kay.'

'Isn't there?'

'No. Darling . . .' He sighs. 'Shall we have lunch now? It's in the kitchen. I'm sorry, I haven't put out the knives and forks or anything. I was working on the picture until you came.' They both go through to the kitchen alcove to bring out the food, and he lays two places at the round table quickly, rather clumsily, she helping him. Once they nearly bump into each other, which makes them laugh, he gripping her shoulder. Then they sit down, start to eat and Ben suddenly thumps his hands on the table, as if calling a meeting to order. 'Now I must know: what have you been up to? How are the studies? How's Baudelaire? When do you go back to college? Oh darling, those weeks at the manor were such fun.'

'Now you have Kay Holden,' she says.

'Darling! I told you what we are to each other.' Ben turns away to look at one of the pictures on the wall. 'Or what we aren't.' He starts to eat again. 'Poor Kay,' he says between mouthfuls. 'No, it's not Kay or anyone else who rules my life at the moment but work: more and more work. There's just so much of it.' He puts down his fork and waves an arm at the picture on the easel. 'After I've finished with the Ruffords, there's a house on Long Island where May Bogwin wants a room decorated with nautical scenes . . .'

Rose interrupts. 'Who is May Bogwin?'

'A friend of Kay's. One of the most successful decorators in New York.' Ben counts off the points on the fingers of one hand. 'Then I have to fly to California to paint the Hopkin family. Julius Hamer wants a picture of his place on Antigua. There's talk of an exhibition next summer in a gallery on Park Avenue. How I'll be able to get enough stuff together for it I just don't know!' His voice takes on a high, agitated pitch. 'Don't think they've forgotten me here, either. The Blake-Murdochs want a whole series of interiors done of their castello near Siena. Then there's the Watsons' house in Norfolk.' His hands fall on to the table as if exhausted. 'I tell you, there's no peace.'

'But that's marvellous.'

'You think so?'

'Better than being ignored.'

He starts to eat again, his head bent over his plate. 'Perhaps.'

Rose sips the sour white wine. 'Now don't start that again!'

'What?'

'About your painting. How you despise it.' She is trying to rid her mind of those cold newspaper reports. 'Why be ashamed?'

'What about that?' He waves his arm again at the easel.

'I don't know the family, so I can't comment.'

'But as a picture?' He laughs. 'Don't you think it's sweet?'

'What do you mean, Ben?'

His voice becomes louder. 'I said don't you think it's bloody sweet?'

'I like it.'

'Why? It's dreadful.' He leans across the table to get closer to her. 'A dreadful picture. Well, not dreadful because of course technique of a kind comes through: the polished technique of a minor craftsman perhaps, certainly not the imagination of an artist. For instance, what can you see in that room apart from the surface details? A photograph, if you like, with a few wiggly lines to make the view just that much less clear. Oh yes, there is beauty, of a kind, stultified of course, inanimate. You should see the family when they are in that room, posing for me. They don't use it often except on grand occasions like parties or when they want to impress someone. God knows how many years it is since any one of those books was ever taken down from the shelves, let alone read. They don't really read, you see, these people. Well, no, that's not quite true, in fact they're quite clever, so I'm wrong, they probably do read but not there.' He almost shouts the last word. 'No, what hits you in the face about that picture is the complete lack of humanity: no feeling, no strength or weakness, kindness or nastiness, cruelty or sympathy. Nothing, just the relentless bloody beauty. No, not even beauty. Prettiness, that's the word. Prettiness. It makes them, the people who live there, so quiet, so pious, as if they are in church. They posed wonderfully for me, never budging or stirring an inch to one side or the other, not even the children because this was what was expected of them. That was what they wanted, you see, to be images of the dead on top of some exquisitely carved huge cold stone monument or tomb, a family sepulchre. That's what all my subjects want: to be killed.' Ben's eyes are alight now. He takes another frantic gulp at his wine.

Rose remembers these outbursts. 'What about these other places: these villas and apartments and castles?' she asks gently. 'Have you killed people there as well?'

Ben shrugs. 'I make them look pretty.'

'Which is what they are.'

'I am a decorator. That is all. My pictures are extensions of the décor of people's houses. It is a harmless and not unprofitable trade.'

He is calm again now and suddenly stretches his arms up in the air above his head. 'Oh, darling, what rubbish! Look, let me tell you what's really been happening to me.' And Ben leans forward, resting his hands on the table, bringing his face nearer to her, and starts to speak in that easy flow, as if either of them might now say or do anything at all, first about Kay Holden's Connecticut farmhouse and his time there last spring. 'I was frightened I might be lonely,' he says. 'But Kay has interesting neighbours, people who work in New York: writers, Wall Street bankers, academics. They're so friendly. Yet she knew I had to get on with my work and I was on my own during the day.' Eventually he stops describing the chintzes in Kay Holden's drawing-room and the view of the river and stands to clear away the remains of their meal. 'Have I told you all this before? Thank you, darling,' he says when she takes through some of the things to the alcove kitchen.

'Some coffee?' Ben asks. There is a bubbling sound and he reaches out quickly to take the pot off the stove. 'Black?' She nods. 'I should have remembered.'

Rose sits down on the sofa again, then thinks, Now Ben will sit beside me once more, which he does. 'Do I make it all sound exciting?' he asks. 'So I was launched into the shark pool of the New York galleries.' Rose smiles. 'Then I came back to England and the manor and the summer with you.' Ben laughs, his face near to hers. She smells the slightly sour odour of his body, which again she remembers from their earlier kisses: so completely Ben that she finds herself quite dizzy and leans back into the sofa. 'You're in love with someone else, aren't you?' he says.

'No.'

'Why not?'

'What do you mean?'

'Why aren't you in love at your age? You should be.' He puts on a stern expression. 'I order you to fall in love, as soon as possible, the moment you leave this studio. That is what you should do. It's crazy . . .' He stops.

'Ben, don't.'

He puts his coffee cup down on the floor. 'Rose, I've missed you so much.' He leans across to put his arm around her shoulders and pulls her closer. At first she resists, but then feels she should be careful not to hurt him because in that instant she senses that he is upset, different to the humorous man who used to laugh, quote Baudelaire and say that he knew he had fallen in love. 'Darling.' He tries a kiss, clumsy at first before a revival of his old self-certainty, the sense that she must follow. 'Ben,' she says, but it does not matter because it is like those afternoons or evenings in the garden at the manor when he had seemed so easy, so full of goodwill, as if you were kissing an older relation, then found suddenly that the process was different, better than friendship. 'Ben, I wanted to tell you,' she says, thinking

153

of what she had read earlier this morning. He kisses her mouth, smothering the story with the truth of this actual moment: a part of life lived before it too joins the great clamouring past.

'Come through, darling,' he whispers. She follows him to the alcove where the bed is, at the other end of the room. 'Here,' he murmurs and undresses quickly, then waits for her until they are in bed together, under a heavy, bright quilt: she close to his thin lithe body which she has never seen naked before, rather frightened now for the first time, all those defences down. 'Darling.' Ben's voice is soft in her ear. He holds her, perhaps aware of her doubts, and then she is reassured by his reputation, remembering that he has done this hundreds, perhaps even thousands, of times before: 'a great Lothario' in her mother's words. She waits, attempting to drive other thoughts away: the fumbling of Simon Pumphrey, her impatience at this, the melancholy lovemaking with Paolo Alessandri night after night in the Via Belvedere. Ben will be sweet, gentle; of this she is sure. So when she allows his hands to do what they want, feels his kisses, she is relaxed, conscious of the slow rise of feelings she had known sometimes with Doctor Alessandri (she still cannot think of him as Paolo) when the Italian had been less tired than usual after his day on the hospital wards, yet never once with Simon Pumphrey who always comes too quickly, occasionally over her thigh or into the bed, once on the carpet in her room in the hall of residence when he had almost wept with embarrassment and shame.

'Darling.' Now Ben is on top of her, that slightly sour smell of his body, which she likes, mixed with the wine on his breath, again sour, not so nice; and she wishes he had waited a bit longer, encouraged her more, although the friendliness and ease is still there enough for her to notice calmly that like Simon Pumphrey he is easily excited, although it might be thought that at his age the response would be slower, more measured, the wisdom of time, not the impetuosity of youth. She feels him inside her, strangely small, a few quick stabs. Then he lets out a low cry, almost a moan, and it is over for him, too soon for her, but she sees she should disguise any disappointment as she gently pats his thin back, whispering 'There' in the way she might comfort a child. She does like him.

They lie alongside each other in silence at first before Ben says in an awkward voice, as if slightly ashamed, 'Come away with me this weekend, Rose. We can meet somewhere, here perhaps, then fly to Paris or take the ferry to France. Please.'

She rests her head on his chest, determined to be loving. 'Yes, Ben.' For a moment she thinks he might be quite brave.

'Ring me. Do try to come.'

Rose murmurs, 'Shall I?'

He draws her head closer into his shoulder. 'Are you happy, darling?'

'Yes. Why not?' So they lie still together for a bit, then Rose runs her hand slowly over his chest. 'Ben, I read something earlier today.' She tells what she has found in the London Library, remembering it all yet not forgetting Ben here beside her and how interested he had seemed that evening when Edward had spoken of the mystery of Alex von Kierich. 'I wonder if it's possible ever to discover what really happened in a case like that,' she says. Then suddenly she remembers about the train home, the public meeting in the village hall, and reaches for her watch, which she has left on top of her clothes beside the bed. 'Oh no!' She must leave. 'Ben . . .'

Rose hears the slow, regular, loud breathing of a man asleep at her side, the occasional quiet snore. She gets out of the bed as quietly as possible, puts on her clothes, glances at his face, the mouth soft in repose: a look of slight petulance. The sound of her dressing wakes him. 'Ben, I must go,' she says. 'If I don't get this train I'll be late. I'll telephone,' and he murmurs, 'Darling, please do,' as she leans over to kiss him goodbye.

Chapter Fifteen

Edward West catches an afternoon train to be back in time for the meeting.

Bill had shown signs of decay: lazy but oddly bitter, those embers flickering in a corner of his dark complacency, a dying glow. Bill's hatred of Alex is the one lively part of him, foolish though it is: an old man shouting at the moon. But Bill at least has a refuge, a family in Italy, or so Edward thinks as he gets into his car at the station to begin the last part of his journey home.

A few miles outside the small town, he turns off the main road on to a narrow lane with empty, wide country on either side, thick spinneys breaking up the rich fields. Once Jane had talked of abandoning her translation of the Paris guide-book to write an historical study of the village. 'What fun one could have, Edward!' she had said one afternoon in the garden during their last visit to England together. 'Think! There must be fascinating material here in the parish registers and James Finch has those family papers, which I'm sure he'd let me see. I do think that's exciting, don't you? Look!'

She had stretched her bare arms towards the church tower, as if in greeting. 'The church, for instance. Think what changes have buffeted against those ancient walls. I must speak to Robert Padstow. One might get up a synopsis, see if a publisher is interested. Just the thing for the Americans! Perhaps Paris has been done too much already.' Then she flared up again. 'I love this place more than anywhere now, darling. Can you see that?'

So he had encouraged her. Would it be a good idea to ask the vicar and James Finch to supper? An evening had been arranged, with Martin and Nancy Riley as well, but Jane did not mention the research, saying afterwards only, 'I didn't like to bother them. I've rather gone off the idea. In any case, there's so little time. We have to go back to Washington next week.'

The arms had stretched out again as they sat in the garden. 'Why can't one just enjoy the village for what it is?' she asked. 'A wonderful place where one can rest and relax. Darling, I want Nick and Charles to love it as much as we do. What's so marvellous is that we can all be here together.' She looked knowingly at him and laughed.

On her way down from London in a slightly later train Rose decides to spend this coming weekend with Ben. It would be dishonourable to refuse, after what she has allowed him to do. She will join him on Saturday, not Friday, and will not show enthusiasm for any proposed trip that is longer than two days. So now she has a new lover at last.

At the manor, soon after her return, she hears the front-door bell ring as she is washing out Trixie's bowl in the new kitchen. She puts the bowl down on the edge of the sink and walks into the hall, the little dog running behind. Samuel Dove is at the door in a dark suit and glossy black shoes, the top of an ironed white handkerchief sticking up from his jacket's breast pocket. In one hand he holds a leather folder. His face shines like the surface of well-polished fruit.

'I hope I'm not too early,' he says, looking at her smart London skirt, then up at the heavy dark blue jersey she had put on as soon as she got back to the manor and its large, cold rooms. 'Your father did say we could have a bit of a chat before the meeting. Are you coming as well, Rose?' Always the use of her first name, said gently as if he is addressing a lunatic.

'Yes.' She glances at her watch. 'It's not until eight o'clock.'

'That's right.' He laughs, still gentle with her. 'There's plenty of time to get into your Sunday best, Rose: perhaps the red dress you wore last year at the opera. My wife said to me that colour suits her down to the ground – and sure enough, it did. That's an evening I'll never forget: the wonderful music in the perfect setting of your drawing-room, looking out at the garden. We were so delighted to be there and your mother arranged the buffet supper afterwards so beautifully. Everyone had what they wanted and no need to queue. What was the name of the opera, Rose?'

'*Don Pasquale.*'

Dove smiles. 'Of course we didn't understand a word. What language was it in?'

'Italian.'

'Oh yes, Italian. But that didn't matter because the way those people acted was so wonderful, it carried you along all the same. We laughed as much as everyone else.' He looks at her in a sentimental way. 'That dress did suit you, Rose. The marvellous red.' He laughs again and brings down one hand sharply on to his leather folder. 'I tell you what: are you going to have another opera soon?'

'Perhaps next summer.'

'Next summer. Will the tickets be the same price?' Dove raises his eyebrows. 'I know it's a good cause and the church needs every penny, but you do make us pay. Never mind. I'll make a bargain with you. If you promise to wear that red dress again, my wife and I will come to the next opera. Not only that: I'll bring my sister and brother-in-law as well, because she plays the piano and they both like music. Is that a bargain? Good. Now where's your father?'

In the drawing-room James Finch, smart in a brown tweed

suit, sits in an armchair reading a copy of *Country Life*. 'Dad, here's Mr Dove,' she says. Her father stands up, vague at first, then offers a smile. She turns to go.

Sir James holds up one hand. 'No no, Rose. Wait a moment.' He looks at his watch. 'Your mother's not back from the stables yet.' He turns to Dove. 'Would you like a drink, Sam, before our ordeal?' His words come in a slight rush. She notices the empty glass by his chair.

'A small Scotch and water, please,' says Dove, his head bowed slightly although he is shorter than James Finch. Then he adds, as if as an afterthought, 'Sir James.'

James Finch turns to his daughter. 'Rose, perhaps you could get it from the Flower Room cupboard.' He hands her his glass. 'And give me a refill, will you, darling? The same as Sam.' He turns back to Dove and laughs. 'We'd better be careful. Don't want to fall off the platform!' He seems to have forgotten about her trip to London.

When Rose returns, the two men are sitting opposite each other on either side of the fireplace, and she hears Dove say, 'The sunlight really brings it to life,' as she gives them their drinks and sits down herself.

'Yes, Sam, it does,' James Finch answers. He smiles at Rose. 'We were talking about the Sun Room.'

'Then the whole room almost jumps out at you!' Dove says. 'Last time I was here, Lady Finch took me in to have a look and you almost had to shield your eyes from the brightness! I thought it was marvellous. All those farm carts and hayricks and little children. The Sun Room. What a lovely name. Was it always called that?'

'Oh no.' James Finch rushes to correct him. 'That was Ben Talbot's idea: the artist who painted it. I don't know if you've ever met him. A shortish man with curly hair. An old friend of mine. The room used to be the old nursery, then the children grew up. I suggested to Ben that he might turn it into something different. The theme is rather charming don't you think? Fun as well.' Suddenly he turns to his daughter. 'Any news?'

Now her face is burning. 'No.'

'Nothing since your dinner with the Rileys?'

So that was what he meant: not Ben. 'I've seen no one today.'

'Well, I'm not too worried,' says Dove, the cheeriness still in his voice. He smiles at Rose and looks again at her father, anxious to get to work. 'Sir James, I hope we haven't made a mistake in asking the vicar to be chairman of the meeting, because he may be biased against us. It's the chairman who chooses the speakers from the floor, Sir James. What happens if he goes for a string of our opponents? I'm as good as certain his wife signed the petition, and I've heard that one of the Miss Horns from the old greengrocer's shop has been boasting they've got the church on their side. To have the support of the vicar is quite something, even these days.' Dove looks at Rose. 'They're going to give the petition to the district council after the meeting. They say it was only fair to allow us a chance to explain ourselves.' He turns back to Sir James Finch. 'How I wish the Reverend Padstow was still here, Sir James. Then there wouldn't have been half this trouble. He had a great gift for calming people down, and with him in the chair you could be sure that both sides would get a decent hearing. She was such a good woman, too.' They are all silent for a moment, as if in tribute. 'We all know who'll be called to speak first, after you and I have said our pieces. The General, of course. Then there's that man in the house next to the church, Mr West. He's very thick with General Riley. All these new people getting together.'

James Finch lets out a bellow of laughter. 'Hardly new, Sam. The Wests and the Rileys have had houses in the village for a long time.'

'Years,' says Rose, in spite of herself.

'Well, I still think of them as new because they've never really been local people, have they?' Dove says, shifting in his chair to pick up his glass off the table beside him. 'They've worked abroad or in London and have rented their houses out to other strangers. The Wests, for instance: I've seen him about, but I've never met her.'

'She's dead,' says Rose.

Dove grins, still patronizing. 'Is she, Rose? Oh well, that explains it. So Mr West lives all alone in that great big house.'

'He has two sons,' says her father. 'Young boys. Well, not that young. In their twenties. Is that right, Rose? How old are the boys?'

Rose looks at Dove, ignoring her father. 'I don't think you'll have much trouble with Edward West. He doesn't want to take sides in this dispute. In fact he's doing his best to calm Martin Riley down.'

'Is he coming this evening?' asks her father.

'I expect so. As an observer.'

Dove laughs, more slyly now. 'We've certainly got all sorts in the old village now, from military men to high finance. Now what was Mr West's profession? I know he used to travel a lot. The trouble with these people is that they haven't got enough to do. They're still fit and full of energy even though they've retired. That General, for instance: he skips through the village like a lamb in springtime. You know, Sir James, they ought to be grateful to us for giving them something to get their teeth into.' He gulps at his almost empty glass. 'The trouble is I don't see how this meeting is going to settle anything. One thing we ought to be thinking about is an improvement to the road between here and the Chilworth crossroads: straightening out a few of those corners! It must be one of the most twisty three-mile stretches in the country. The council has been wanting to do something about it for years, or so someone in

County Hall told me, but they've never been able to justify the expense. My lorries can manage all right now, but if the new mill really takes off and we start to get bigger loads coming in there could be trouble.'

'Improve the road!' cries her father.

'No no, Sir James. It's really nothing to worry about,' Dove says quickly, leaning forward in his chair. 'All that's some way off. We've got to get the operation going first and when the work is done on the road, it will only be a question of straightening out a few corners, as I said. That should make it easier for Lady Finch's horsebox as well! There's no need for a great motorway or anything. We've been through all this before.' Even Dove's control is starting to slip. 'You must remember our previous conversation about the increase in traffic. Lady Finch said there was going to be some advantage in being deaf at last! We laughed at that. Then I was able to say that you will hear nothing up here at all and the people who live near the church and down that end of the village will hear nothing, either. The only houses which may be slightly affected are those on the edge of the council estate, nearest the site. But most of them will gladly accept this small inconvenience in return for the new prosperity and jobs the mill will bring. There's no need to worry.'

'Are you sure?' asks Rose.

Dove's face settles once more into that smile of condescension. 'Why, yes, Rose, or as sure as anyone can be. You see I grew up in the village, and although I've moved on since I still know what people are thinking. After all, I've got relations in and around the place, two or three of them on the council estate itself, and they tell me what goes on. People are getting fed up with the way some of these newcomers have only been here five minutes before they start telling us how to run the place. It's all very well for them, with their jobs in London or their nice fat pensions.

They don't mind what happens to the young people of the village as long as everything is neat and tidy and there are nice open fields where they can walk their dogs. Talking of dogs, Sir James, I was on the site the other day with the contractor when I saw that golden retriever of General Riley's loose, running towards the wood. He seems to let that animal go wherever it wants. Has it ever chased your sheep? They all have dogs, those people.' Dove shakes his head. 'The Rileys, the two Miss Horns. The new vicar has a chow.'

'Edward West,' adds James Finch.

'No. Edward does not have a dog,' Rose says.

'If you say so, darling.' He looks at his watch and then at her. 'Are you coming to the meeting? Of course, you've changed already.'

'Dad, I've been in London.'

He seems to think for a moment, frowning. 'So you have.'

'I'll put Trixie away.'

Rose gets up and walks to the door, which opens suddenly to reveal her mother elegant in a dark green skirt, black jacket and cream blouse with pearls strung tight around its high neck. Isabel Finch's hand goes straight to her ear to switch on her hearing-aid, as if cocking a gun. 'Rose, where's Trixie? There's a perfectly vile smell in the hall.'

They stand facing each other, mother and daughter. Rose fights back. 'The smell couldn't be anything to do with Trixie. She's here with me. Before that we were in the kitchen together.' Rose shouts, 'Trixie!' The little dog runs across.

'Isabel!' James Finch's voice is loud, agitated. 'Where have you been?'

'Changing.' She turns on her daughter. 'Where are you going to put that dog?'

'In my room.'

'Please try to keep her away from the hall. Some people are coming back for supper after the meeting and the smell won't be a very nice welcome! We may be depressed enough as it is.'

'Will you have a drink, Isabel?' her husband calls out. 'Sam is here.'

'So I see. Good evening, Mr Dove.' She stays with Rose. 'How was your lunch?'

'Wonderful.'

But her mother seems not to have heard or to care because she walks into the drawing-room, leaving Rose by the door. 'Well, Mr Dove, are we ready for the fray?'

Chapter Sixteen

Cars are parked near the village hall, lining the street from the crossroads up towards the end of the village where the fields are dark green in the fading light.

Edward, walking alone from his house to the public meeting, thinks of Martin, the vigour with which the General is prepared to defend their adopted landscape from the supposed ugliness of the saw mill. It is the new imperialism, he decides: these conquerors with their civilizing mission, determined to save the village from savages like Dove. He smiles, satisfied with the analogy, pleased also to have trumped for himself Bill's facile use of it earlier on. Tonight he will watch. There may be shouting, anger, even hysteria, in contrast to the calm which the protesters say they wish to preserve. The girl Rose will be there, uneasy perhaps but essentially detached as well.

He should be too old for fantasies, or so he thinks: fantasies that involve the living and the dead. What happens, he wonders, to men like Bill Higginson and Martin when they are alone at night with their wives? Most probably a great calm descends, a sweet oblivion, a foretaste of death itself.

'Evening, Mr West.'

He turns to see Bob Gifford, the husband of his cleaning lady. 'Why, good evening, Bob.'

'Going to the meeting, then?' Bob Gifford asks. He has just emerged from the Bell, the village pub.

'Yes. Are you coming?'

'Oh yes. We all ought to take an interest, oughtn't we?' He laughs, the lines deepening in his tanned face. 'I said I'd meet my wife by the door. We thought we'd better be at the hall nice and early to get good seats.' He pats his ear. 'My hearing's not what it was. Too much tractor-driving, I expect. We both think the mill would be a good thing for the district, Mr West.' They walk together towards the crossroads. 'There's nothing here for young people now. They're even cutting back at the manor.'

'You must have known Mr Dove a long time.'

'Sam Dove? I should say so. I've got a lot of time for old Sam. He's built up the business started by his father and done well for himself. Of course you'll always get those who run him down. A lot of people don't like to see other folk make money. Sam and I grew up together, right over there.' He points to the other side of the crossroads. 'Well, not quite, because my old father lived further out, in one of that pair of cottages by Barrow Wood. He worked for the Finch family as well, for Sir James's grandfather, as a stockman. I started off with the cattle too, but you had to do a bit of everything by the time I finished. A real jack of all trades I was at the end.'

There is a crowd by the doorway of the hall, a low red-brick building that stretches back to a grass field in which three or four horses stand silhouetted against the trees. Edward stops briefly. 'Whose are those horses?' he asks.

Bob Gifford stares into the field. 'Lady Finch's,' he says. 'You can be pretty certain any horse around here is hers. They're the cause of the trouble, I reckon. Sir James can't afford to keep them, so he has to go to Sam Dove for help — old Sam who grew up in those labourers' cottages. Funny, isn't it?' He laughs again and makes for the crowd. 'Now if you'll excuse me, my wife will be getting worried. Ah, there she is!'

They join the crush. Mrs Gifford comes up and Bob

suggests Edward should sit with them, but he refuses politely, saying, 'No, I'm all right, thanks,' and goes alone into the badly lit white room, making his way between the rows of chairs, glancing at the large portrait of the Queen to the left of the door. At the front, in the centre of a raised stage, is a solitary table covered in a green baize cloth with three chairs behind it and an easel to one side. The easel displays a huge plan of the village, a section shaded in grey to show the proposed development.

Edward looks at his watch: only a few minutes to go before the start of the meeting. How strangely phlegmatic these people are, he decides. Surely an issue like this should interest the whole community, yet there seems to be a large predominance of what are often called newcomers. Apart from the Giffords and perhaps a dozen others, the older inhabitants appear to have stayed away. Those who have come sit at the back of the hall, far from the stage.

He moves forward, hears a cry of 'Edward!' to his left; it is Martin Riley. He smiles at Martin and Nancy, who waves, pats an empty chair next to her and shouts, 'There's a spare seat here!' He shakes his head and looks back at the door where people are now entering the hall, a mixture of old and new villagers at last.

Another arm beckons from the front row. Isabel Finch looks straight at him, whilst beside her Rose faces sideways, apparently staring at the bare white wall. He wants the girl to keep her head in profile just a moment longer so he can watch her expression: that young disenchantment. 'Edward!' Isabel's voice is shrill, the pearls at her neck dull in the dim light. 'Come and sit with us.' Rose turns, embarrassed but smiling as well. He walks past some empty chairs and sits down between Isabel and a thin young man called Godfrey Webber, who is the Finches' agent. 'Well, what do you think?' Isabel whispers. 'There seem to be a lot of people. Is that good or bad?'

They have assumed that he is on their side. 'In what way?' he asks.

'For us.'

'Everyone likes James.'

Isabel gives him a sweet smile. 'Edward, I've been meaning to telephone you. We hope you'll come to the manor afterwards to have something to eat. Just a sandwich, I'm afraid, but it would be lovely to see you. I know that James will want to have your views on the meeting.' She laughs, her charm pledged to the service of her husband. 'Did you see Martin's ridiculous manifesto?'

'Look!' says Rose before he can answer.

Three men have come on to the stage: Sir James Finch, the vicar and Samuel Dove. Gradually the sound of talking in the hall fades. Edward looks round. The room is full; people are standing at the back by the door and along the walls at the sides. He sees Martin Riley's face, redder than usual, those fierce eyes unnaturally bright. Oh Martin, for God's sake! Even Nancy must be frightened when he is like this: even the Beacon with her Boy. He suddenly remembers Jane saying, 'One never really knows what goes on in other people's marriages, does one? Take Mummy and Daddy, for instance. Even I don't really know.' She had never taken the Rileys seriously, had mocked them behind their backs and gently to their faces. This was wrong: another example of that odd, twisted naïvety which had made it impossible for her to survive.

Rose and her mother stare at the stage as if expecting a divine revelation, Isabel's hand raised to adjust her hearing aid. The vicar starts to speak. 'Louder, louder!' comes a shout from the back of the hall, followed by a few claps. The vicar, a large bald man in a black suit and a dog collar, smiles in the direction of the heckler. 'Of course,' he says. 'Of course.' Then he turns towards the centre of his audience. 'I am new to your village,' he says, the voice high, a smile weak on his narrow mouth, his anxious face pale above the sombre certainties of his dark clerical clothes. 'You must forgive me if I have not yet mastered the acoustics of your hall. What is important is that tonight we should listen to all sides of the argument: the point of view of Mr Dove here and Sir James Finch who is supporting him, then the various objections to the proposed development which have been raised by others.'

'Hear, hear!' comes another shout, this time from one of the boys standing along the wall to the right of the stage. Some of the audience may be drunk, probably the rowdy element of which Mrs Gifford speaks so often. Edward turns again, sees a group of youths standing at the back; then, further forward, Martin Riley's wild furious eyes.

'Hear, hear, indeed,' says the vicar. The flustered clergyman sits down, turns to Samuel Dove on his left as if for reassurance but receives only a cold glance as Dove stares at some notes of his own. Next he tries Sir James Finch on his other side. James smiles, places a hand on the vicar's shoulder and says something which makes him nod vigorously, the top of his head a dark crimson. The vicar stands again, with panic in his eyes. 'We will start the evening's proceedings with a short statement from Sir James Finch,' he says.

James Finch stands to an outbreak of whistling, hooting and shouts. Isabel stares ahead, possibly not hearing the worst of it. Rose looks at her hands, but Webber the agent is applauding. Edward claps several times as well, thinking that the heckling is not vicious because most of the faces he sees are laughing as if out for an evening's fun. Martin Riley looks towards the back of the hall and puts a finger to his lips. As if in response, the noise fades, ending with a loud imitation fart from near the door.

Damn Martin: he has fixed this. No, surely not. Edward whispers 'Poor James' to Isabel, then sees a collapse in her face, the frozen calm thawing in eyes bright with tears. Beyond her, Rose does not look at the stage, still studying those tightly clasped hands.

'Ladies and gentlemen!' James Finch begins. Immediately there comes another shattering imitation fart and a shrieking whistle but also shouts of 'Let him speak!' and 'Quiet.' Isabel's eyes are dry now, Rose's lips parted in wonder as she stares at her father. 'That's better,' the young agent whispers. The hall is quiet again. James speaks, oddly contained, as if he is announcing minor variations to a timetable. 'I am most grateful to the vicar. Thank you, Peter.' The clergyman smiles up at him, his bared false teeth absurdly bright. 'Now let us turn to the evening's business. Mr Dove will explain his proposals in a moment. I don't want to make you wait too long for that. As you know, this meeting is the last stage in a process of consultation which has been going on for some time. A part of this was the article which Mr Dove and I wrote for the parish magazine, to which those opposed to the development replied in the next issue. Then came the publication of the plans and scaled drawings in the local paper. We also distributed a short explanatory leaflet throughout the village. This led to the counterblast of the recent so-called "manifesto".'

James Finch stops. There is good-natured laughter. His pause is slightly too long. 'Mr Dove and I have already spoken to the council's planning department, although we have not yet been given permission to go ahead. However, we are fortunate to have secured the support of the councillor for this village, Mrs Upcher. I believe she is here tonight.' He stops to a further outbreak of whistling and jeering, beaming at the audience until silence returns. 'That is all I have to say. I hope we can air our differences without unpleasantness. At least let us keep the debate calm and courteous in the best English tradition.'

This time there is polite clapping, the only real enthusiasm apparently coming from Isabel, Rose and the agent, who slaps his knee. The vicar gets to his feet. 'Thank you, Sir James, for those few words, in particular for your remark about the need to keep to the courtesies of civilized debate. Every issue has more than one side to it. We should remember that this evening. Now I welcome Mr Samuel Dove.'

Almost complete silence follows as Sam Dove stands, shorter than the other two, more compact, his face red but reminiscent of good health. 'Thank you, Reverend,' he says, the slight accent slurring his words. 'My job is to make your flesh creep, after these two gentlemen have dealt with the nicest parts.' There is laughter, particularly from a few rows behind, but Dove is one of them: old Sam Dove. He must again be making the Giffords feel proud of their old school-mate, for he speaks easily, without apology or doubt, not at all in awe of this large gathering. He says that as someone who grew up in the village he is worried about its future. 'I don't want to destroy the place but to help it.' He points out features of the plan on the easel to help his argument. Soon the monotone becomes dull, again a natural quality; there is no rhetoric or emotion. 'He's lost them,' the agent whispers. Edward says, 'That may be a good thing.' Dove is cunning enough to know the infinite uses of boredom. 'That's all I have to say, Mr Chairman, thank you.' Sam Dove sits down to muted clapping.

The vicar stands, seems about to speak, then thinks it might be better if he remained seated, so sinks once more into his chair. 'Now we come to the time for questions,' he says. 'Will you please rise if you have anything that you wish to ask? Please do not put your question until I have pointed to you.' He smiles, displaying those bright teeth again. 'Unfortunately I do not yet know all of you, so I must ask each person to call out his or her name before he or she speaks. Forgive me!'

About half of those in the hall leap to their feet. Peggy

Upcher is standing, Martin Riley and both the Miss Horns. Webber the agent, Isabel, Rose and Edward make an island of apparent indifference. 'Oh dear,' whispers Isabel. 'Yes!' the vicar calls out, pointing to Mrs Upcher in the middle of the hall, to be answered by hoots and groans, soon countered by cheers. The councillor for the village is stately in a blue dress and white cardigan. 'Peggy Upcher,' she says, her voice steady for she is used to public speaking. 'I want to ask Mr Dove how many local people he hopes to employ at the mill. He has told us there will be ten jobs immediately, perhaps rising to twenty in a few years' time. How many of those will be from the village and how many from his existing workforce in Chilworth, which it is rumoured is going to be cut back?'

Dove smiles patiently. 'May I answer that, Reverend?' he says to the vicar, who seems startled, then nods his head. 'You know, Peggy, that I want to help the village. I want to take on as many people from here as I can. In any case it will be much easier for me if they've only got to walk up the road to work rather than come all the way from Chilworth. Then they'll have no excuse for being late! There can't be many folk here as haven't heard what a strict timekeeper I am.' There is laughter.

The tone of the speakers who follow Mrs Upcher is that of interest in the proposal and a wish to know more. The agent whispers, 'Where is all the opposition?' Then, as if in answer, comes the gentle, soft voice of one of the Miss Horns.

Avril Horn speaks of heavy lorries, a vision of devastation, the noise of the mill, the end of peace 'in this beautiful corner of England'. Why is it necessary for Mr Dove to move from Chilworth? Chilworth is a large town much more suited to factories of this kind. Why cannot Mr Dove build his new mill on the outskirts of Chilworth, where there must be suitable sites available? If Mr Dove is so

173

interested in the village, why doesn't he lay on transport to take the young people into Chilworth every day, so they can work for him there and come back in the evening to the same lovely unspoilt place that their parents and grand-parents knew? Why should these villages be spoilt in this way, just on the vague promise of ten more jobs? Why?

Her frailty seems to suggest that anyone who disagrees with her is a brute. There is applause, at first not great but then growing until it seems to come from all sides of the hall. In the shouts of 'Hear, hear!' Edward hears Martin Riley's voice above the others and turns to see his old friend smiling and laughing, now standing as well, trying to catch the vicar's eye. But the vicar looks down at James Finch, apparently in search of an answer. Then the audience is quiet, as if straining now to catch each possible new word. How polite they are, Edward thinks: all that barracking was just high spirits, young people letting off steam. This is a decent community: an English place. 'Sir James?' asks the vicar. James Finch sits still, staring out into the hall. 'Sir James?' the vicar repeats, perhaps pleased to have found a name he knows at last. 'Sir James?' Now the cheers start again, accompanied by the stamping of feet, whistling, shouts of 'Answer!' and 'Hear, hear!' James Finch turns to Dove, who seems unmoved, and quickly back because the vicar is whispering something to him. He nods, then shakes his head. 'Answer!' comes another shout and more hooting. Isabel stares at her husband, perhaps willing him to be strong. This time it is Rose who seems upset, her face set in agony, probably near to tears. Edward shifts in his chair; he cannot bear this hurting of innocence, an end of youth, the start of a path towards disappointment, bitterness, defeat, anger with an ungrateful world. Surely these need not follow. People must strike out, keep themselves sharp and young. He is sure of this.

Silence comes gradually over the hall: a new, clear wave.

Again he sneaks a glance at Rose, her face firmer now, set like a cool, sculpted head. What beauty: yes, it is that, or not quite perhaps, but enough for him. He remembers his rash invitation to this shy girl, thrown off so crazily at dinner with the Rileys. Quickly a whole imagined visit passes before him as if in a sudden delirium: the flight to Hamburg, arrival at the airport, a drive across a flat, grey landscape south-east to the small town near the old border where Alex von Kierich lives, to be greeted by Alex's forgiving wisdom, that special intensity, an ultimate seriousness: the man who knows. Rose too would be fascinated by the experience of evil, the terrifying Gestapo interrogations when one wrong word might have led to death. Again Alex would pose that unspoken question: how can you or most people ever hope to understand me, you with your dull little lives? Then von Kierich might look at the girl and remember Jane, the one bright part of this awkward Englishman, and think, No, there is more to Edward after all. Back in the hall, he hears a small voice call out, 'Clara Horn.'

It is the second of the two spinsters from the old greengrocer's shop. Her tone is not quite the same as her sister's, just a little slower, the fury less disguised by that fanatical gentility.

'Mr Chairman, may we please hear what Mr Dove is going to pay Sir James Finch for this field, because if it is a large sum of money then at least the people will know that their village was ruined for a good price?' She pauses, breathing deeply. 'Naturally, I recognize that we owe it to our families to earn a decent living. Sir James has more than any of us to keep up in the way of houses, pictures, furniture and land. What a burden it all must be!' There is silence, perhaps shock at the hatred behind the muddled words.

'I know that in certain circles it is thought vulgar to talk about money. But my sister and I were only able to buy our little house with great difficulty, and we have slowly converted it from a shop into a quite comfortable dwelling for the two of us, using our small savings and the sale of a few beloved family heirlooms to pay for the work done by our friend Jack Carter, a builder in the village who has worked on the cottages around here all his life. I have no doubt that if Mr Dove goes ahead with his saw mill, we shall have to move. We are just across the field from the proposed site and our back garden will look straight on to it. We will be deafened by the noise of machinery whenever we step outside. The lorries delivering and collecting the timber will come right past our front door. At our ages this is too much for my sister and me. We could not bear to see the ruination of our little house, which we love and have spent so much time and what money we had in improving and, we hope, creating a front and back garden that is a credit to the village, which has a reputation for its lovely displays of flowers.'

Here she seems to swallow, her voice trembling, apparently about to break into sobs and tears. Trying to push Alex out of his mind, Edward senses the sympathy in the hall. The Miss Horns are liked in the neighbourhood. The silence is a form of tribute; also pity for the defenceless old women, admiration for their courage in speaking out.

Clara Horn speaks with a new tenderness, her voice softer. 'It is the flowers I will miss most: the lovely way they return each April, then more in May. The hollyhocks we put in front of the cottage, the sweet williams and the pinks, the dear little pansies and the roses on the other side that faces the field.' She stops, as if reminded of something terrible, almost too odious to mention. 'That is why I would at least like to hear what profit Mr Dove and Sir James Finch are going to make out of this development, so that my sister and I will have the small satisfaction of seeing that someone has done well even if our lives have been ruined.' She bows to the platform in fake deference. 'I recognize that in Mr Dove's case the profits are only a projection at the moment because he cannot have a more precise idea until the new mill is working. But surely the question of the rent for the field itself has already been discussed, or should have been. I mean of course the money which Mr Dove will pay the Finch family for the right to build this great saw mill on their land!' She finishes in a forthright voice, almost a shout. 'That is what I want to know!'

Clara Horn sits down and turns to her sister who puts a hand on her shoulder. Then she raises her head to look out at the room, her eyes bright in triumph. At first there are only a few claps, some subdued shouts of 'Hear, hear!' More applause follows, the noise rising slowly into an ovation accompanied by whistling and stamping of feet. There are cries of 'Answer, answer!' Menacing and angry, the sound of a mob.

Edward glances at Rose and sees that perplexed look, the mouth slightly open, the sadness back again, a melancholy acquired through early disappointment. He thinks of that evening in Bath, the saga of Dr Alessandri's obsessive attempts to reclaim his youth, the sorrows of the Via Belvedere; then his own snatched kiss before she had run away, those recurring thoughts, the phantoms of elderly lust. Alex will like her as he had liked Jane; well, not quite, because Jane and Rose are so different, the one with her sharp, nervous, glaring beauty, the other softer, more feminine, the sort of quietness Edward admires, not like practical Judith in Delhi or cool-eyed Barbara from New York. He had loved beauty, its soft, strong light.

The vicar speaks. 'Thank you, Miss Horn. The best I can do is to refer your question to one of our two speakers. Mr Dove, I wonder . . .' Dove looks up at the clergyman with courteous surprise. 'I wonder, Mr Dove . . .' The voice falters. 'Mr Dove, perhaps . . .' Now a sentence comes at last. 'Mr Dove, might you be able to set Miss Horn's mind at rest?'

Dove stands. He gives Miss Clara Horn a crafty smile. 'Ah, Miss Horn,' he says, 'you're a great one for details, and why not? Now I can answer any question about the building, the mill itself and the sort of trade we think we might get, even the projected figures for the first two years of operation or the number of lorries a day, because I know many of you are worried about the traffic. I can answer all these with the greatest of pleasure and tell you in this hall tonight more about the way my company is run than I've ever told anyone, even including my dear wife!' He stops for a moment. There is polite laughter. 'I'm quite happy to tell you all these things, and if there's anything else you forget to ask tonight or don't understand then just telephone me in my office in Chilworth tomorrow or any day and come round to see me and I'll show you the books and the plans personally. That I will. But one thing I cannot do is to talk about the rent. This is something which involves two parties: myself and Sir James Finch. So I must not disclose any of the figures without Sir James's permission. I'm sorry, Miss Horn.' He sits down to silence.

Clara Horn, that small, round figure, gets up again. 'Mr Chairman, I did not really intend Mr Dove to answer my question,' she says with a smile like a floral print. 'Cannot Sir James Finch himself enlighten us? It would seem only fair to let him answer because his family is to be the chief beneficiary of the scheme. He may say that such information is a private matter between him and Mr Dove, and in that case we cannot force him to tell us what he wishes to keep to himself. But I feel he should be truthful and open with us tonight. We are all going to be affected by what happens. The value of our houses will go down if this scheme goes ahead. Who is going to want to buy a property that is within sight and earshot of a working saw mill? Who will want to live in a house that has these huge lorries going past most of the day and night as well? Perhaps Sir James will at least tell us how much he and his family are going to benefit from what he has described as "progress".'

She looks around the hall as if overcome by doubt. Perhaps she thinks that she may have gone too far; but then she summons up a last ounce of bile. 'Sir James does not hesitate to hark back to the old days when it suits him. In the old days surely the Finch family would have felt some responsibility for the village. Even if they took advantage of a business opportunity of this kind, they would have put some of the profits they made from it back into the community. So I want to ask Sir James what he is going to get out of the scheme. I would also like to know if he has any ideas of giving some of it back to the village, perhaps in the form of a new hall or centre for the young people or sports field or tennis court, just something to make up for the damage he has brought upon us all!'

She sits down quickly. There is a solitary shout: a thick, brutish sound, the cry of the ignorant or the drunken. 'Answer!' Another voice cries out from a different part of the hall, 'How much? Tell us how much.' Two or three more join in, chanting, 'Answer! Answer!' These must be Mrs Gifford's 'young hooligans' from the council estate, the ones who vandalize the telephone box by the Bell and let Isabel's horses out on to the road. Suddenly it stops. Everyone is staring at the stage, some apprehensive, some mystified, others scowling, Martin Riley with that wild smile. Edward thinks, You started this, the Finches are good people who think of you as their friend. Remember those long summer evenings with Ben Talbot, Nancy, Isabel, James and Rose in this lovely place. Remember that friendship, sympathy, even love.

James Finch stands. No voice comes; he is so still that it

seems as if he has been petrified, cast suddenly in stone or ice. There is absolute silence. The vicar leans towards him, puts one hand on his arm, but James does not move, although now there is a strange, almost mad mixture of fear and fury in his eyes. Still the silence lasts: not even a cough or shuffle of feet. Then an extraordinary thing happens. Rose leans across Isabel, not caring if her mother hears, to say quite loudly to Edward, 'Please say something now, anything. Just speak!' and after first withdrawing slightly, as if ashamed, she comes even closer so that her mother has to move a few inches back. 'I'll come with you tomorrow if you do. Quick, before they start shouting again. Please!' Her look, the hint of tears (like Isabel earlier), forces him to stand, then call out his name as a sign to the vicar that he wishes to speak. James Finch sits down and covers his forehead with one hand, hiding his eyes. It is humiliation, the rout of a diminished man.

People are watching Edward, waiting. He sees the Miss Horns, Avril smiling gently, Clara's head raised in triumph; Martin Riley now angry, a look of contempt; Nancy at that moment whispering to her husband, probably astounded; then Rose's imploring eyes and Isabel's look of relief. The vicar repeats his name. 'Mr West.'

He starts with some innocuous words, a bid for time. 'Mr Chairman, I am perhaps a newcomer to the village. At least I feel a newcomer. My wife and I bought our house here almost twenty-five years ago.' He stops, looks round, then continues to ramble. 'I feel a newcomer because at first we were seldom here, thinking of the house more as a place where we would retire when the time came. You must know it well: the house next to the church which is believed to have once been the morgue because of its position so near the cemetery. I wanted to change its name back to the Old Morgue, but my wife, who died, didn't agree, so the name on the gate still says Church House, which was the name when we bought it.' He stops again, to a few laughs, the atmosphere lighter. 'The Old Morgue.'

Now he smiles, more sure of himself. 'How long does one have to live in a village like this to become accepted? I don't know. But I feel that I cannot speak as a true villager, partly because, as I said, I did not come to live here permanently until quite late in life. Before that I was working abroad, in the United States and other parts of the world. Naturally I still regarded this country as my true home and the place to which I hoped eventually to retire. We chose this village because some friends of ours, Martin and Nancy Riley, who were with us in America as well, had bought a house here: the Old Poor House, just next to ours, one up from the church. Their predecessors had kept the original name, so the Old Poor House it remained, unlike the Old Morgue, which had been changed to Church House, although, as I said, I would have been happy to have gone back to the old name.'

Then comes the first interruption, a male voice from the back of the hall. 'Get on with it!' Another joins in with 'Hear, hear!' There are a few claps. The vicar lifts his hands in an appeal for quiet. Edward sees James Finch's face, raised from his papers, relaxed, smiling slightly, the worst over. He almost leans down to Isabel and Rose to say, See what I have done for you. But he must finish his task.

'It may be asked, Mr Chairman, what I am trying to say,' he shouts. 'It may be asked and with justice, too. I felt it necessary to establish my credentials, to make it plain to those of you who do not know me the history of my connection with the village, which is shorter than some of you have enjoyed, but' – and here he looks at the two Miss Horns – 'longer than others. I feel, however, that I have a clear idea of the atmosphere of the place, which is so very English in its slow evolution, in that pragmatic mingling of the present and the past, the absence of rancour and hysteria so envied by the rest of the world.' He shakes his head, grasps the lapels of his jacket in the pose of an orator. 'In England we have a reputation for level-headedness, for tolerance. To be honest, Mr Chairman, I do not have strong feelings on the issue of the field. I can understand those who think that to build a saw mill would be a kind of sacrilege, because of the damage that could be done to our beautiful and peaceful surroundings. I can also understand others who are concerned for the future of our community. Of course we do not want a dead village without opportunities for young people. The saw mill would provide jobs; of that there can be no doubt. I am sure that those who wish to see it built have the best of motives. Of course the Finch family is moved by far more than mere profit. But perhaps like many others in this room I find it hard to judge between two such well-reasoned points of view. Therefore I feel I must stand up and speak for that part of the audience which has until now remained silent: the don't knows.'

He has lost most of his audience now, probably because of the tedious drone that always enters his voice when he speaks in public. Jane had remarked on this, sometimes in a sweet, teasing way, occasionally with a sneer: 'Darling, public speaking simply isn't one of your talents.' The hall is quiet; even Isabel looks bored. Then Rose stares up at him with the clearest, most open smile he has ever seen, a look of love. He must end. 'So let us be tolerant of one another's opinions. Let us remain friends inside and outside this hall, remembering that we will have to live together long after this particular dispute has ended, whatever its result. There should be no victims or scapegoats. No enemies or bristling lines of battle. Surely in this country, in this beautiful corner of England, we can do better. Here we can conduct a courteous, civilized debate without acrimony or wild charges against individuals. No, please, I beg of you, stick to the issues, not the personalities. That is all I have to say.'

He sits down to a few polite claps, even a shout of 'Hear, hear!' Isabel smiles at him, obviously pleased. 'Well done,' she whispers and then leans closer as if anxious to be heard by no one else. 'Thank you.' Rose reaches across her mother to pat his hand. 'Thank you, Edward,' she says, her voice louder. 'Thank you.' Now she must keep her word. Oh Rose. Suddenly, towards the end of the clapping, he hears a shout of 'Rubbish!' It is Martin Riley; he does not repeat himself, but leaves the word there like an unpleasant memory.

Edward does not move again. The debate continues, much gentler now, some speeches in favour, others against, but none with that earlier aggressive tone. People describe the beauty of the field, others speak of the new life for the village that must come with the saw mill, one man mentions the pride they should all have in the success of Samuel Dove, a local boy. Sometimes there is applause, now of a polite kind; it is as if the audience is in a state of mild shock. The vicar calls Martin Riley, announcing that this must be the last speech of the evening from the floor. Edward crosses his arms tightly, pressing them into each other, but to his surprise Martin says how much he agrees with his old friend. Those who are against the proposal wish only to preserve the character of the village, which the previous speakers have evoked so well. Now the scheme must go to the planners who will have the final say. The petition will be sent to the council so that it should know the strength of local feeling. No doubt Mr Dove and Sir James Finch will make their own submissions as is their right. All opinions must be heard, with courtesy of course. On that note Martin ends, a smiling, calm, elderly man.

The vicar asks Sir James Finch and Samuel Dove if they have anything more to say. No? Well, in that case – and, ignoring several raised hands, he thanks the audience for coming and declares that it is time to go home. There is clapping before the chairs scrape against the floor. The audience begins to depart.

'You will come back to the manor, won't you, Edward?' says Isabel. She calls to the agent. 'And you too, Godfrey. Have you got Fiona with you? No? Well, perhaps she can spare you a bit longer. I know Sir James will want to have a word.' Then she speaks to Edward. 'I've asked the Rileys as well, in spite of his line. After all, we've been such friends and he did try to be reasonable at the end, didn't he?' She takes her daughter's arm. 'Rose, can you go ahead and see that the glasses and food are laid out in the dining-room? Mrs Marsden said she'd come in, but you'd better make sure. Let's see: there's the Rileys, Edward, the Upchers, the vicar and his wife, Mr Dove . . .' She turns again to him. 'Perhaps you could go with her, Edward. I'll wait for James.'

Then Isabel puts her hand on his arm. 'You were absolutely marvellous, my dear. I thought for one awful moment things were going to get out of hand.' She scowls. 'That beastly little woman.' She glares at the Miss Horns who are amongst a crowd of people by the door, the sisters talking with great animation. Suddenly those who are with them raise their heads as if in unison and let out great guffaws of laughter.

'Godfrey will come with you,' Isabel says. As they join the queue to get out he curses Webber, for he had hoped to walk with her alone, the darkness pierced only by the few street lights of the village between the hall and the start of the manor's drive.

Chapter Seventeen

Out on the road they smile and say goodnight to people whom they know. Godfrey Webber starts to talk. 'Well, it could have been much worse, don't you think, Rose? I thought the vicar did a first-class job. It's not easy to control some of those people and there was no real disruption apart from a bit of heckling. All fairly good-natured stuff!' This is not true. He does not mention Sir James's collapse.

'What about Miss Horn?' Rose says.

'I wonder why she feels like that.'

'It's my family,' Rose answers. 'She hates us.'

'Surely not.'

'Yes, she does.' She kicks savagely at a stone as they turn into the manor drive. 'Oh . . .'

'It might be a good idea for some one to call on the Miss Horns,' Godfrey Webber suggests. 'Your mother or you if you have the time.'

Now they are beside the tennis court, a reminder of summer outlined through the darkness, and the low branches of the lime avenue. 'Perhaps I could have a word,' Edward says.

Rose walks fast, as if anxious to reach the safety of the house. 'Don't go and see Clara Horn, Edward. You'll only have to put up with all her pathetic little complaints about this and that. Why should you get involved? You've done more than enough already. He was marvellous, wasn't he, Godfrey?'

'Marvellous.'

'I felt sorry for him.'

'Sorry?'

'For your father.'

The humiliation has been mentioned at last. It seems to lie heavily between them, for no one speaks again until they reach the manor. In the hall, the agent says to Rose, 'I'll make sure that everything's laid out,' and then, 'If you'll excuse me,' before he goes into the dining-room. Now they are alone beside the rows of boots and shoes and the tall wooden stand on which hang the great mass of coats and hats, far more than one family can possibly need.

'You are kind, Edward,' she says, her voice tense as if straining at the leap, then softening as she lands. 'What can I say? Yes, I'll come tomorrow, I promise.'

He clasps her arm briefly, then Webber returns and starts to speak to him, something again about the Horn sisters, but the words seem only a series of meaningless sounds until the agent says, 'Oh, here they are.' Isabel enters first, followed by Martin and Nancy Riley, several other women, Mr and Mrs Upcher, the vicar and his large wife, and James Finch, who looks oddly cheerful, not at all cowed; he may see a strange justice in this public degradation, believing it to be the natural consequence of greed and money. Soon the narrow hall is full. Isabel shouts to Webber, 'Godfrey, open the dining-room doors and ask everyone to go through! Rose, the drinks!' They move slowly into the dark dining-room. 'More lights, please, Rose!' Isabel calls. Her daughter obeys, banishing the darkness. He finds himself next to Nancy, who says, 'You were superb, Edward,' and he smiles at her red face, the face of the Beacon, as she takes a glass of wine from a tray.

The food is laid out on the long wooden table in the centre of the room: some sandwiches, bowls of salad and fruit. Rose talks to the guests whilst Godfrey Webber, Mrs

Marsden and James Finch take round the drinks. Nancy says to James as he passes, 'Let me help, James.' He shakes his head and hurries on, now awkward. 'Oh dear, I expect he's angry with us,' she says to Edward. 'Do please try to make him see that Clara Horn was speaking entirely for herself. I'm sure Isabel knows, but men can be so much more difficult. Martin, for instance!' She sips at her drink. 'Where is he, Edward? Can you see?'

They look round the room. 'By the fireplace, talking to Mrs Upcher,' he says. Martin Riley is excited, gesticulating with one hand, a drink in the other. Peggy Upcher nods as he speaks, then they both laugh.

Nancy stares at them. 'Well, at least they're not at each other's throats. Do you think I ought to go over in case he explodes?'

Rose is busy. 'No. Come and get some food.' Nancy glances at him, anxious for a moment, then they walk together to the long table and help themselves before moving away to the edge of the room, underneath the high lattice windows.

'I had my fingers crossed all the time Martin was speaking,' Nancy says. 'James and Isabel are our friends, after all.' She glances across the room again. 'Look, Edward, I think I must see what Martin is up to. There's quite a group gathering around him. Come with me.'

She sets off towards her husband and he follows, nodding to the vicar, smiling at Isabel who is talking to an old man whose face he knows but cannot place. 'Yes, Rose is still at university,' he hears her say before their eyes meet. He is not embarrassed. The Finch family should be grateful to him for what he has done this evening.

Martin Riley has three people listening to him: both Upchers and the fat-faced publican from the Bell. 'Hello, Nance,' he says. 'We were just saying how splendid it is that we can all disagree about something like this yet still remain friends: an important aspect of civilized life, don't you think, Edward?' Martin's laugh is high-pitched, a false note. He turns to Peggy Upcher. 'What did you make of Edward's contribution to our discussion this evening, Peggy? Do you think he made some good points? Can you remember what he said?' Again the laugh, this time shorter, almost smothering his last words.

Mrs Upcher smiles tolerantly, thinking perhaps that Major-General Riley is having another of his little jokes. 'He calmed us all down very nicely.'

'Calmed us down!' Martin laughs, more of an explosion this time.

'Martin . . .' Nancy begins.

'No, my dear, Peggy is right. Edward played a great role this evening: that of the anaesthetist. The person who puts the patient to sleep, thus avoiding the pain of a great operation: the pain and the terrible sight of those surgeons and doctors clustered round the operating table. The anaesthetist!' He roars with laughter again.

'And what are you, Martin?' asks Edward.

'Me?' Martin Riley looks surprised. 'You say, Edward. You tell us what you think I am.' He beams at the group.

'A retired army officer,' Edward answers.

'Oh, I see.' Martin turns to Nancy. 'I was expecting rather more than that, weren't you, Nance?'

'Martin . . .' she begins again.

Once more he cuts her off. 'Do you think I made a fool of myself, Edward?' he asks. The others watch uneasily. 'Do you think I made a fool of myself this evening in the village hall? Do you think I went too far?'

'No.'

'That is something.' Martin Riley looks at the publican. 'I need not feel ashamed, then, eh, Tom?'

At first no one answers, then the publican's deep voice says, 'That Clara Horn's a sour old woman, make no mistake about it.'

'But why?' asks Martin. 'It's often neglect that leads to such bitterness: neglect or personal slights. Perhaps she believes that Sir James and Lady Finch have not paid enough attention to her. And why should they?'

'Yes, why should they?' echoes the publican.

'Did Clara Horn speak to you about this, Edward?' Martin asks.

The idiocy of the question astounds him. 'To me? Certainly not!'

'Perhaps her sister, Avril, has been more forthcoming?'

'Martin, I hardly know the Horns.'

'Hardly know them!' Martin is shouting. 'You must have seen those two women thousands of times: in the shop, on the street, walking in the woods and fields. They're great walkers, Clara and Avril. Great walkers! Then they do the flowers in the church. Jane used to help with the flowers. Do you remember?'

'Sometimes.'

Martin Riley presses the point. 'She gave flowers from your garden.'

'Martin . . .' Nancy is still trying.

He smiles at them, still pleased. 'Now let me ask you once again. What do you think Edward said in his speech?'

Mrs Upcher answers. 'I think he was trying to calm us all down, General Riley, that's all.' She looks beseechingly at him. 'Is that right, Mr West?'

'Quite right.'

'No no no!' Martin's voice soars once more. 'But dear lady, what did he say about the saw mill?'

'He said we shouldn't get so worked up about it all,' Mrs Upcher answers.

'Was he in favour of the development or against it?'

'That I can't tell you, General. He didn't seem to mind too much one way or the other.'

'There you are!' Martin let out a guffaw of triumph.

'That's what I've been trying to say. Here we have an intelligent man, a man of achievement and taste, a man of education, who, to quote your very words, does not seem "to mind too much one way or the other". Why? I will tell you. It is because he no longer bothers about the present. It seems dull to him, irrelevant. So let the whole village be wrecked. It does not matter to Edward West.'

'Martin . . .' Nancy says.

'Oh I know, Nance, I must stop. It quite spoils the evening, doesn't it?'

This time Edward wants to fight back. 'What are you trying to say, Martin?'

Martin's eyes are bright, almost unbearable. 'That we would like to feel that you cared more about what happens here, in the place where you chose to make your home: you and Jane together.'

'Jane?' He tries to be fierce as well.

'Yes, Jane.' Martin's repetition of her name is louder.

The publican joins in. 'You can't help admiring her, though, that Miss Horn. The way she spoke up. That takes some courage, eh, General?'

Martin turns to Nancy. 'You know who Edward is going to see, don't you?'

'Alex,' she answers.

'Excuse me, General,' Peggy Upcher says. 'Gordon and I really ought to be getting along. We'll find Lady Finch and thank her. It's been a lovely party.' She looks worried. 'Goodbye, Mr West. I'm so glad you were able to have your say.' They walk off towards Isabel, who is on the opposite side of the room, two people fearful of a row neither of them can understand at all.

'You've driven them away,' Edward says.

'Are you talking to me?' asks Martin.

'Yes.'

'When are you going?'

190

'Tomorrow.'

'On your own?'

'No.'

'Who is coming with you? Your boy Charles?'

'No. I told you, Martin. Charles is in America. I told you that the other evening.'

'So you did.'

'Are you going on a trip, Mr West?' the publican asks.

'Yes I am, Tom. A short holiday.' He feels his face begin to flare up. Then Rose comes into their group to stand next to him and Edward almost takes her hand in his, so great is the relief at finding an ally at last. He says the words: just two of them. 'With Rose.'

The publican bows to her. 'How nice for you, my dear.'

Martin glares at the girl. 'You will find a small town, quite frankly rather a dull place, near where the frontier used to be,' he says. 'I understand that Alex lives in a hotel owned by some relation of his. He fills in the time by acting as a guide in the set of medieval cloisters which is the town's only sight of interest. He has some friends: two women called Frau Schneider and Frau Hartmann, and the owner of the hotel, Otto Friesen. One of the women he likes; the other he thinks is silly. I imagine he is apt to ramble when talking about the past. What do you know about von Kierich, Rose?'

She lies. 'Hardly anything.' Then she speaks quickly to Edward, almost a whisper. 'I've spoken to my mother.'

He nods. 'You never told me any of this, Martin. How long have you known?' he says.

'Not for long. You see, he wrote to me as well. I didn't like to encourage you, Edward.'

'You lied to me.'

'No I did not.'

'By not telling me you had heard from Alex. When you sat and listened whilst I spoke about him: all the time you knew.'

'I did not lie. I said nothing.' Martin turns to see Isabel Finch who has come across the now almost empty room. 'Ah Isabel, welcome.' Her eyes have narrowed; for a moment he seems to shrink before them. 'You are kind to entertain us all.'

'Is James upset, Isabel?' asks Nancy.

'Upset? Why?' Then she realizes that the question comes from Nancy whom she does not blame. 'Oh I don't think so. After all, most people must have been appalled by that dreadful woman.'

The publican nods. 'She went too far, Lady Finch.'

'But Isabel,' Martin says, 'surely you must respect strength of feeling.'

Her look would burn him if it could. 'Strength of feeling, General? So that is what it was. Strength of feeling. I see.' Her laugh is a mere gurgle in the throat. 'To me it seemed more like bitterness: the pathetic frustration of a mean old spinster.' She laughs again. 'Well, tonight she had her moment of glory. I must say you have some strange allies, Martin.' She turns to Rose before he can answer. 'Where is Trixie? You won't forget to let her out, will you? At least the fortunate creature has missed all this. Sometimes one despairs of one's fellow humans and is tempted to spend much more time with horses, cats or' – here her mouth droops in distaste – 'dogs. Have you spoken to your father? I think you should go to him, don't you?' As the girl moves away, Isabel looks at Edward. 'I hear you're taking Rose to Germany. No, don't worry!' She laughs more easily now. 'She's quite old enough. She tells me that you hope to see your old master.'

Master? Is this really the right word? 'Perhaps.'

Martin explodes. 'Perhaps! Perhaps! It is the sole purpose of the visit. The sole purpose!'

Isabel glances contemptuously at him. 'Why not?' She smiles at Edward, her face soft again. 'Personally I should be fascinated to meet him.'

'Ha!' shouts Martin. 'The fascination of the sinister!'

And Edward, unable to stand any more, clasps Rose's hand briefly and walks across the dining-room into the hall, then hears footsteps on the stone floor behind him and turns to see her anxious eyes, like those of a fugitive. 'What time do we leave?'

He waits. They are almost touching again.'Quite early. Nine o'clock. I'll pick you up. We'll drive to Heathrow and leave the car there, just for two nights. Are you sure . . .?'

'Yes.'

Suddenly Martin Riley is with them both as well, touching him on the shoulder. 'If you come back with me now, I will tell you what you wish to know.'

Chapter Eighteen

So they sit in Martin Riley's study, just the two of them because Nancy has gone upstairs to bed, leaving her husband to tell what he knows at last.

'I was sworn to secrecy,' Martin says. He stares ahead, as if unaware of the other's presence, a full glass of whisky in his hand, the dog at his feet. 'I take such promises seriously, even if few other people do these days. That is why I could not tell you what was known at the time. There was another obstacle. I knew what Alex meant to Jane, how she had found in him some one whom she trusted completely, enough for her to give both admiration and love. No!' Martin looks straight into Edward's eyes, raising a hand. 'I want to be truthful. She thought there was some of this in you as well, Edward: that mixture of idealism and strength, the heroic virtues, examples of what we should all try to be. God knows how many times she told Nancy and me about those evenings in Rome: the way she inveigled you to dinner at the embassy, the first conversations, her hopes that at last she had found a cause to which she could devote her life, a man who might lead her into a great adventure! You were so much, Edward. She made that plain. Jane never showed disappointment, or not in her words. That was not a part of what she told us: only a hint behind the silence at the end of her story of those first few months, then years as remembered the move to Washington, finding the George-town house, the births of Nick and Charles, the start of your time with von Kierich. She liked to rake through the past, as

194

if searching for some pleasure or thrill, some excitement she may have missed the first time through. Nancy knew this. It was to Nancy that Jane talked whilst you and I were at work or away. Your absences hurt her more than you knew, Edward. Of course they became a part of the great romance: your splendid life, the dedication, the ideal of service, self-sacrifice, that burial of the self in a cause greater than any individual, more deserving than the commonplace needs of a wife, a home, a family. It consoled her that you were with Alex, a true hero. Did you know all this, Edward? I expect you did.'

'Yes.'

Martin drinks from his glass, several gulps. Now he seems sad. 'I wonder if she ever felt betrayed by him,' he says. 'Perhaps briefly she may have done. Very briefly. She had an immense capacity for belief, didn't she?'

'What if the rumours were all lies?'

'You believed they were. Do you still? Yes, I think you do. What loyalty!' Martin puts his glass heavily down on a table beside his chair so that there is a sudden noise.

Edward speaks louder. 'Martin, Alex told me about the shooting incident when we were in Africa. He never denied that he saw the massacre. But he killed no one himself: not then or at any other time. You forget. He was a civilian. A bureaucrat in their Foreign Office. Why should he suddenly seize a gun and start murdering people?'

'I know,' Martin says, staring again at him. 'Von Kierich told Jane the same story. Didn't she tell you? While you were ill in hospital that time, when you got back from Africa, he told her about the massacre, the way he wanted to step forward and kill the woman, the wife of the man he called the schoolmaster. It was the horror of this which she couldn't forget. She vowed to preserve it for herself alone: a great and terrible secret, a glimpse of hell, the extreme at last, what she needed to prove she could face the worst. She sought extremes, Jane. "You don't know how far I might go," she said to me once. Yet the excitement bubbled over. She told Nancy, not you. She may not have trusted you by then. No, that's not true.' Martin shakes his head. 'She wanted a piece of Alex all to herself: that was why she told no one apart from Nancy. With Nancy Jane felt no reason not to share. Nancy was fond of Alex. Quite fond. But not bewitched by him. Not like you or Jane.'

'What happened, Martin? Why did Alex have to go?'

Martin Riley watches him. 'He wasn't quite what you thought, your Alex. All that inner spirituality, that soul. I remember you told us how he had spoken of the traditions of his ancestry, the withdrawal into a fortified inner self, a forswearing of external loyalties. Then I thought, What arrogance! As if his own personal purging of evil helped anyone else! Such selfish introversion, such conceit, such vanity! Oh I know he took part in those plots. But he survived, didn't he? At least the others threw themselves on to the wire of the monster, cancelled out whatever part they may have unwittingly played in its creation. They at least added to the great tally of victims that would be used in the end to bring about its extinction. It is the victims who ensure such a regime is held up as an example of wickedness. It is the victims who bring about the downfall of tyranny, Edward; not the survivors, however harrowing their stories. It is the thousands, the millions, of often nameless dead. Von Kierich may have detested the regime. But he survived it! You might call that a victory. To me it is a surrender.'

'I don't understand you.'

'Don't you?' Martin looks briefly away, as if distracted. 'Let me tell you this. Von Kierich's sacrifice was not so great as you think. The Americans had him watched. I don't deny that there was impatience in some quarters with the activities of the Survey. Alex was getting quite shrill at times in some of his public pronouncements. That wasn't very diplomatic, Edward; not perhaps fair, either, to the richer nations who were just starting to do more for the Third World. The insults, that endless goading, irritated them. They couldn't be seen to submit to the pressure put on them by a megalomaniac, hysterical German. That wasn't on, Edward. Surely you can see why.'

'So you had him watched.'

'Not me, Edward. The Americans.'

'Did you have me watched as well, Martin?'

'I had no one watched. It was the Americans.'

'You didn't need to. You were with us for so much of the time in Washington, with Jane and me. Were we under surveillance during those trips to the beach, the suppers in Georgetown, the summer barbecues? You're never off duty, I suppose, in the sort of job you used to have. Never. Always snooping and prying, storing up what you see in the little computer in your head so that it can all come spewing out when it's needed. I'd give a lot to see the reports you wrote about us. That was your trade, wasn't it? A nasty little spy. I understand your anger now. The frustration. Those early dreams of military glory all ending in grubby little eavesdropping.' Unused to speaking at such length and with such vehemence, Edward is out of breath. 'What did they say about Alex?'

Martin smiles. 'Mostly trivial stuff. Where he went, who came to see him. There were women, you know. Usually in Germany or Austria when he was on leave. Not much, I suppose.'

'I knew all that, Martin.'

'How?'

'Alex told me. He said the most important thing was that no one should be hurt.' Then he adds, not sure why, 'Did you tell Nancy?'

'No.' Martin smiles again, a look of infinite cunning. 'Once I nearly did. When the Americans said the same woman had come to his apartment on Q Street several nights running. Then I was more interested. This seemed different. Even the Americans were surprised. They got in touch with me to ask if I knew anything about this visitor. They had taken photographs: the usual routine, from a van parked near by, I believe.' Martin lifts his glass to his lips. A window shakes; the wind has blown up. The dog snores, a rough, regular sound like the idling of an old engine. The pause is theatrical, perhaps sadistic. Has Martin secretly loathed him all these years? 'So I glanced at the snaps, calling them that just to annoy the rather earnest young man who had brought them round. Snaps! He looked at me as if I was incurably frivolous, yet another example of the decadence of the old country. But you can imagine my shock, Edward. They were of Jane.'

Edward smiles now, as if relieved. 'When were the photographs taken?'

'Morning, afternoon, evening. All times of day.'

'No. What date?'

Martin's eyes leave Edward's face, a small victory. 'After the African incident. While you were in hospital.' Then he looks at him again, fiercer now. 'I remember so well. It seemed to add a particularly unpleasant dimension to the whole business. That was one of the things von Kierich used to boast about, wasn't it, his skill as a conspirator? This was a conspiracy of one: just himself. A conspiracy to steal your wife. Does that please you?'

'Please me?'

'Yes, Edward. You gave the man everything else: mind, loyalty, trust, devotion. Why not give him your wife as well? Why hold that part back?' Martin stops briefly, as if stifled. 'No doubt von Kierich will play the old game with you. A certain nobility: that was what he wished us to believe he had. He was a fraud, Edward! I don't give a damn what happened in Russia: if he shot the woman or not. In fact I'm sure he did nothing. Absolutely nothing. Just watched, that's all, thinking, goodness, how awful this is. A poor show, don't you think? If I'm right, that is. But he cheated you, Edward. Wouldn't you agree?' Martin is breathing fast, the crimson spreading from his cheeks across the smooth, bare skull. 'Don't go. And don't take that poor girl with you.'

Edward stands up. 'Is that all, Martin?' he asks.

'Yes. That's all.'

'Tell me one more thing. Did she stay the night?'

Martin looks confused, the breath still coming quickly as if at the end of a race. 'What?'

'Did Jane stay the night with von Kierich?'

From above comes the sound of movement, a door closing, footsteps in the passage: Nancy preparing for bed. Martin shouts, 'Why not ask him? Damn you. Now get out!'

Rose does not sleep for a bit, lying in her bed, listening again to the steady breathing of the little dog. Last night her father had kissed her goodnight without referring to the meeting at all, so she had offered no comfort, not even one kind word, thinking, Let us pretend that it never happened, this will be the cure.

She thinks, Ben and my father represent beauty and gentleness but these are too weak, whereas Edward is old, brave certainly, secretive as well, someone who deserves help, yet without Dr Alessandri's black melancholy and remorse. That is interesting: a man's mystery, his knowledge of the world. She thinks of Ben's pretty pictures, the life of fashion, of her father's failure, then Edward, the serious man in the photograph of the disgraced von Kierich. Surely it is weakness against strength, frivolity against seriousness, death against life.

Then she is shocked by the coldness of her perceptions,

the cool rationality. Is this what she has become, someone for whom love and romance are as strange as the fantastic colours of a tropical bird? No. There is still time. She sleeps fitfully, wakes early and makes a decision. Then she sleeps again before going downstairs to telephone Ben Talbot.

On to the line comes the staginess of his answering-machine voice. Where can he be?

'I am not in at the moment, but if you leave your name and number I will ring you back as soon as possible. Please speak after the bleep. Thank you!'

She speaks slowly at first, then faster. 'Ben, I can't come this weekend. I'm sorry. I'll call you again to explain what's happened.' Then she adds, 'Don't worry. It's not serious: just something that I can't get out of here.' She remembers that she has not given her name. 'It's Rose, Ben. Don't ring today. I've got to go out. We'll speak soon. Goodbye, darling.'

Her parents are already at breakfast in the kitchen, sifting through the debris of yesterday's explosion. 'That bloody little woman,' her father says.

'So bitter,' adds Isabel.

'After all these years.'

'I know.'

'It makes you think.'

'It does indeed.'

'Edward did his best,' James Finch says. 'He refused to be bullied by Martin.' He seems quite recovered, although Rose glimpses a restlessness in his eyes.

'But Martin has no malice,' his wife declares.

'Oh no. Absolutely no malice. You know, that's one of the things I've always liked about Martin: the fact that he has no malice.'

'Yes.'

'The vicar did well, didn't he?'

'Very well.'

'Very well indeed.' Her father raises his voice, clearly excited. 'I should say he did very well. I had a longer speech prepared: more stuff about the history of the village, the importance of each generation leaving its mark, that sort of thing. But I thought. No, not tonight. Do you think that was wise, Isabel?'

'Very wise.'

'One does not want to say too much.'

'Precisely,' she says.

'You know how I hate it.'

Suddenly Isabel Finch turns to Rose who has sat down beside her. 'When are you leaving?'

'At nine o'clock.'

'Oh darling,' her father begins. 'Are you going away? I'm sorry, I'd forgotten. We've been so tied up with this wretched field that everything else has slipped from my mind. Has term started already?'

Isabel answers for her. 'Term does not begin until October. Rose is going to Germany for the weekend with Edward West.'

'Oh.' James Finch makes a joke. 'Is this his reward for speaking out at the meeting last night?' His laugh cuts roughly through the tension.

Her mother's smile is quick, utterly false. 'I don't think so.' Then she smiles again, with a new warmth. 'I envy you, darling. There must be so much going on in Germany now. And Edward will be a good guide.'

'Why?' asks James.

Isabel's voice is soothing. 'I imagine he has been there before.'

'When?'

Her mother turns to Rose. 'Darling . . .'

'We are to visit the man for whom he once worked,' Rose says.

'Oh yes.' James Finch's eyes leave her, now lost. 'What is he called?'

'Alexander von Kierich. We spoke about him, Dad. Don't you remember?'

'I remember.' More seriously wounded than she had thought, he needs solitude and stands up, holding a newspaper. 'I must be off. Goodbye, darling.' Rose stands to kiss him, then sits again. 'Will you be here for lunch, Isabel?'

'No. Jack and I are driving to a show near Salisbury. You'll find the ham in its usual place.' As James Finch leaves, his wife looks again at their daughter. 'Darling, has Edward booked you into hotels? Do you know?'

'He hasn't told me.'

Her mother does not seem to mind. 'You are brave.'

'Why?'

'Going off with him alone like this. What happens if he ...?' She stops, then rushes out the words. 'Well, if Edward should forget himself.'

'Forget himself! At his age? Oh Mum.'

'Yes, darling.' Isabel looks towards the open door, as if frightened of eavesdroppers. 'He is a man, after all. And he does seem ...'

'What?'

'Quite spry.'

'I think I can cope.'

Isabel smiles again: a sweet look. 'Darling, you know how James and I want you to have all sorts of different experiences whilst you are young: travel, friendships, new places, new people. Of course you must go to Germany with Edward if you want. He is a kind man.'

Should she say, I'm doing it because of what he did last night? Edward saved my father, whom I love. 'Thank you, Mum.'

Isabel stands now and glances at her watch. 'Good heavens, I'm supposed to be meeting Jack at the stables in two minutes' time. We've got to box up two horses and get all the way to Salisbury by twelve o'clock. Well, I'll say goodbye now. When will you be back?'

Rose realizes that she does not know. 'Probably Sunday night. Perhaps Monday.'

Her mother raises her hand to her ear, stops and says something extraordinary. 'Kiss me, darling.' Rose gets up, kisses Isabel's soft cheek and feels her mother's arms around her, the hands pressing just below her shoulders so that the two of them are close enough almost to seem like one body. 'Have a lovely time, won't you?' Then they separate and Isabel leaves the room.

In Church House Edward also wakes early and wonders how he will explain matters to this shy young girl.

'They felt betrayed, Rose: Martin Riley, Nancy, Bill, my old friend from Rome – even Nancy who has never known an illusion in her life. Alex had this odd power: the ability to make us feel that we were in touch with something almost elemental, a force . . .'

No, that is wrong. She will not understand. He must talk about love, which is what young people want to hear.

'I think Jane loved me at the start, or loved an idea of me. At the start her idea was not so far from the truth. I was idealistic, keen to work for the good of the world, to see millions of wretched people have better lives. But I saw my job also as an escape: a way out of poverty and boredom. So there was this tension. We spoke sometimes about it at the beginning. Jane wouldn't hear anything against me in those days.'

Then Rose might ask, Did you love her?

'It was an obsession more than love, I think, one which has never died. She found out soon that I was not so exciting, just a man of figures and charts, someone of finite limits, not infinite dreams. Then her pulse slowed, the devotion ebbed, to be replaced by what she felt she should be in her marriage: some concept of duty. Jane drew back from me yet tried to stop herself. She fought hard. Her father had taught her to fight.

'Later there were two women, Rose: after her death. Two points to my compass, you might say: Judith in Delhi and Barbara in New York. Sometimes when I think of them now, they merge into a single self, a gigantic feminine apparition that rears up in my dreams, or when I sit on my own in the garden or lie in bed as I am now – as we are now together. They were different but so similar: professional, serious yet fun as well, calm, not obsessive, each dark like Jane, like you. I seem always to like dark women.

'Everyone's life has a high point, a few years, months or days when everything seems right. Sometimes we are conscious of this whilst it is happening, sometimes not until afterwards. I felt a hint of it whilst I was working for Alex, travelling, believing we might do something for those pathetic millions. These trips were hard work but more than just that, because then I would be alone with him quite often during the hours between meetings, the journeys in aeroplanes.

'It wasn't safe, Rose. Once in Africa Alex and I were ambushed by guerrilla forces. They kept us prisoners in the bush; we thought we were going to be killed. In our prison hut we spoke of what seemed important; or rather Alex spoke and I listened because I did not have much to tell. I heard what he had seen, part of the great tragedy of his life.

'Then we were free again and flew back. But I nearly forgot, Rose. I was sick, taken ill during our captivity, an invalid for a short time. I lay in a Washington hospital, exhausted, weak. Never had Jane been busier, she said later. She came often, bringing the boys, although the doctors allowed only short visits. The head man, Dr Blumfeld, told me how fortunate I was to have such a wife. "She spoke to me about Dr von Kierich," he said. "Already he is back at his desk. What a man!"

'I took the inference, probably not meant by Blumfeld: von Kierich had withstood so much in the past and again had not succumbed, whereas I, younger and previously unblooded, had taken to my bed. I thought of that bachelor apartment on Q Street, the great wall of books, the hired furniture in its hideous green, yellow and red, the rough covers that must feel so uncomfortable against bare skin.

'In the hospital, looking at Jane across the room, for she was not allowed to come too close, I told her she must telephone Alex. He must not become lonely, desperate enough to think of leaving Washington and his job. She should see he was properly fed, cared for. This was important. He had suffered as much as I had. Maria, the Italian maid, could look after young Nick and Charles. Jane had agreed, blown a kiss. The next night, she said, she would ask him to the ballet. "How nice," I murmured. She smiled, blew me another kiss.

'Rose, I left hospital after three weeks: much too long. I noticed no change, yet I see now that Alex was more in our lives, not much more because the work took him away often at that time, sometimes with me. At first my life seemed the same: still a sense of rightness, of things slipping into place. Jane never saw Alex alone then, I think – just during those three weeks of my illness. She took the place of his family: the sisters in Salzburg and Mainz. I'm sure that's what happened, Rose.

'The first rumours amused me: laughable stuff about the Survey being run by a German who had served and survived the Hitler regime in spite of his supposed opposition to it. A columnist who specialized in paradox wrote this in a short piece on famine and agricultural development: no statistics, just a few prejudiced paragraphs, some predictable stuff about the Survey's arrogance, profligacy, utopianism; its wish to help some of the most brutal and unpleasant regimes in the world. Was this so admirable, the writer asked? What if this great hero were a false god? Other attacks followed. Much of what went on in eastern Europe during the Nazi conquest, they said, had still to be uncovered.

'I read this in the office. Later that morning Alex called me to his room. It was just the two of us, seated at a table strewn with maps, details of some scheme in Bangladesh. I knew the truth; remember our talk in the African bush. He spoke first. "You will have seen the piece about me this morning, Edward. I will not answer it. You know what happened." After Africa we were conspirators together against an ignorant world. "Yes, of course," I said, "but why not come out now with the truth at last?" "Where is the evidence?" asked Alex and I saw that he meant for his own story, not for the rumours.

'Jane thought Alex should stay quiet, allow the poison to subside. How shocked she was when he decided to go. "We must get him here alone," she said, and one evening Alex came to our "last supper" as he called it and repeated the story of the massacre. He had told her this before, although I did not know it then. "Some old friends in Munich have offered me a job," he said. Then the anger. "It seems that merely to have been alive in Germany at that time is wrong."

'When he left, Jane said, "I believe him, Edward. What will happen now?" Then the old English plea, "We mustn't lose touch," and silence for months, she not mentioning Alex or seldom, perhaps, I thought, trying to practise some vague ideal of self-denial. I said often how well Alex's successor, Vittorio Falconi, was doing at the Survey.

'The new accusations came, the documents in *Der Spiegel*. Jane started to talk of him again. I watched her as she spoke: the excited face, the glistening eyes. She stood to fetch a dish from the sideboard, laughed at some memory. I almost asked, "Did you sleep with him?" Once so nearly. That night we talked in bed together. I held her, made love, her reluctance gone at first, then flooding back to make me think of a dead body, or dead to my touch, alive only in a mystery of her own imagining.

'"I must see him," she said one day. "I won't be long. If it takes more time, you can join me. People go to Munich all the time. Vittorio cannot mind. It might be a holiday." She left for the airport in the rain. Two days later Alex rang. "Edward? Jane has been killed in a car accident. She collided with a lorry. Her death was instantaneous. When can you get here?"

'He shook my hand at the arrivals gate, his face still thin, ascetic, those faint white scars, some signs of age, tiredness around the eyes. He arranged a hotel, the identification of the body. "You will have her ashes flown home, I take it, Edward?" Home? Where? I remembered the village. Alex guided me through these matters. In the evenings we sat together in bars or restaurants. I never saw the place where he lived. "The truth is what I told you in Africa," he said. "What a good friend your wife was! The best for me: the best. Now I cannot work here any more. I will go north, to a friend who owns a hotel. This is what I want: just a room, quite small. No visitors. Do not come yet. Some time in the future, maybe. All right?" He sighed. "Jane hired that car. I said, 'Drive south to the mountains, to the great church at Ottobeuren. Take your time.' I could not believe it when she came." The lips drew in. Then he disappeared.

'A year later I was in Germany on Survey business: some work with the Foreign Ministry. I finished in Bonn late on a winter afternoon, early enough to take a fast train through the Rhineland in the dark towards Bavaria and the south. I had asked the hotel in Bonn to find me somewhere to stay, which had been difficult because there was a winter congress in Munich; finally they booked me into a small place near the station.

'I could stay four or five days, I thought. Then I must return to Washington, perhaps stopping over in England to take Nick and Charles out from boarding school, visit Jane's parents with whom I should keep in touch for the children's sake. I felt vague, full of confused excitement. Snow fell, only a few flakes in the sharp, clear air. I slept, the window open, woke early, the sun bright through the thin curtains, and saw the absurdity of the trip. This sudden decision to go in search of a part of her, to stir some sweet memory, was pointless; there could be nothing to find.

'The day was cold: ice, footprints in thin snow. I thought of taking a taxi to the scene of the crash, a fast approach to an autobahn on the edge of the town. Instead I walked through the city, the wind penetrating my thick overcoat, past the chestnut-sellers in the Marienplatz, along the Residentzstrasse and the barren Hofgarten to the large, grey block where Alex's friends' company had its offices.

'In the small front hall on the first floor, a girl came through a wooden door, and I asked about Dr von Kierich. She answered in English, cool and polite, quite inhuman. Did she know his present address? She excused herself, went back through the door, returning soon to say, "Dr von Kierich no longer lives in Munich." I said I had once worked with him and was a friend, to be told again to wait whilst she fetched a typed piece of paper with the name of the town which I already knew. How near I was then to taking a train north, straight to that place where Alex now lives. But I pulled back and returned to my hotel.

'So we have kept away from each other all these years. I had my house, the village, the boys, nothing else: two lives really, one hidden, the other visible and bland, but now with the chance of being brought together, so perhaps it is not so bad after all, especially as I will make this last journey with you, Rose, I hope.'

Chapter Nineteen

Of course it is awkward in the car at first.

That morning he had spoken to the airline and will pick up their tickets at the airport. He can arrange a car at Hamburg. They should arrive in time to drive to the town where von Kierich lives tonight.

Edward looks stern, and, as if determined to fight this, Rose talks quite frantically. Soon they are remembering together last night's meeting, the atmosphere in the village hall, Dove's outward serenity, the Miss Horns' bitterness and anger, the measured pomposity of General Riley, James Finch's collapse. They laugh, shake their heads, lean back, laugh once more, even at her father, although only slightly because both feel guilty at mocking him, Rose through her love and pity, Edward because he does not wish to hurt her. Rose says, 'He's bad at public performances. No, that's not true because he can talk so brilliantly. It's the deviousness he can't manage. Of course he was arguing for a scheme that will bring profit to himself. He would feel that was wrong: an act of selfishness, no matter how cunningly Dove and others might disguise it.' She hits her forehead gently with the palm of one hand. 'I can imagine how the guilt must torment him. The sleepless nights, the long hours of worry in his study: all because of the money he is going to make. Crazy, isn't it?' She laughs outrageously, stifling the sound almost immediately, the control restored, a smile lingering like the memory of carefree days.

Then Edward seems to relent at last and asks about

the garden at the manor, wondering why neither her father nor her mother has ever really taken it in hand. Perhaps they have not had enough time, what with the children, James's management of the estate, Isabel's horses. Now he is back amongst his flowers, suggesting some for Rose to mention to her parents. The names cascade out of him: the shrub roses, 'Penelope', 'Buff Beauty', then 'Mermaid' the climber, so good for the manor garden's old brick walls. He speaks also of wisteria, jasmine, myrtle and lavender, of philadelphus, potentilla and viburnum, of buddleia for the butterflies.

'But you must leave the yew hedges, the border round the house, the species roses, the *moyesii* and the *Rosa alba*,' he says. 'Do not tidy too much away. James and Isabel must know this. Is there method behind the chaos?' Rose laughs and says that she thinks there may be. 'What about your brother and sister?' he asks. 'Are they keen?' He thinks of money pouring like liquid from holes in the old manor house.

'They take an interest,' Rose answers.

He waits. 'Are you close to them?'

'Oh yes. Quite close. We are . . .' She waits as well. 'Well, rather different.'

'In what way?'

'Lucy is more ruthless. I envy her that.'

'And the boy?'

'Hector?' She laughs. 'Oh, he just slops about.' That does describe him. 'Not that he's stupid or slow. It's a question of attitude, temperament perhaps. He's a dreamer.'

'You're more practical.'

She laughs again. 'More ordinary.'

'No.'

'It's true. I'm not really very interesting, you know.' Now it is her shyness that is on display.

'Quieter.' He feels a stab in his forehead, an unexpected

pain. In an instant it is gone, but already he seems to have lost control and drifted back into his own solitude, away from her and that first laughter. It is as if the frustration of the last months, even years, stands like a huge earthwork, barring the way to the fertile, calm plain of which he has dreamed.

'Does he write to you often?' she asks.

'Who?'

'Alex.'

'No. Not since my wife's death. We drifted apart after that.'

'Was your wife with him when she died?'

'She was alone. Surely I told you that?'

'You did. But had she been with Alex in Munich?'

'Yes.' He touches her knee. This might be another way. Shocked, he sees that he is prepared to use Jane or her dead self, his strange, self-made dream, to get closer to this girl, an exchange of remembered coldness for the prospect of new warmth or friendship. Not so wrong really, because it will be at least partly a return to that time in Rome, the first unforgettable love from which all else has followed, even this journey eastwards. 'I wasn't with them.' He stops and then lies. 'My work kept me in Washington.' Then he says, half truthful at last, 'No, I could have been there. She died alone.'

'And you reproach yourself?' She stares at him.

'Yes.' He shies off again. 'Do you remember Jane at all? Of course not. You're too young. Jane liked your parents. She loved the village.'

Rose does not return to his dead wife, perhaps from tact or fear; he does not know which. 'Do you like it?'

'Oh yes. That's why I spoke up at the meeting last night.'

'Wasn't it just out of kindness to my father?'

Edward laughs. Now they are speeding along and he speaks again, still strangely voluble, as he had been during an earlier evening with her. 'No. I'm not like that at all. Mind you, irritation with Martin would have shifted me over to your side. But the village is different. I don't get attached to a place just for its beauty. There has to be more. Happiness, pleasure, delight, friendships. Good memories, perhaps. Look, I'll tell you something. I grew up on the Kent–Sussex border – not so nice now because the suburbs have crept out, but still not bad, or so I'm told. It was beautiful when I was a child, quite remote, too. The way of life hadn't changed that much for years, in spite of the coming of the railway and the motor car. Yet I have no feeling of nostalgia or even affection for it at all. None whatsoever. The beauty I can remember. Even at that age I was conscious of it: the early-morning walk to school in the summer, perhaps the sharp brightness of winter frost, the return at evening, the shadows of the trees.' He dignifies his early life with these high-sounding phrases. 'All that sort of thing. As good as the village in a way, perhaps even better. Less self-conscious. Less preserved. A paradise, you might think. But not for me. All I think of now is that grim, grey loneliness, solitude, harsh silence, boredom, frustration, my determination to get out as soon as possible. At school I worked hard. I won scholarships, prizes, came top time after time. My father once said, "You're like a machine." There was no love in his voice when he said it. A bit of pride perhaps, but no love.' Edward laughs again. 'So here I am.'

'You escaped.'

'To what?'

'A wife,' she answers. 'Children. Money.'

'In that order of importance?'

'But she was rich, wasn't she?'

'Jane? Yes, quite rich.' He speaks of her almost imperson- ally, as if describing a historical figure: someone pieced together from reading or research. 'It came from her mother, you know. The same pattern. Mother and daughter both married beneath them. One chose a poor but well-born diplomat, the other an ambitious young civil servant.'

'Civil servant!' Rose sounds amazed.

'That's what I was before I went to the Survey. Not very glamorous, I'm afraid. In fact the work didn't change much in essence, not even under Alex von Kierich. I still had to draft memoranda, prepare reports, submit briefing papers. I travelled more, I suppose. I lived abroad. Does Washington sound exciting to you? I can assure you it is not.'

'Yet you became devoted to him,' Rose says.

'To Alex? Did I tell you that?'

'More or less.'

'He may have been a monster,' Edward says suddenly.

'Will we find out?'

He turns to her, puts his hand on her knee again. 'Perhaps.'

It is quite chaotic at Heathrow.

They leave the car in the long-term car park, take the coach to the terminal, aware suddenly that he has misjudged the time needed for the journey from the village to the airport and only if the aeroplane has been delayed will they be able to catch it. The day has become warm. Rose watches the sweat appear on Edward's reddening forehead as he lifts their two suitcases out of the coach. Now he reminds her of Dr Alessandri, the way Paolo too used to sweat in the Florentine heat, then dab his face with a white handkerchief ironed into a neat square by his wife whom he would betray in that melancholy fashion.

It is difficult for Edward. Rose senses he is worried by her: someone much younger who might become impatient or cross. She decides to be especially kind on this trip, to comfort this man who has suffered yet is willing to reveal his past to her slowly, gradually, as if opening the shutters of a great, dark gallery. So she follows him to the airline desk, stands silent at his side whilst he questions a polite girl who soon shakes her head. The flight has left on time. The girl is so sorry. Yes, there is another flight to Hamburg in three hours. She will check the availability of seats. She taps the keys of her computer, stares at the screen, taps some more. Again the head shakes. The aeroplane is full.

What else is there? Edward leans over the desk, his creased forehead almost touching the bowed blonde head of the airline girl. There must be other flights to north German cities – not Berlin or anywhere too far east. He mentions Frankfurt, Dusseldorf. The girl taps at her computer. Again the head shakes. He turns to Rose. 'Oh dear,' he says. Then almost a shout. 'This whole trip seems to be doomed!'

'No, Edward.' She pats his arm.

The airline girl looks up at them, waits before speaking as if reluctant to enter their private world. 'There is a flight to Cologne about to close, with several seats not taken. If we are quick you will get it. Where are your bags?'

The rush makes the start of the journey easier because there is no need to consider what should happen next or the right thing to say. On the crowded aeroplane, the doors shut behind them almost immediately. After take-off, Edward asks, 'Are you hungry?'

'Not really.'

'Anything to drink?'

'Just orange juice, please.' Rose hears him order a gin and tonic for himself. He gulps at his plastic glass, winces as the aeroplane gives a slight jerk. A few drops of the colourless liquid fall on to his grey trousers, growing into small dark patches. Already the glass is almost empty. She cannot remember if he drinks quite heavily; it would not be in character, she decides, in spite of his obvious disappointments. But on the evening in Bath, after the theatre, he had drunk too much, talked obsessively and made her intrigued, then frightened of the drive home. She had spotted this although her eye is usually slow to pick up details. It is the great broad impressions which lodge in her mind: these and the odd recurring features like the way Edward is different, more irritable or aggressive, when Martin Riley is there. Now he stares at her, the lean face tense. The aeroplane bounces again, yet they are in a clear blue sky. 'Rose, why have you come with me?'

'Curiosity.'

'About Alex?'

She glances out of the window at the bright endless blue. 'Partly. Then there is the place. I like to see new places. Does that seem odd?'

'No. I suppose there was also the question of my reward.'

'What do you mean?'

'For speaking up at the meeting. Defending your father.'

'You didn't defend him. You merely suggested that the best course was to have no opinion at all: to support neither him nor the protesters. The middle ground, in fact.' They are back behind fortifications, each suddenly surrounded by a stark stockade.

'A fair compromise.'

'Certainly fair. To do nothing is fair under these particular circumstances because you will not be furthering the cause of either side. Yet inactivity is not always fair. By standing in silence, turning away, you give implicit support to what is happening: to the dominant force.'

He shakes his head. 'There is always internal resistance: the battle within oneself.'

'That sounds like vanity to me.'

'Not at all. It is a struggle that has to be fought. How else is any kind of rationalism to emerge unless each individual takes care to debate the arguments in his own mind first?' He is almost shouting.

'*His* mind?'

'Or hers.'

'That's good of you.' She laughs. 'Tell me, Edward: what should happen when the argument has been internally resolved, when you reach a decision?' She laughs again. 'When should the internal become the external?'

'When you think you can do some good. When it is not useless to speak out.'

'Until then it is better to keep silent?'

'You're a romantic, Rose. You'd have us all die a hero's death.'

'No. But there are more important things, surely, than simply to live and think alone.'

'Of course. There must be kindred spirits, like-minded people,' he says. 'But everything starts with that first inner certainty. That is where a revolt begins. Do you see?'

The meal interrupts them. Edward has wine; again Rose takes orange juice for she wishes to be absolutely clear-headed, without any excuse to miss whatever may lie ahead. The stewardess has handed out newspapers and, after they have eaten, both Rose and Edward read; soon he drops his paper and sleeps, his mouth open, the breath coming in short snarls, his forehead now dry, the anxiety vanished. Old men sleep often in the afternoon, she has heard, then lie awake for hours at night or wake early in the morning, a long, empty day ahead. Edward is not that old. In spite of his early retirement she cannot think of him as a pensioner, the recipient of long-service awards, free butter sometimes from the vast Common Market dairy stores. No doubt he can still make love. Then the engine note changes and their descent begins, through the clear blue into those soft clouds and the grey sky over Germany. The aeroplane bounces several times; the announcement comes that their landing is imminent. She tightens her seat belt, nudges Edward, worries for a moment when his inert body suddenly convulses like that of a dreaming dog. 'Here already!' He makes as if to stand up. Rose restrains him with her arm.

'No, no. Just landing. Your safety belt . . .'

'Thank you, Rose.'

In the terminal at Cologne Airport, all is quite quick: the arrival of the luggage, the hiring of a car. They walk towards the car park, he carrying both their cases, to find a small white Ford Fiesta. 'How nice,' she says vaguely, looking up at the sunless sky.

Then the rain begins. He puts the suitcases down and rummages in his pocket for the key. There is a burst of lightning, thunder sounding over the low airport buildings. He is inside the car now, leaning across to the door of the front passenger seat, pushing it open. 'There!'

She looks again at the black sky, the blurred airport buildings, row upon row of parked cars as the rain beats hard on the roof. 'What shall we do?'

Edward seems anxious at first, then excited. 'We have a choice,' he says quickly. 'Wait a moment. There must be a map amongst all this.' He searches among some bits of paper and brochures. 'Yes! Here we are. Now look.' He unfolds the map, rests it against the steering wheel so that she has to lean across to see where he is pointing, their faces close enough for her to smell the remains of the gin and wine on his breath. 'Here is our destination. Look! Right the way over and down along there.' A long finger, slightly turned up at its end, draws an invisible line. 'See!' His stiff face collapses into a smile. 'I have an idea.' He glances at his watch, his eyes focusing quickly on her again. 'It's quite late. Well, perhaps not late now, but it will be by the time we reach our destination.' The smile vanishes, to be replaced by a quick frown, then returns, apparently still confident. He looks at his watch again. 'Tell me what you think about this. Presumably you are in no particular hurry. Or have James and Isabel imposed a time limit upon this expedition? No?' He laughs. Now she senses his anxiety even more, the fear of a man who has endured so much. Surprised, she feels powerful: someone who can bring dismay or pain. She must check this, use it with care. 'We could stay the night here,' he says. 'Not here at the airport but in the city. We could catch our breath, so to speak, before setting off eastwards tomorrow. What do you say to that?'

The rain goes on. Inside the protective box of this small car they are isolated, as if in quarantine: not ready yet to mingle with the rest of the world. Rose feels free, unaffected by past influences, ties of any kind, remembering only loosely that voice of Ben's on the answering machine: a moan from a dead part of her life. She wonders if some days ago Edward had embarked upon a cold series of moves that should end with her seduction: this surprising old man. No, it is for her to help him. 'Yes.'

They drive out of the car park, slowly at first so that he can master the new car, pausing at the start of a broad highway where traffic rushes past in the spray of the wet afternoon. He goes faster, jerking through the gears, but still she feels safe, secure in this capsule they seem to have made for themselves. She has so much, even the sense of joyful comparison. Ben would talk about himself, a long whine of self-pity. Simon Pumphrey might show off, boast, drive too fast, try to impress her with what he knows about existentialism. Paolo Alessandri would brood in silence, preoccupied with a sense of shame, Catholic guilt, an adulterer's sorrow. Edward is better: proud and brave.

So they enter the outskirts of the city, long straight streets where trams glide down the centre. She studies the high buildings, the posters in a strange language indistinct in the rain which has slackened into a dull drizzle. Edward peers at the windscreen. She remembers that he needs glasses for reading; perhaps an old man's vanity will not allow him to wear them in front of a young girl. Is this partly why she is drawn to older men: because her youth gives her power, strength and superiority? No, she seeks to learn from them, to glimpse the great world of grown-ups, so mysterious and inviting. Young people show too much of themselves. You know them within hours, even minutes. After that there is nothing left to explore, to imagine.

Now they are on a long bridge over the Rhine. The old city of Cologne is ahead of them: the huge, grey cathedral clear through the lifting rain above small streets of gabled houses coming down to the river's edge, where a lighted cruise ship is tied up beside a high railway bridge further upstream.

They discover an open route at last between pedestrian precincts and one-way streets. Near the bridge is a large new hotel. 'What about that?' he says. 'No, we want somewhere different. Don't you agree? Let's drive on. Look!' He stops and points to the other side; a horn hoots behind him. Set back from the road, about halfway down an alley forbidden to cars, is a more modest house with a hotel sign outside. 'Isn't that the sort of place? Perhaps, Rose . . .'

She gets out, runs towards the sign whilst Edward waits in the car. In the small dark hall of the hotel, a fair-haired young man in a grey suit sits behind a wooden desk reading an illustrated magazine. She asks for a room, speaking slowly in English. He answers, rather faster; they have one. Then she remembers. 'No. Two rooms, please.' Single or double? 'Single.' The young man stands, puts the magazine down, turns to take two keys off the rack on the wall behind him. He looks at her. His lips are thick, the eyes interested, and on one smooth, feminine cheek he has three pockmarks. 'Have you a car?' he asks, not smiling. She nods and thinks, As a race they have no charm. Those eyes seem amused, slightly repulsive. Suddenly she feels a stab of fear. There is so much she does not know about this place: the town, the country, the man she is with. Her strength slides away; then she grasps for it, pulls it back. 'You can park round the corner in the big car park. Come. I will show the direction to you out-side.'

They park the car and the young man shows them to their rooms. He takes the two cases towards a small lift, in which the three of them stand in silence as it rises slowly towards the third floor; Rose thinks of a resurrection from the dead. 'Unfortunately it has not been possible to give you rooms that are next to each other, but there is only a small gap in between.' He opens one door, then moves quickly along the passage to open another. 'Sir?'

Each room is oblong-shaped with an adjoining bathroom and a colour print of an impressionistic picture on the wall opposite the single bed: one of the twin-spired front of the great cathedral, the other of vine-covered hills descending towards the Rhine. 'Which one . . .?' Edward starts to ask. She smiles, enters the first, followed by the youth, whom she tells which of the two cases belongs to her. 'What about a short walk whilst it is still light, perhaps to the cathedral?' Edward suggests. 'Shall we meet downstairs in an hour?'

The door shuts. He has left her. At first Rose sits on the single bed, looking vaguely at the television set, the squat fridge like a small altar beside the window, the view out to a gabled house on the other side of the street. Then she gets up, opens the fridge door to see a collection of miniature bottles and small cans. On top is a price list and a suggestion in German, French and English that guests should make full use of this 'mini-bar'. One is never quite left alone. But she feels a drink may help to relax this odd stiffness; so she pours herself a strong vodka and tonic, takes two or three sips before lying on the bed, leaving her case unopened. The thrill of adventure swells, almost pushing the breath from her body.

She will tell him this evening what she has read about von Kierich: a sign of her interest not only in the German but in Edward's past as well. So she tries a few sentences in her head.

'Edward, you remember yesterday when we met on the train going to London?' Yes, that is a start. 'Well, I had a particular purpose, or two really, I suppose: one to do with you, the other something different but linked also in a way to us both. I'll get to that in a minute.' She drinks some more vodka. 'I was going to the London Library to see what I could find out about Alex. I looked him up, you see, in *The Times*. Can you tell me what happened? That's what we're after now, I suppose, on this journey: the truth. Then there was the second reason for my London day. After a morning spent in the library, I took a taxi down to Fulham from St James's Square to have lunch with Ben Talbot. We haven't talked much about Ben, you and I. But you ought to know that he made love to me yesterday, in his studio at three o'clock precisely, which I know because there is an alarm clock on the table beside his bed. So there!'

Rose lies back, bending her long legs up towards her waist. Her heart slows. She is suddenly tired, closes her eyes, feels heavy in body and mind, as if a huge smooth stone is strapped to the top of her head, and sleeps, a haze coming over her. Then the telephone shrieks like a hysterical child. She snatches the receiver from the bedside table.

'Rose?' Edward sounds worried. 'Are you coming? I'm down in the lobby.'

'Yes, of course. Sorry.'

Outside it is bright now, a fine late afternoon. 'I fell asleep,' she says at his side in the carless street, remembering that she has left the half-drunk vodka and tonic in the room. What a waste. Yet to drink more would have been an error, for she needs to watch and note so much, to catch every inference or hint.

Edward smiles. 'Why not?'

He wants to approach the cathedral from the west, to get a clear view of the façade, so they walk quite fast through the pedestrian zone, up towards a complex of modern buildings. Rose wonders if the other people notice them: men in business suits or well-dressed women emerging from the shops, occasionally an older, heavier figure, one fat woman with a bulging shopping bag who stops to rest or regain her breath. At the square in front of the cathedral, they try to keep their eyes away from the huge edifice until they can have a full view of it, then turn at last from the flat-roofed offices built on the bombed land around to see the great grey-brown west front, the twin spires rising out of fantastic octagonals into high, tapering peaks. 'Well?' he says.

It is so extraordinary that she cannot answer. They go in and stand at the end of the middle and broadest of the five long aisles to stare at the vast recesses, the soaring emptiness. He buys two guidebooks in English at the bookstall. They walk slowly forward. She thinks of the relief that will come when she tells him the truth, the cathedral still somewhere on the edge of her mind.

So Rose falls in behind Edward, hoping that he will not turn to talk to her yet. He may feel that, as an older escort, he should instruct her, pass on knowledge and experience. Is he interested in art? She does not know; as so often, her picture of him has huge bare patches of canvas, unfinished sections. She tries to remember the essentials of the Gothic style. In Florence this had been part of the course she had done, and then it had seemed fascinating, so appropriate, to be told of such things by a kindly, rather effeminate young lecturer at the British Institute. All that remains now is a memory of that high voice swooping and fluttering like a nervous bird, speaking of a 'reflection of God's universe, a gigantic hymn of praise'.

A shadow crosses the long nave, a cloud over the sun. She stares upwards, stands still, her eyes leaving Edward for some time, conscious at last of the huge height: the great space of an imitation heaven, a paradise of cold, curved stone. She thinks of Ben returning to the studio, turning on the answering machine, then her voice and its short, cruel message: a lie as he would quickly guess, another example of what he had once called 'the cruelty of youth'. Hadn't he said that young people want really to kill the old, bury them, get them out of sight? Her broken promise will cut into Ben like rough-edged glass.

Rose shakes her head. Her eyes search for Edward again, as if seeking comfort. But he is not there, or not where he had been in the aisle three or four paces ahead of her, studying his newly bought guidebook, a frown on his thin, austere face. She looks round, calmly at first. Four Japanese men are in conclave next to one of the pews on the right, their heads together, cameras slung over their shoulders; beyond them stands a solitary nun. Other visitors are further away, by the intersection of the nave. The cathedral seems quite empty; probably it always does because of its vast size, even when thousands come. There he is, seated on the left some ten pews up. He must be anxious to concentrate fully on his guidebook, to see what he should look for before starting out on the long walk round, unlike Rose who feels suddenly ashamed of her self-absorption, her laziness in not also trying to find out all she can about this extraordinary place. Edward has his head in his hands. He seems to be praying.

She is sure that she should not disturb him. Certainly not. Then he puts out his right arm, grasps the back of the pew, raises his head (which she can see only from the back) as if to look at the roof, turns slightly to the left, revealing the odd pallor of his cheek, then lowers it again on to a supporting left hand. Suddenly Rose thinks, He is sick. She rushes to the pew, bends low so that her head is next to his, that pale cheek now turning grey; there is sweat on his forehead. He bites his lips together, frowns, swallows hard. 'Hello.'

'Edward, what are you doing?' she asks.

'Just sitting down for a bit.'

'Are you all right?'

He shakes his head, those lips still tight, a defence against pain. 'Some sort of trouble. Just tiredness, I expect. Nothing to worry about. Shall we get out of here?' He smiles. 'It feels rather oppressive suddenly. I don't know why. We can come back tomorrow, before we leave. There should be time.'

'Yes. Of course.'

'Wait a minute.' He grasps the back of the pew more tightly, seems to push at it and stands up, tall again beside her. 'There. Now what about some fresh air?'

Chapter Twenty

Perhaps the huge cathedral has in some way impressed upon him the immensity of his risk: to bring a young girl out of England to almost certain disappointment, disillusion and disgust. Those burnings in his head, the flashes of pain, the same symptoms as a migraine or so he imagines, have echoed this worry. Not too persistent during the first part of the journey, providing merely an odd lightning stab like the lunge of an assassin's knife. Then in the long centre aisle came what he thought might be the *coup de grâce*: a pain so intense that he had to sit down. Soon she was with him, but by that time he had recovered. How odd; he has never suffered from this before.

They should leave. An impatience, or worry about the unknown, makes it impossible to concentrate on this great building, its monuments and stained glass, the gold monolithic shrine of the Three Kings, which he knows from the guidebook is in a case behind the high altar, the long views back towards the entrance doors, then up to the dim distant roof. Even something so enormous, supposedly so imbued with historic spirituality and selflessness, cannot silence the whispering anxieties inside his now painless head. Meekly he follows her to the door, then out into the grey, modern square.

'Can you walk?' she asks. Her dark hair falls forward to cover her cheeks as she looks down at his slightly shuffling feet.

'Yes. Look, what about a drink?' He glances up at the sky

which is now clear, the darkness still some time away. They go down to the river and take a table outside one of several almost empty restaurants or bars. A waiter comes, and Edward orders a beer for himself, some white wine for her.

'What was it, Edward?' she asks. Her round face is near his at the circular table, those huge eyes anxious, almost, he thinks, in tears.

'Just exhaustion.' He laughs and taps his forehead. 'Old age, I expect.' He lifts his beer, laughs again before drinking. 'Some sort of tension.'

'Yes.' Her voice softens to that of a comforter. 'Of course you must be worried. So much anticipation. So much conjecture.'

The words sound odd coming from her, redolent of some cold background briefing. 'Conjecture?'

'About how he will be. This great Alex.' Her smile teases him.

'I am expecting nothing. You forget my age, Rose. One learns to accept things, to roll with the punches.' This is a lie. 'One seeks calm. Rest.'

'That can't be true. If it was, you wouldn't be here.'

'No. You're wrong. By this journey, I am hoping to resolve various doubts and uncertainties. Some unfinished business, you might call it. Without this settled, I cannot have the rest of which I have spoken.' As in the past, that pomposity creeps into his speech when he is agitated, unsure. It had begun as a protection from the more self-confident and urbane of his colleagues, continued as a defence against Sir Roger and is now ingrained, an ineradicable part of him.

Rose seems to come nearer. 'Edward, I must tell you something. When we met on the train yesterday I was on my way to do some research on Dr von Kierich. I went to the London Library, to look at the old copies of *The Times*.' She stops, withdraws a little from him, her eyes staring at the surface of the table.

'Was that the only purpose of your visit?' he asks.

'Almost.' She looks at him, then shies away.

'Don't worry.' He glances at the great, slow river. A freight train trundles across the railway bridge, as small as a toy at this distance. 'What did you find?'

'He left your organization in disgrace. Does Martin know, Edward?'

'Know what?'

'The truth.'

'Why should he?'

She speaks slowly, with great measure. 'Martin was involved with that sort of thing in Washington, wasn't he? Secret work. Undercover stuff. The Survey was an important international body. From what I have read, its campaigns were much more aggressive in those days, more shrill.' She tries to sound knowledgeable, grown-up. 'The richer countries must have been interested in the people who ran it. After all, the Survey was attacking them for their greed and selfishness, the inadequacy of their efforts to help the poor.'

'Where did you read this?' he asks. 'Surely you're too young.'

'I looked up von Kierich in *The Times* index.'

'What did you find?' His voice is angry, even after all these years.

'You must know the story so well.' She tells it slowly, raking through the remembered details, the saga of rumours and denials. 'Extraordinary.'

'Why?'

She blushes. 'Because of what you have told me about him. His experiences during the war. His courage.'

'Alex was brave.'

'Strange too. That solitude.'

'Yes,' Edward says. 'Did I give you that impression? I'd forgotten.'

'Was he a homosexual?' Rose asks suddenly.

Edward is astonished. 'Good heavens, no! Why . . .' He stops for a moment. 'There were women. But not . . .' Something stops him again, an odd shame, as if he were about to shout obscenities in that great cathedral. 'Jane loved him, I think.'

'Jane? Your wife?'

'Yes.'

'Did they have an affair?'

'No.' He tries to smile. 'But there were others: old friends in Germany, when he was on leave. Sometimes they visited him in Washington.' The waiter comes again and he orders more beer for himself, more wine for Rose. Then he turns back to her. 'Why are you interested in Alex?' Now his voice is so loud that some people at the next table but one turn to look at him. He glares at them as she lifts her head, the mouth and chin set, only the eyes showing a slight distress. 'Rose, I'm so sorry.'

'That's all right. It's just that —'

'What?'

'I felt I had to come with you.'

'To see him?'

'Partly.' She takes a small white handkerchief from her bag, dabs at her eyes, manages a smile. 'I couldn't bear it yesterday in the hall when they were shouting at my father. I know we laugh at him: Hector and Lucy and I. Dad is such a creature of whims. Do you remember the market garden?' She laughs. They are back in the village, on familiar ground, and Edward sees how much she loves her father as she speaks of the purchase of expensive equipment, vehicles in which to transport the flowers and vegetables, architects' drawings for the shop and wholesale centre, then the slow subsiding of his enthusiasm, the realization that the scheme had failed and there was still just enough time to get out before bankruptcy and personal ruin. 'It must seem odd to you,' Rose says.

228

'Why?'

'Your own background is so different.'

'Yes.'

'Tell me about it, Edward.'

So he speaks for rather a long time, thinking at first that he will get it over quite quickly because she cannot really be interested and is surely just asking out of courtesy. The one thing the Finches have taught their children is good manners, far more than he and Jane ever did with Nick and Charles, who are still often inconsiderate, even boorish, in spite of those years with the urbane Sir Roger and his coolly polite rich wife. Yet she asks questions, seeks to know more. Can he describe his father, give some physical details? What about the farm? What did they grow there? She wants also to know about the schools: the village primary, the grammar school, the winning of the scholarships. Then the London School of Economics: his time there must have been the heyday of its socialism. She has heard of the Webbs and Tawney, even if she is not sure of their dates. It is not all cold fact, either, for when he mentions his childhood asthma, those bouts of breathlessness which had prevented an active, careless youth, she becomes solicitous again, as she had been that evening in Bath.

'The trouble vanished, just like that!' he says, clicking his fingers. 'Strange, don't you think? Nerves, I suppose. The cause must have been psychosomatic. I believe it often is with asthma. A break with the past, the chance to work abroad, in Washington and Rome. These might have done it. Then I married.' Edward seems to stiffen. He looks at his watch, then towards the river and the dark buildings on the opposite bank, dull under a cool, grey sky. 'Aren't you cold out here? We could go inside and eat.'

'If you like.'

They sit at a table in a large bright room and a waiter takes their order. They face each other. 'All right?' he asks.

Rose laughs, a soft sound. 'Yes. How's your head?'

'Completely better.'

'Does it happen often?'

'Never.'

She seems to pause for a moment. Then the words come in a calm, clear voice. 'I noticed how tense you seemed at dinner with the Rileys; then some days before when you came to the manor and we spoke about Alex. Had you received his letter then?'

'That evening when we sat outside on the terrace?' He remembers how she had watched the artist Talbot, staring up at him like an amazed child. 'Yes. The letter had arrived. But don't worry.' He taps the side of his head. 'I have prepared myself for anything. One must realize that the man is old, perhaps already in his dotage. The shock of our arrival may well do for him completely!' He laughs. 'Let us hope not. How old was Dr Alessandri?'

'Fifty-one.'

He leans back to make way for the plates of food that the waiter has brought. 'I've been intrigued by him since that evening. In Bath, when we went to the theatre. Did you sense my interest?'

'In what?' She looks at her food.

'Have you ever been in love?'

She is cross, her eyes bright as lightning, and he thinks she might leave the table, run back alone to the hotel. Then she changes, as if under control again. 'No.' She pauses. 'But I have a friend.'

'Who?'

'A good friend.' She waits. A roar of laughter comes from the group by the bar. 'Ben Talbot.'

Edward smiles. 'Dear Ben. Are you fond of him?'

'He is an old friend of my parents.'

'Is that how you think of Ben — as a sort of honorary uncle?'

Rose smiles, her eyes easier, quite calm, and ignores the question. 'This summer I watched the Sun Room take shape, from the bare walls to what it is now: the children playing in the fields, the hayricks, the carts and all the rest. He worked so hard, yet none of it seems to please him.'

'The true creative spirit is never satisfied.'

'Is that what Ben is, do you think?' she asks.

'I wish I knew him better.'

'What do you see?'

'In Ben?' Edward speaks slowly. 'I see charm, facility, glibness, glamour, superficiality, technique, repetition. Ben likes comfort. He likes warmth, praise, admiration, beauty. As he sits on the terrace of the manor, looking out across the garden at twilight, a glass of wine in his hand, people loving him and his gentle perception, he thinks this should be heaven: I am free yet loved, solitary yet in demand. I have my independence. But I am wanted, even needed, as well. Then Ben's gaze turns inward because he is always looking at himself. Now comes a sharp beam of self-analysis. He thinks of regret, disappointment, the failure of his ambition – for I am sure Ben once had great dreams about how his art might change the world. Don't all artists have to settle for less than they really want or need?' He stops. 'Am I being too cruel?' Then he snaps, 'Ben is vain. Weak.' She does not answer. 'It upsets me to think of him with you: a man of that type.'

'Upsets you? Oh Edward.' She will not give way.

'Have you slept with him?'

'What if I have?' She looks coolly at him. 'Why should you care?'

'Because I love you.'

'Don't be so ridiculous.'

'So you have,' he murmurs.

Rose stares at this old man, a look of infinite sadness on her young face, the insouciance gone: a form of capitulation. 'Only once.'

'When?'

'Yesterday afternoon.'

He smiles at her, trying to look wise and kind. 'What made you succumb?'

'Succumb?'

'To Ben.'

She shakes her head. 'It happened so quickly, so easily.'

'You take pity on these old men, Rose: Dr Alessandri, Ben Talbot, Alex von Kierich.'

'I've never met von Kierich!' she cries. He waits, expectant, longing. 'I know what he means to you.' Her voice seems to thicken, to descend. She puts her hand on the side of her head. 'Did she kill herself?'

'Who?'

'Your wife.'

'No.'

He does not speak, shaming her into avoiding his eyes, until she says suddenly, 'Edward, can we go back now? I think I've had enough.' She points desperately at her plate, then looks in the direction of the bar and the laughing group. 'The noise . . .'

'Yes. Of course.' He stays seated for a bit, watching her get to her feet. 'Rose,' he says involuntarily, the word slipping away like a small, smooth stone.

She looks up. 'I . . .'

'Wait for me. I must pay.'

Now they are at the door of the restaurant together, Edward about to put an arm around her shoulder, then thinking, No, not now, wait because she needs more time. He knows this tension: the sense of a taut, stretched body at his side. 'Which way?' she asks.

He has a good sense of direction. 'Up here. Then to the right. It's not far.'

They walk in silence. On the narrow, pedestrian streets people seem to move aside instinctively to allow them to take a strong, straight line. Edward looks up. The sky is dark: not black but a deep blue, the stars sharp on its surface, the housetops rising in ghostly outline behind the lamps and bright windows of the city. He takes her arm, guides her round a corner. Barbara would pat his hand when he did this, but with Judith such a move had seemed wrong: too sentimental or old-fashioned, likely to be mocked. Rose may feel his interest to be paternal, an inept attempt at protection or reassurance. Slightly embarrassed, he lets his hand fall once more to his side.

At the desk in the hotel there is a new face: a stern old man wearing a white open-necked shirt and a dark grey cardigan who puts down a newspaper and seems to recognize them. Quickly he takes their room keys from the rack, without a smile, just a slight narrowing of the eyes. Edward thinks, If she says 'Thank you' we will sleep together tonight. Rose looks at the man, smiles and speaks English. 'Thank you.'

He remembers the lay-out of the building. There is a lift but Rose walks to the stairs and they will go up three flights: then comes the passage, the rooms numbered from the stair end so that her room is first, before his: three numbers in between. He stands back slightly, allowing her to go first, and on the stairs watches her long legs in their dark tights, the pale skin vague beneath. In the passage he is still behind her. She turns her head slightly and he thinks she may look round, perhaps to say something, but it seems that she wishes only to see the numbers on the doors of the rooms, for she glances down at her key, as if to check. Edward walks faster and comes level with her. They reach her door together. She turns, holding the key so that it points at his chest like a pistol. 'Well,' she begins.

He must move now because he loves this girl. 'Darling,' he says and puts a hand on her waist, feeling the hardness of the bone. Their faces are almost level; she is quite tall.

Rose's eyes regain that anxiety but her hand, still clasping the key, falls to her side. Then she turns away and he suspects the beginnings of a rebuff although it is to open the door, which she does quickly without speaking or apparently responding to him except by not flinching or retreating at all with the rest of her body. Glancing along the passage, cautious even now, he kisses her twice, on either side of her mouth, before they go together into her room. She turns on the light. The interior seems cold.

Inside, she shuts the door, tries the lock again to make certain it is secure. He is still close, jammed up against her in the narrow entrance with the bathroom behind them before the space broadens out into the main part of the room and the bed with its creased dark green cover on which Rose had been lying before they left for the cathedral. No one has turned the bed down, an example, he thinks vaguely, of poor service when one considers the rate for the night, which is not cheap. How slack! He frowns, puts an arm across Rose's back, pulls her even closer, tries to kiss her again but this time she draws away. 'Wait, Edward,' she whispers, her breath almost smothering the words. They step further into the room, now more apart, and stand by the bed, where she takes the lead, reaching out to him, making the kiss long and sure at last. 'No,' she says, perhaps involuntarily, a reaction natural for any shy girl. He ignores this and soon they are together on the bed, the light of the house across the street like fire through the window where the curtains have not yet been drawn. 'Edward,' she murmurs again, then surprises him by standing up and pushing her hair back briefly before she walks across to close the curtains, her movements quick, the shutting-out of the rest of the world accomplished sharply and well. For a moment he feels alarm at her practical power. She is so young. There is no contempt so strong as that of youth for age.

Then the fear goes, as it had vanished all those years ago in Rome when he and Jane had first made love together in his large, quite cold apartment one winter Saturday afternoon. This is no time for awe, no time either for those other memories, although he knows that it is at least partly his past which has drawn her to him – that and a sudden wish to protect her father.

So he sits, waits and then she is back beside him on the bed, drawing him closer, saying, 'Edward,' softly so that there seems to be a tightly drawn circle now around them both, within which is only her sweetness, her wishes for him. Nothing else, not Jane nor Alex von Kierich, the ostensible object of her quest. He hears himself say, 'I love you.' She smiles between kisses, again whispering, 'Wait.'

Edward knows her so little, and he sees this now as they begin to make love in the bed which is not meant for two people at all. Now it is she who seems to move back, slightly timid after that first sweet, brave advance, but he does not allow this, having recovered his strength. She clings to him, as if frightened that they may be parted, so he clasps her in return, feels her young, tight body soften again, then respond to his older self, of which he is no longer ashamed because there seems to be nothing half-hearted or contrived about the way she is with him. He senses that strange melancholy; then she thrusts this aside as well and gives up everything, relaxing completely, much quicker, much more than he would ever have dared to hope she might when they had been together on those innumerable imagined times during his lonely hours in the large dark village house.

Afterwards he strokes her cheek, lifts her thick hair away from her ear, traces his finger down the side of her slightly smiling mouth. Always he has wanted this. Always. 'Darling,' he says.

'Edward.'

'Did you enjoy it?'

'Yes.'

As he looks up to the grey-cream ceiling of the small room, that sense of quiet delight covers each part of him: the surprise resurrected again after the dead years. Then he sleeps.

Chapter Twenty-one

It is Rose who wakes first. This morning she hears the noise of distant traffic, becomes aware of the light of day through the thin brown curtains. Then she sees him again, his life here in the slightly obstructed breathing of an old man asleep. Edward.

She turns towards him, instinctively covering her breasts with the loose top sheet. He lies on his back, turned only slightly away from her, on the edge of the narrow bed. If he moves only one inch to that side, she thinks, he will fall out on to the floor, waking quickly in a state of shock. He must be beginning to feel his age: that face pale and angular, with no spare or slack flesh. But his open mouth, which in old people can give an impression of pathetic collapse, has an odd rigidity as if alert even now, so different to the way Simon Pumphrey's thick, childish lips pout in sleep into a look of spoilt discontent. Paolo Alessandri had been more like Edward: alert as well, the fine intelligence showing always, yet also suffused with an apparently accepted defeat. Edward has fought back. He is brave.

She puts her hand on his smooth white shoulder. At first he stays still, then moves his whole body slightly further away from her across the small bed. This she will not allow. Like last night, she will take the lead, not of course too flagrantly; the difference in age and his obvious anxiety dictate this. She wishes to make him happy, to see also that they both enjoy this trip into a strange country. In the future, Rose feels, she will look back in wonder on this odd interlude. 'Edward.'

He moves again, opens his eyes and she edges towards him, the sheet falling away. At first he seems uncertain, even lost as perhaps the events of the last two days rush back in some disorder into his awakening consciousness; then he sees Rose and reaches out to her. 'Darling.' The word comes quickly, like the response to some coded challenge. He is awake and now, in the slight chill of the room in the morning, they make love as happily as the night before, Rose wanting to hold on to this moment for ever, forgetting that future which waits in the dull corners of home, glimpsing the way ahead to the small German town and the old man who waits for them there. Afterwards, she wonders what Ben had planned for her: probably nothing beyond his own desire and a few vague hopes. Ben must hate scenes, involvement, any glimpse of the depths.

Edward sleeps once more. She stays awake but does not move or get up because she feels he must have more rest. Soon he turns, so thin but not too old in appearance, and holds her, kissing her shoulder before whispering that he will go back to his room and dress, for they should not leave Cologne too late.

At breakfast, Rose asks if it is far to the town where Alex lives.

Edward smiles. 'Darling. You asked me that yesterday. Are you worried?'

'No.' She turns away.

'Rose.' He reaches out and holds her hand briefly. She smiles at him, then looks across the room to see that the dark-haired young waitress is staring at them, an expression of amused superiority on her round, pretty face. 'Are you glad you came with me?'

'Yes.'

In the car he feels as if he wants to tell her so much and for

the first time wishes that there was not the prospect of Alex
at the journey's end. His old obsession has been pushed to
one side by this girl who entered his life much later but now
might grow until everything else vanishes at last. Last night,
the way she had come so quickly, surely that meant he
might fill an emptiness for her as well: unbelievable now, at
his age, like a second spring, so strange here as they leave
the outskirts of Cologne on the autobahn on a clear bright
day and enter the wooded hills of the Rhineland.

But he talks of Alex, or the Alex he remembers, and she is
not shy but quiet as usual, calm with her hands together on
one knee. Today she wears a pair of black jeans, a dark
green jersey. Sometimes she stares out of the window, looking
at the thick mass of trees in the morning light, as he tells her
about Africa, how they were captured in the bush, then von
Kierich's story of the massacre. 'I believe him,' he says.

Again there is that conflict: the strength of her present
against the power of his past, a lost age of agony and
heroism. She looks at Edward's lined face, the skin etched
by years of sunlight. 'Is Alex an imaginative man?' she asks.

'Not imaginative so much as obsessive.' Edward's voice is
louder. 'That is part of the reason he made such a success of
the Survey. He left nothing or nobody alone. Every proposal
or plan had to be justified, argued over. There had to be no
mistakes. The Survey was his life.'

'A form of retribution, perhaps?' she suggests. 'A way of
atoning for what he had seen and been a part of?'

'That is the simplistic explanation. No doubt there is
some truth in it.'

'Did he ever love anyone?' she says suddenly.

Edward does not turn to look at her. 'I don't know.'

There is a silence: ten, perhaps fifteen minutes. Then
Rose says, 'What shall we do after we have seen Alex?'

'We could go off somewhere together.' He puts one hand
on her thigh, then takes it away again quickly.

239

She sighs, fending him off. 'Term starts in a few weeks' time. I've got so much work to prepare.'

'In the holidays?'

'Yes, even in the holidays.'

'I can't see you properly at the manor.' For the first time that morning his voice sounds strained. 'What will your parents say?'

She laughs. 'You're a family friend.'

'Precisely. Not their daughter's lover. At my age, one should not try to combine the roles.'

'You mean you wish to be respectable?'

'I want to see you again.' Then suddenly he says, 'Marry me, Rose.'

She sinks lower in her seat. 'Edward. Not now.'

'Never?' Looking ahead at the great straight road, he feels he can say anything. 'Oh darling, I haven't got much time left. I see it falling away: the days, the months, the years without you.'

'Why didn't you find someone after Jane?' she asks.

Then he tells her about Barbara and Judith, and she laughs and talks of other things: the saw mill and Dove and her mother's moods. They stop at a bright clean service area for lunch and it is as if he has not asked her the foolish question at all. How clever she is, he thinks. On the way into the restaurant, at the door, he puts his arm on her shoulder, pushing her gently ahead of him; on the way out he does the same, this time leaving it there for longer so that they walk together towards their small hired car like a romantic couple or, more likely, a father on holiday with his favourite daughter. So they start off again and after a few miles leave the wide autobahn on which they have been since Cologne for a single carriageway road, which is quite straight at first as it passes through the flat fields and small groups of trees and occasional larger woods, mostly of thick conifers. Now there are fewer cars, few houses too outside the small villages where the empty streets add to the sense of an echoing space, even that slight threat of the unknown. It is dark; the clouds show no glimmer of a break. Edward puts a hand up to his forehead. 'About ten miles more,' she says.

No life that he can see: no people. Suddenly a car roars past them, as if it has descended from the sky, the driver alone. A mile or two later they reach a crossroads. Edward stops, starts to edge out, looks to right and left when again there is an unexpected sound, the low blast of a horn as a huge truck carrying logs comes quickly towards him, swings out and away just in time: an apparition apparently from nowhere, for he could have sworn that the road had been clear.

These shocks, the strange darkness. Rose sees the sign with the name of the town first and reads it out to him as if in triumph. 'Better make for the centre,' she suggests, so he drives down a small hill with detached houses on either side, the lighted windows showing signs of life at last. Two elderly men walk together on the pavement, one in a cap. They move slowly but with regular movements, as if in thrall to an unseen hypnotist. On the right a red and white neon sign announces a hotel.

The building is quite large: four storeys high with the familiar gables, like those illustrations for *Hansel and Gretel*, *Struwwelpeter* and the Brothers Grimm. The sky stays dark, making even the bright white of the window surrounds dull in the late afternoon of this warm autumn day.

Edward stops by the back entrance. Of course they might have to stay the night here and he has not thought this out at all or mentioned it to her, a reflection perhaps of the curious other-worldliness or sense of wonder he has felt since yesterday in Cologne. 'We must go in and ask for him,' he says and adds, 'No, I'll go in.' Then he says quickly, 'I love you.'

A woman of about forty-five waits behind the desk. She wears a dark green suit, a white blouse with a frill at the neck and pale pinkish-rimmed spectacles. She has greying fair hair tied up in a bun at the back of her head. Behind her, on a pink wall beside a half-open door, hangs a dark-painted landscape of woodland and heath. Her lips are closed tight. '*Bitte?*' she says in a low, sharp voice.

'Dr von Kierich?' Edward asks.

The woman looks at him with a slight smile, and speaks in English, having guessed his nationality. 'He is at the Kloster, where he sometimes guides tours. You know the way to the Kloster? Or you can wait here.' She looks at her watch. 'He will be back in two hours.'

'Is the Kloster near?'

'*Ja.*' She takes a folded map from a stand on the desk, lays it out in front of them and points at the street plan of the town with a long finger, the unvarnished nail lifeless. 'See, it is up here. Turn down to the right, then left. About five minutes' drive. You have a car?' He nods. 'Then it is easy.' She smiles again, a quick way of telling him to go.

He drives slowly to a crossroads, turns right on to a main highway, past the last few houses of the small town, then left beside a small lake next to some empty tennis courts. A few yards further on, there is a sign to the left marked 'Kloster'; clearly the place is of historical interest as Alex had said. A few older, detached houses line a street that leads to a complex of obviously monastic or ecclesiastical buildings where several cars and a coach are parked by the roadside. Edward stops beside a brick chapel with a short spire and an adjoining two-storey stone block in the form of a quadrangle. 'Here,' he says.

They get out and walk towards an open door. Beside this stands a short-haired woman in a tweed skirt and cardigan, probably over seventy but quite straight, small

and with a comfortable shape. She greets them. *'Bitte?'*
Again it is like a request for the password.

'Herr von Kierich?' Edward adds, 'Dr Alexander von
Kierich?'

She stares at him, at the girl, and suddenly raises her
hands, as if overcome. 'Ah . . .' The German words flow,
then change to English.

'He is inside. Why do you want him? I know. Oh, how
wonderful. I know your face and I am rude to say this.
Please forgive. But Alex will be so pleased and happy. It is
Mr West? Oh, I hope so. How lucky. I was here in case
more tourists came, to see if I could help Alex, and now
this!' Edward steps back. The old woman puts her
hands up again to clutch at him, as if to prevent his escape.
'I am rude! Oh no. But I want to show how pleased I am for
Alex that you are here. You must say. I am Mrs Schneider. I
told him to write to you. How lucky! Is it Mr West?'

'Yes.'

'And your daughter?'

He almost says yes to this as well, but shakes his head
instead.

'Wait!' Still she is smiling, her eyes those of a delighted
child. 'Please.' She stares at them both in silence, her breath
coming quickly. 'Oh I wish!' She looks up at the darkening
sky, as if appealing for help. 'Come in, please. We can wait.
I have a room.' She turns to Rose. 'Are you well?'

'Yes, thank you,' the girl answers, and as they follow
Frau Schneider through the wide stone doorway Edward
reaches across to clasp Rose's hand.

The hall is dark, lit only by dim lights placed subtly in
the vaulted ceiling so that they do not disrupt its shape.
Ahead is a stone-flagged passage; to the left, the beginnings
of another. 'Do you know the history of our Kloster?' Frau
Schneider asks.

'No.'

She laughs, opening her mouth to reveal dark yellow stained teeth behind the bright red lipstick. 'I hear often Alex give it in English so I can say a bit, probably not too well but enough. At school and college I studied your language. Then with my husband I would read in English. He was a priest but that was a long time ago because Klaus died.' She looks at her large-faced watch. 'Alex will finish soon. Today he has a group from Gifhorn: some club, I think. Old people. Always afterwards he comes to me, in my room: just to talk. We can go, Mr West.' She smiles at Rose once more. 'Please follow!' They walk behind the old woman down the long stone-flagged passage ahead, then turn left at its end, passing closed wooden doors every few yards. Of course: this is some kind of convent. Yet Frau Schneider is not a nun but the widow of a priest, as she has said. He tries to hang back to explain at least some of this to Rose, but Frau Schneider stops and turns, still smiling, to make sure they are still there. 'My home,' she says and opens one of the wooden doors. 'Please.'

The door leads into a cream-painted room with two wide windows which look out on to a fountain and dark trees beneath what is now a clear evening sky. Between the windows hangs a small wooden crucifix. To their left is a shut wooden door and beyond this a blocked fireplace. On either side of the fireplace is an alcove with shelves of books and china ornaments. Small wooden shields with coloured crests hang above each alcove, the symbols of various towns: Kiel, Munster, Celle.

By the door, against the wall, is another bookcase: long, with a narrow top shelf of older books, some thick and with heavy bindings. On the broader lowest shelf rests a pile of about ten albums stacked flat, leaving space for some other large volumes. Edward stares at those albums bound in blue, red or dark green leather with gold bands. They belong to Alex, to the old photographic record. 'Frau Schneider . . .' he begins.

She is by the wall to the left of the door, beside a copy of a Dürer self-portrait. 'My bedroom,' she says, pointing to another closed door to her right. 'I have also a small kitchen. Do you like tea? I can do it now!'

'We have eaten only a short time ago.' He spaces out the words to make it easy for her to understand. 'We must not disturb you.'

'Please?'

'We can wait outside for Alex. In the hall.'

'Oh no!' She looks horrified, then raises one hand to her forehead. 'I am forgetting. It is possible Mrs Hartmann, a friend who lives also in the Kloster, will come to see me. She knows Alex as well but they have not much to talk about!' Frau Schneider laughs. 'No, Frau Hartmann will perhaps come. Please. We will sit.' There is a sofa on one side of the fireplace, an armchair on the other and a harder, wooden chair between these in the centre of the room. Frau Schneider takes the wooden chair and points Rose and Edward towards the sofa, where they sit beside each other. 'You know about our Kloster?'

'No.'

'Then I can say something.' She leans forward, waits a moment, tense as a crouching athlete. 'It was founded in the thirteenth century by the daughter-in-law of the Herzog von Sachsen. Now listen! He was married with Mathilde, daughter of King Henry of England. There! At first only twelve monks, then the Kloster was burnt so they built it once more, this time not for monks but for nuns. A great change. Now we have another change in 1540: no longer Catholic because the Herzog von Braunschweig was a follower of Luther.' She tries a joke. 'Like my man! See!' She points to a small table near the sofa on which there is a framed photograph of a grim bald man with a strong mouth. 'He was a pastor. Seven years ago he died. Then I came here. Now we have no nuns but old ladies without husbands: twelve people. I tell you about the building. Parts of the old place are left. The rest was done in 1730. One interesting thing! The church is of bricks, not stone like the rest of the house. You must see the great picture by the altar: of Jesus and his sufferings. Alex will take you. Ah!' They hear footsteps outside in the stone passage: at first far away, then nearer, a great crowd of people. The noise stops. Edward listens. Someone begins to speak, the roll of words like a distant storm. 'You know that?'

'What?'

'Alex is telling them about the fountain. We have so much water here. Through there is another pond. So many fountains we have!' She points to the door in the wall on the other side of the room. 'We sit in the garden when the sun is out and I have a small table and chairs. Really, this place is wonderful in summer. Now also, if the weather is kind – not like to–day when we have not seen the sun at all, I think. In this part of Germany we have two kinds of summer: the English and the Russian. Really, when the English summer comes it is bad: cold and wet. Me, I like the Russian winter better as well, with snow and more snow, not warm rain like with you.' She holds out a hand in the direction of the wall. 'He and I speak of this.' She laughs, her whole face bright. This is marvellous. She has hoped for it so often over the last few years.

'Frau Schneider . . .' Edward says.

But her joy is too much, and once more she interrupts. 'Listen, Mr West!' She looks at Rose, a quick kind glance. 'And you too, please!' The footsteps in the stone passage fade as the crowd walks away. 'Ah! They go. You can hear? Now we shall see. Some days he takes them to the church first; at other times, on the way out when the rest of the tour is over. If he is going now, he will be a little bit longer.

They must be told about the altar picture and the carved basin and pulpit. He does it so that each person is interested, from the oldest to the little children. With the children he is so good. I like to go and listen myself to him as much as I can, but he says it is silly for me to be there too many times.'

'Has Alex told you about me?' Edward shouts.

'You? Oh, Mr West!' Frau Schneider shakes her head and speaks directly to Rose. 'What I have heard! And he has shown me the old photographs as well. I know so much of his life, but I do not try to make him say more than he wants. We speak sometimes of the first years, before Hitler's war. All that has gone: what Alex knew then, and even now in our new country, it cannot come back because his old family home was too far east, in what is now Russia. And if it does come back, the great house is not there. The Russians burnt it on their way to Berlin in 1945: everything, all into flames! How terrible.' She stops to allow a moment's silence. 'You know what I think?' she says. 'This is why Alex has taken these photographs.' She points to the lower shelf of the long, low bookcase. 'Yes. That is why. He took them to try to make for himself a new past: a fresh history! Do you see that, Mr West? Something to keep, to make into those books so that this time it will not all go. Like that!' She throws her hands up in the air, as if to release a captive bird. 'Pouf!' Her breath comes more heavily: all this excitement. 'Now he uses his camera no more. It is over.' She smiles suddenly. 'I remember the photographs of you: that couple. Mr and Mrs West. Is she called Jane?'

'That was my wife's name.'

'Yes.' Frau Schneider looks embarrassed. 'She is dead. I am sorry. To him she was so much. Like a daughter, I think. It is sad he had no children because he is so good with the school parties.' She points to some other framed photographs on tables or on top of the bookcase. 'See, my family. Some grandchildren, too. Heidi is in Koblenz, the wife of a lawyer. My son Gerd has been sent to the east with his firm of accounting: to Rostock. Then the other boy, Thomas, is in Bremen. So clever he is, with computers. They are good but all far away. It is sad I do not see them more. But poor Alex: only one sister is left, the one in Salzburg, and she is not well. Herr Friesen in the hotel is kind to him. Did you know he lives there? They are cousins, not very near, but friendly so that is good and the Friesens have a family which Alex likes.' There is a knock at the door. 'Ha!' She shouts in German. '*Herein!*' The door opens. Edward turns almost reluctantly. It is not Alex but a tall, thin, slightly stooping woman of about the same age as Frau Schneider, her longer grey hair down to her shoulders, a face stretched into a careless smile. She wears a white cardigan and a dark blue skirt and in one hand clutches a magazine. Frau Schneider looks impatiently at the newcomer. Without even acknowledging her high-voiced greeting, she says to him, 'It is Frau Hartmann. Do not worry. I will be quick.'

'Please . . .' he begins.

But she is already speaking quickly to the old woman, not allowing any excuse, driving the other back with her words, amongst which Edward catches his own name, then that of von Kierich, until Frau Hartmann is almost pressed up against the wall, Frau Schneider now standing alongside her: a shorter, more dumpy figure but charged suddenly with an unstoppable power as she leans even closer to Frau Hartmann as if about to leap and bite her in the neck. She seizes the magazine, which Frau Hartmann gives up easily, saying only a few words of weak protest. '*Ja!*' It is a shout of triumph. The woman leaves and the door shuts once more.

Frau Schneider turns back to her English guests. 'See!' She

248

holds up the magazine and points at the cover, on which there is a photograph of a middle-aged couple sitting on a bench in a sunlit garden. 'The King and Queen of Sweden. I can read it later.' She puts the magazine down on a table by the window and goes back to her seat. 'Frau Hartmann has no English. But she is a good soul. I tell her Alex will be here soon and she goes.' She leans forward, putting her hand to one side of her mouth in a gesture of mock secrecy. 'She is frightened of him. You see, he is not so interested in what she thinks: that sort of thing! Now many people are like her and want to hear only the silly things: not much else.' Frau Schneider points again at the albums on the lower shelf. 'That is so different. The story of one man.'

'How is he?' shouts Edward.

'He? Alex? Oh quite well.' She pats her shoulder. 'Like us all who are old, he has some problems. Just a few pains, nothing too terrible. For his age he is marvellous. You have children, Mr West? I think I have seen some photographs.'

'Two boys.'

'Sons? Good.' She smiles at Rose. 'And you are a friend of those boys?'

'Yes,' says Rose.

Frau Schneider laughs. 'I do not mind.' She glances at her watch. 'Where is he? He should have told me you were coming, then I could have done a nice tea: just the thing you would like. Have you travelled far?'

'Alex is not expecting us.'

'Oh?' Perhaps she has not understood.

'I did not warn him.'

'But surely he wrote! Alex told me . . .'

'Yes.' He remembers to speak slowly. 'I received his letter and it is because of the letter that I have come.'

'Mr West, he loves you.'

'Frau Schneider . . .'

She leans forward, her eyes very bright. 'You and your

wife: these are the people he speaks of again and again. Others too, but always he comes back to Edward and Jane. Those other English he remembers also: Mr and Mrs Riley. They are in the photographs. And Vittorio, the Italian who took over from him at the Survey and who still writes: Vittorio Falconi. But to him they are not like you. Not so much. Oh!' She stops, puts a hand to one ear in the gesture of someone listening. 'I can hear. Perhaps. Listen, Mr West. How pleased he will be but so surprised.'

Outside, there are footsteps, faint at first, quite fast, the shoes surely tipped with steel to judge from the sharp echo, then slower, each blow of the shoe on the stone regular as if in time. He has expected the shuffling pace of an old, tired man. It cannot be Alex. But Frau Schneider knows. 'His walk!' she says and looks at Rose. 'You have heard it!' Suddenly she seems worried. 'I hope that the shock – Mr West, you should have warned him. Oh!' The door opens and a tall man stands in its frame. He stares at them and steps back: just one short pace.

Alex will be old and this is what Rose sees, imagining it first before she looks towards the door, having granted herself a lightning extension of her imaginary view of the German: that soft sepia print of suffering and an epic life. Old age, yes, then clear, surprised eyes, the scars beneath, a straight thin old man flinching briefly, quick to regain control. It is this potential for dominance that she feels too, for her idea is more of the way he must be, whereas Edward concentrates on the exterior: the large Adam's apple, the long chin, the thin arching line of the pressed lips, the broad nose, then the mystified eyes. So she is searching too hard to be surprised, whilst Edward finds the tautness of the face strange, each line set rigid, the mouth a downward crescent above the prominent chin, then the eyes partly hidden in small, tight slits. These have changed – no, not changed. He should have remembered them. Yet Alex has survived: a stoop barely noticeable, still the smooth hair, now all silver. There is that neatness: the dark loden jacket, polished brown shoes, a white shirt, a maroon and green Paisley tie. 'Marietta.' The voice is a quiet cry. Then Alex says, 'Of course.'

Frau Schneider cannot bear to see him so helpless, even for an instant. 'Mr West,' she says in English. 'With a young friend.'

Von Kierich stares. 'Edward.' The eyes relax, revealed properly at last as he lifts his brows in apparent pleasure. There is the urbanity, the way that great, smooth machine could absorb almost everything. 'So you have come.' He walks towards the Englishman. The skin of the handshake is dry, like soft leather. The hard bones are unyielding beneath. The rough, broken bones. 'My dear boy. Why didn't you say? Where did you meet Marietta?'

'Outside. By the gate. You were doing your tour.'

Alex laughs, the eyes wrinkling up. He looks at Rose. 'Yes, I was doing my tour. And . . .?' He waits.

'This is Rose Finch. I am travelling with her.'

'Rose.' Alex bows slightly. She inclines her head also, then sees his useless fingers, the deformed thumb; of course there had been torture, then the deaths he had seen, the pain. He shakes her hand, those two useless, bent fingers touching the palm. 'I thought it might be your daughter, Edward. Then I remembered that you have only sons. How are they?'

'Very well.'

'I want to hear it all.' The voice rumbles; surely it has become lower. The old man looks so relieved as he raises his eyes briefly towards the windows of Frau Schneider's room. 'I never thought you would come. And you didn't write or telephone to warn me. But why should you? Better by far, more wonderfully impulsive, to leap into your car and come across the Channel to an isolated continent.' He laughs and turns to Frau Schneider. 'You know, Marietta, in England they still think really that we poor Europeans are on the edge of things.' Then he looks worried for a moment, the stiff courtesy returning. 'Can you understand us?' He speaks a few words of German. '*Ja? Ist das vielleicht zu schnell und undeutlich?*'

'Oh no,' she reassures him. '*Nein, bitte.* Oh Alex.'

'May we sit?'

'*Natürlich.*' She adds quickly, 'Yes, please.'

'Edward, why don't you and I take the sofa?' He puts a hand on Rose's arm, as if about to push her away from where she had been sitting beside Edward. She flinches, ashamed to feel fear, physical and instinctive. 'You have the chair on the other side of the fireplace. Frau Schneider likes the wooden seat, strange though it may seem. Sometimes I tell her that it has assumed her shape over all the years she has been sitting in it. You see, this furniture accompanied the Schneiders all round northern Germany to the different places where Herr Schneider was a priest: from Kiel to Bremen, to Celle and then to this town. She is lucky, though. I don't know what the Kloster could have provided, but I am sure it would not have been nearly so good.' Already he has taken charge. 'Now, Edward, how did you get here? I want to know every detail.' The laugh is louder this time. 'I can assure you I have not changed in that respect. It is the details that make our lives. What is the time?' He raises his thin wrist close to his face. 'I cannot see. Marietta!'

'Nearly seven.'

'Nearly seven!' Alex addresses her again in German and she looks embarrassed as she answers, shaking her head. He turns to Edward who is beside him on the sofa, so close that the thin outline of the old scars is clear on the white, lined skin. 'We should have a drink to celebrate. Unfortunately Marietta has only some bottles of the fruit cordial that she makes. It doesn't matter. We can go back soon to the hotel where I live and sample Otto's hospitality.' He smiles, now curiously shy. 'Are you free? I will introduce you to Otto Friesen, who is a distant cousin of mine. They do not live in the hotel, you know, Otto and Klara. He has bought a small property with some woods about ten kilometres away, a nice place, more quiet for her than the town. Poor Otto! The hotel is a burden for him now but they must keep it going to pay their bills. Shooting is his great love. Some years he goes to Africa for the big game, often to Scotland, occasionally England. It is his passion. You do not shoot, Edward?' He laughs to show that it is a joke.

'No.'

'I thought not. As a boy I did. Never since then. Some women are keen now. Does it attract you, Rose?'

'Not at all.'

'Where do you live in England?'

Rose names the village, adding, 'My parents have a house there,' in case he might think that she is Edward's resident mistress. Quickly she imagines his cold, courteous surprise, the chilling embarrassment, if she were to tell him about last night in Cologne.

'Near Edward?'

'Her father and mother live in the manor,' Edward says, rather awkwardly. 'The big house on the edge of the village.'

'The manor? Is it an old mansion?'

He answers for her. 'Parts of the house are early by English standards: fifteenth or sixteenth century.' He turns to Rose. 'Isn't that right?'

She smiles at him. 'Mostly sixteenth,' she says, and adds 'darling' for she feels braver now, determined to fight back. Edward tries to smile.

Alex ignores the provocative word. 'Good!' he says. 'Now, Edward, tell me how you reached our dear old place. Don't

you think it is a fit occupation for your old friend: a part-
time guide in an almshouse? You know, sometimes the
tourists try to tip me.'

Rose sees the wide forehead, the brown eyes often ob-
scured for a moment in laughter by folds of tight tense skin.
Disapproval or dislike could come instantly in a glance, a
gesture of contempt, a silence. Is this his power? Again she
feels Edward's unease. 'I love the Kloster,' she says suddenly,
then regrets her gushing tone. The words will not come in
the way she wants.

Alex swings angrily towards her, as if to prove her right.
'Do you? I am so glad.' He looks away, then back at
Edward, his rebuke now past. 'So you have plenty of time.
Isn't this pleasant?'

'Do you take it?' Edward asks, the words falsely cheerful.

'What?'

'The tip.'

'Take it!' Alex lets out a bellow of a laugh. 'Oh my dear
fellow! Look, Rose: what sort of a monster does this man
think I am? Has he told you about me?' Once more he is
sympathetic, a gentle old man.

'A little,' she answers.

'A little? Come on, out with it!' That laugh again. 'No, I
won't embarrass you. You know, Rose, Edward and I
worked so closely together. Can you imagine what this
means, to see him again? It is a dream come true. I thought
it would never happen: that I would die without that chance
to talk and remember and make everything clear. Yes, that
is what this meeting will allow us to do: not in talk alone,
for one can say only so much. There is also the physical
presence, which is incommunicable in words, a reminder of
what we once knew.' He looks at Rose, yet does not seem
to need an explanation of her or her presence here. Perhaps
he knows; such omniscience does not seem impossible:

either that or an arrogance that ignores anyone outside his own deep past. Now Alex turns to Edward. 'First I must ask how are Martin and Nancy?'

'Very well.'

'Still living in the same village as you?'

'Yes.'

'I wondered about that. I wrote to them too but there was no answer. I thought they might have moved, then Vittorio Falconi told me they had not. I suppose he hears of them from you. Vittorio is a most reliable correspondent. Twice a year, once in the spring, again just before Christmas, so I get some of the gossip about the old firm. It's changed. Bernt Kristiansen has given things a new direction. The campaigning side has gone. It's all much quieter. They try to persuade gently, behind the scenes. Bernt's right of course. People are much more sceptical now, less trusting. The perception of Africa in particular is one of increasing chaos, hopelessness, despair. To fight this, Bernt has opted for accurate balance sheets, financial probity. That is his chief boast – not our cry for a new world, that great transfer of resources.' Alex smiles, as if resigned to human folly. 'Vittorio complains of a loss of idealism. But I believe Bernt is right. He has no choice. You know Vittorio is working on a book. I have encouraged him. One should have something in retirement: some great project.'

'Are you writing, Alex?'

'I?' The German touches his chest and laughs in mock dismay, looking now at Rose. 'What could I say?'

'You could give your view of the Survey. Or go back further. You should do it.'

'And tell about my life? No.' Again he looks at Rose who has been watching, trying to grasp his real new self as opposed to her old idea of how he might be. Her breath heaves; the fear lingers, then drifts away. 'We have too many of these memoirs here now. Is it the same in your country: old men refighting battles?' Alex turns to Edward. 'Also I am in disgrace.'

'Oh, Alex,' Frau Schneider says.

'It is true.' He leans forward, raises one hand, a gesture from the Washington days. 'Here in this town I have peace: blessed anonymity. I love it. The hotel, my walk to the Kloster, this time with the visitors.' He lifts an arm towards the ceiling. 'I love this place, Edward, Rose. It is wonderful. Before we go I will show you the chapel, perhaps one or two other parts of the building. I feel here there is a link: the last link. It is the peaceful contemplation of what was and what is to come: an unwinding. Marietta knows about this. Here I have privacy.'

'But they must know who you are,' Edward says. Rose watches him with the German: his slight eagerness, a false emphasis perhaps, but no real difference, just that courtesy, a cover for feeling.

'Who?'

'The people around.' Then he adds, 'Here and in the hotel.'

'Some of them.' Alex smiles, puts a hand down on the sofa. 'But it is so quiet. You have no idea. No one tries to probe. If you wish, you can talk and they will listen. But they will not ask you. They may watch you, wonder about you, but always in silence. What peace! So different to what I knew before. Am I right, Marietta?'

'Yes, you are quite right.' Frau Schneider laughs rather hysterically, so happy to see that her beloved Alex has at last what she feels sure he wants more than anything else: a living reminder of so much that was good in his life. Surely nothing can undo this.

'You know I had to leave Munich?' Alex asks, the smile now one of complicity. 'It was after Jane came out, wasn't it? Forgive me. My sense of time is not so good.'

'Yes, it was.' The old man must be watching him for a reaction, a blush or flinch. This is another reminder of the past: the oblique exercise of control. Edward strikes back. 'What happened to the man who testified against you?' Rose waits, her breath still tight. At last.

Von Kierich delays. 'Which man?

'The one in Chicago.'

'The Ukrainian Nazi?' Alex shakes his head. 'It was pathetic. He died in prison, awaiting trial.˙ They had not really got good evidence. No eyewitnesses. Wiesenthal was involved –'

Suddenly Rose interrupts, her words banishing fright, seeking truth, even command. 'What killed him?'

He stares at her. 'Did you hear of it?'

'Edward told me.'

'Ah yes. Well, that I can understand. It was a heart attack, I believe. There was another rumour of suicide but I do not give much credence to it. Why should the man kill himself when he had started this new line about me? People were interested, you know. It was just my word against his. No other witnesses came forward. The victims could not, of course, because they were all dead. Then my friend who had taken me there. You remember him, Edward? He was sent to the eastern front by the Nazis to be killed. There were the guards. But none of them have spoken out.' Suddenly he turns to Frau Schneider. 'I have told you.' She nods, her face stern, and looks anxiously at him as he speaks, his voice higher now. 'So the Ukrainian might have pursued me. He could have had me called as a witness. In Munich I lived with this. The newspapers got hold of it. But do you know, Edward, my new friends have been so good!' He touches Edward on the arm, a lightning move. 'The Friesens in the hotel, Marietta in the Kloster, the others whom I had got to know since moving north. You see, there is great tact. That is one of the things which divides the civilized from the uncivilized in my view: tact, the ability to know when to be silent. I wanted to speak of it, not straight away but quite soon, so I talked with Marietta here in this room for hours and hours: not only about what happened in the east on that day but the rest of the past as well. We looked at the photographs. She was not shocked, perhaps because there are hundreds, thousands, of stories quite like the one I have to tell. What makes mine different, I suppose, is my attempt at redemption. The years you and I went through together, Edward, when I thought I might be able to make some sort of amends – not to forget myself or what I had seen, for that must always live within me. That I owe it to the victims to keep alive, almost to cherish as a unique inner suffering. My God, how I needed that!' Alex taps the side of his head. 'No. It stayed here. Always. In Washington, on those journeys, at meetings, conferences, interviews, during conversations with friends, enemies. It stopped a complete immersion in whatever I did. Always there was this protected area: the inner sanctum. Only one person could reach it: myself. Yet I had to share the horror, just occasionally: when I could not bear to be alone with it any longer, when the sense of overcrowding, of claustrophobia, became too great. Then it grew in my mind. It grew until everything else, each aspect of me, my life, my hopes and ideals, felt crushed, suffocated by it, almost dead until a little air could be let in by opening a door or window to some-one else by talking about what had happened, watching them as they listened and seeing perhaps forgiveness or at least sympathy in their eyes, the healing sound of their words. In Africa, Edward, I told you. Do you remember?'

'Yes.'

'We were to be killed.'

'A last confession?' suggests Rose. Then she blushes, looking so young.

Alex smiles at her, the eyes tight again, almost invisible. 'Perhaps.'

'Alex,' Edward says. He senses already a complicity between von Kierich and the girl. 'Were you frightened?'

'Oh certainly. But calm as well. One could do nothing. There was no decision to be made. No moral dilemma. You helped me, Edward.' Alex smiles again at Rose. 'We were helpless prisoners, at the mercy of our captors. We could do nothing. Once I had believed that solitary redemption was possible. I believed that salvation and peace could come through an inward struggle, that one might arrive at serenity through a long argument, forcing oneself to confront the truth and to bow down before it: a triumph of reason, you could say. Why had one seen so much inhumanity and still survived, still lived and prospered in its aftermath, risen high and splendid out of the ruins? I thought of my friends who had gone: the victims. I thought of my own cowardice and subservience: of my life, the way I had held myself back and emerged at the end from behind the corpses of much better men and women. I argued all this in silence. Peace did not come. So I spoke first to Fredericka, the eldest of my sisters, the one who is dead. To her it meant little. Her husband, a surgeon in Mainz, had served on the eastern front. His unit had taken prisoners and killed them. It was a rough war, Fredericka said. One should think of what the Russians did. It was a war of creeds, one without chivalry. Fredericka was not sentimental. She hated nostalgia. Dietrich, her husband, is a most practical man. Yes! He took her away from her past: our parents, the old home, her memories of the war. So from Fredericka I received a brisk command to forget: to live now, not then. Josephine, the younger sister, is different. She is still alive in Salzburg, but sick, her mind loose within itself. She is cared for in an old people's home, visited much by her children, sometimes by me although I find the journey a chore with the train, the airports and the flight. Sometimes she knows me. On other days there is nothing to say because she recognizes no one, not even her own children, and just talks about matters of which I know nothing, perhaps some past incident with her husband, Wolfgang, who died ten or fifteen years ago: a good Catholic lawyer, an Austrian. They were good men, Dietrich and Wolfgang: dependable. Josephine I did tell once, before her illness. She listened and tried to help. She had that intuition which rises above language; also tact. But she never raised the business again although she had listened, like Marietta. Salzburg is so far away.' Now he smiles.

'Alex, you were a hero,' Frau Schneider says.

'Not here,' he answers.

'In this town?'

'No. In Germany. Many people thought not. There are those who are shocked that I went against the state, that I was disloyal. There are those also who see my survival as a form of cowardice. They think I did not go far enough. Of course after the war I was useful: the good German whose scars of torture could be inspected and found to be genuine. In that way I could help.' He looks at Rose. 'Now perhaps —'

Edward interrupts him, the impatience breaking out. 'Alex.'

'Yes?' The German turns to him, crouched on the edge of the sofa, about to stand.

Edward seems to falter, then retreat soundlessly before Alex's tense, short word, which is almost a hiss. Rose feels a sudden pity. She speaks for him, an artless, trite question, bringing relief. 'How does it feel to see each other again?'

Alex looks at her, the surprise buried by a new sympathy. 'Why, I am so pleased. I think I said. But what about you? I have been speaking so much of myself and things that concern only Edward and me. Do you have a job? Or are you still at college? Please tell me.'

His eyes feign interest. It is condescension, not courtesy, she decides. 'I am at university, studying languages.'

'German?'

'No.'

'Which languages?'

'Italian and French.'

'I am so glad.' His smile is fixed. 'You know, I owe Edward so much –'

'What does it feel like?' Rose asks suddenly, trying to force the banality away.

'*Was . . .?*' Frau Schneider begins.

'I don't understand,' says Alex.

'Rose,' Edward murmurs.

'To see him again.'

Alex straightens his slightly bent back. 'Why, I think I have said.'

'Not really.'

'At one time we worked closely together,' Edward begins.

'Oh, Edward!' Alex's tone is one of gentle exasperation. He turns to the girl. 'I owe so much to him. We travelled all over the world, then in Washington too. There were the meetings and conferences, trying to bludgeon more money out of stubborn bureaucrats. Governments are not generous, you know, unless pressure of some kind is applied. What one hoped was to create a crusade, or at least the atmosphere of one. The richest nations were all democracies, supposedly responsive to popular wishes. If one could somehow reach over the heads of the governments to the people . . .' He raises his arms. 'It was exhilarating.' He laughs. 'We took risks. Do you know the story?'

'Which one?' she asks.

'Of our time of captivity?'

'I told her,' Edward says.

'You did?' Alex smiles at her, the eyes wrinkling again. 'Edward was a hero.'

'And you?' she asks.

'No.' He holds out one hand, points to the crushed

fingers. 'It was not my first time. Then we were friends, too: Edward, Jane and I. Such friends.' He smiles again at her, that thin, patronizing look. 'Now surely I have said enough.' His light, strong laugh means to push Rose to one side.

She stands firm. 'Did you sleep with her?'

'With whom?' His smile is still there.

'Jane. His wife.'

It is Frau Schneider who speaks first. 'No! How can you? Please!' She turns to Edward, her head up like a raised axe. 'Herr West, please, you must understand that Alex adored your wife. I know this because of all that he has told me about her. You and she are like icons to him: no, not icons, because they are holy.' The strange words come faster. 'It is more a question of memory, the way he thinks of you both. You know Alex's story. You know!' She purses her mouth as if about to spit. 'Surely this is not why you have come here, to ask this kind of question.' She puts contempt into the words, turning on Rose. 'And what are you? How insulting! For the benefit of whom? You young people, you can never understand. Leave him alone! Can you not see that he deserves some rest after all that has happened?' She looks up towards the ceiling. 'Why should he have to suffer more?' Her eyes glare at Edward. 'Oh, Herr West, when I saw you this night at the gate of the Kloster it seemed like some influence from Heaven. That you had come after what I had asked Alex to do again and again: to write to England, to his beloved Mr West or perhaps General Riley, although I knew the General would be more difficult. One could not expect much from a soldier! They want everything to be clear, or so my late husband used to say both during and after the war. I felt General Riley must be like this, from an idea I had of him partly through the photographs and also my imagination. There is no room in the army for light and shade, for those shadows. But Herr West I thought was different, perhaps partly because of the sadness of his beautiful wife. You have a sense of tragedy, I thought. Is that the word? An idea of what poor Alex has suffered. Now you come here with her!'

'No, Marietta,' Alex says.

'It is bad!' Frau Schneider is exhausted. She breathes heavily and glowers at Rose, who looks down in instinctive shame.

'Alex,' Edward says.

The old man smiles at him. He knows what the Englishman needs: just a few words about her. 'Edward, Jane tried to help me. She was so loyal to her friends: to you, to me. To us all.'

'She went to your apartment, when I was ill: after we got back from Africa.'

'She was lonely. So was I. We talked. Nothing else, of course. Why, surely . . .?'

'No.'

Alex laughs. 'At least spare me that.'

'Did she kill herself?'

'It was an accident.'

'Was it?'

Alex looks round the room. He seems in no hurry. 'Whom do you believe?'

Edward does not answer and Rose stares at him, scarcely heeding Frau Schneider when she searches in her handbag for a handkerchief with which to dab at her wet, tired eyes. But he sees the old woman's confusion and remembers the grim face of her dead husband in that faded photograph. She is in love in a way that she has never been before. As if to echo this, she says the name quietly to herself. 'Alex.'

Von Kierich waits, then moves on past the silence, his words sharp and clear. 'Now what shall we do? Although I hesitate to leave the comfort of Frau Schneider's room and her hospitality, we should at least see the chapel. You must not come all this way without that.' Alex speaks to Frau Schneider in German. She answers, nodding her head, almost recovered, dabbing her face one more time. He looks at Edward again, quite affable. 'Shall we go?'

The old woman stands and holds out her hand to the English visitors. 'Mr West.' She bows to him, catching his eye only briefly. Rose's name she does not say, and for the girl the handshake is quick, a reluctant gesture. 'Alex.' She says the name once more.

Outside, their footsteps crash on the stone. In the colder air, Edward feels suddenly that he is in the presence of the two women he has loved: Jane here in his mind, still strong yet wounded and unhappy even after death; Rose now beside him, an absolute reality but at moments apparently no stronger than the intangible force of his dead, betrayed wife. The girl's question, 'Did you sleep with her?' Only the young can intrude in that brash, quick way. It is a weakness, forgivable as well. He should not mind.

They reach the hall. Edward has fallen back, leaving Rose and Alex together, and as he comes level with them he hears the old man finish some joke about the bad behaviour of one of the local princes towards the nuns in the Kloster. 'He was a naughty man!' Alex speaks to her as if she is a child – perhaps a form of punishment. 'But it did not last. On the whole they were fortunate in their rulers in this part of Germany. Now, come this way.'

They follow him into the dark, the fountain at the centre of the courtyard an outline on their right. By the corner where the courtyard turns in another right angle, there is a small entrance into a passage and it is through this that von Kierich leads them, out of the cloisters to the thick door of the chapel of dark red brick. He has a key. The lock clicks smoothly; then Alex reaches inside for the light switches to reveal a high rectangular room with panelled walls, a wide stone floor, great clear glass windows reaching up to a series of gothic peaks. 'This afternoon a schoolboy from the town played the organ. Wonderful!' he says, pointing to the spread of richly painted pipes at one end of the room, opposite the altar. They stand beside him. He starts to talk, at first a dry drone, then with more enthusiasm.

'This is early Gothic, but now much restored, principally in the eighteenth century. However, the form is the same as it always was, and the basic idea. They built in brick to show the modesty of the order – the humility, if you like. That is the reason also for the flat ceiling, without decorative beams or any flamboyance. Before the restoration too the windows were much smaller: less grand, so in a sense their present size is a betrayal of what the original builder wished. Outside too, in the cells where the nuns used to live, like Frau Schneider's present room, things were quite different in the early days with no fires, such small windows too in order that nothing should distract them from their work and meditation. Wouldn't you call that a hard life? Certainly few people have the strength or the faith for it today. Now come this way. Walk slowly. First you will see the font with its wood carvings of the seventeenth century, representing the baptism of the infant Jesus in the River Jordan. Then the wooden pulpit, a little earlier than the font, held up here by the representation of Moses, the man of law: most appropriate, I think you will agree, for the place of instruction and teaching. Here on the pulpit's upper part are the angels bringing their message to earth, also the four evangelists: so in this structure the New Testament and Old are combined. See the stalls and their carved panels in the choir, still sat in by the residents of the Kloster like Frau Schneider when there are services here, although these are now open to anyone and are conducted by one of the pastors from the parish church, which you may have seen on your way through the town's central square. Chairs are brought into the chapel for the congregation. For the rest of the time they are not here so that visitors can have a better sense of the building's architecture. Let us move on. Come!'

He leads them to the raised altar covered with an embroidered cloth, on top of which rest the three large wooden, painted panels of a brightly lit triptych. 'See, Edward. It is quite early, yet late compared to other works in Germany: probably the beginning of the fifteenth century, damaged slightly over the years, not at all in the last war, strangely enough. Two years ago it was cleaned. I think the colours are now too clear, but experts say that they must have been like this when the picture was first painted. What do you think, Rose?' He seems to have forgiven her.

'There's often a problem with restoration.' Her voice is loud in the high space.

'You are right. But this picture is too clean. I like to be made to search a little, not to have these symbols flung in my face. You know what they are? It is the suffering of Christ on the Cross, a link also to the start of our time on this earth, or so the Christians wanted then to believe: the wood of the Cross coming from the Tree of Knowledge in the Garden of Eden or from another tree grown from its seed. For them the site of the crucifixion itself was also the place where Adam had been buried. See the skull at the foot of the Cross, which means not only Golgotha, the place of the skull, but Adam's own remains spotted with the blood from Christ's wounded body. Look how red it is! The restorer's art has not improved that, I think: the bright red against the white bone and the green of the hill itself. Now the other figures. But first note the wound on the right or "good" side of Our Lord: blood and water came out to be the sacraments of communion and baptism, caught here in the angel's chalice. The head too bows to the right, the side of the thief who seeks forgiveness; on the left is the bad side, the other thief still unrepentant. Did you know this,

Edward? I am saying my piece. But this picture is important. People come here to study it. Are you interested, Rose?'

'Yes.' Here in the chapel she has linked her arm to Edward's, who stands between her and Alex.

'These symbols fascinate me. Of course in medieval times they were a way of teaching the people, a form of simplistic code, if you like. Then there is another explanation. The Crown of Thorns, for instance, began to appear more in pictures of this kind from the middle of the thirteenth century when King Louis IX of France came back from one of the crusades with what he claimed was a relic of the original. Henceforth one might say that it was a reflection of his vanity or pride of possession: an extension of the King's temporal power. Until the Counter-Reformation the crown featured often, the result of the arrival in Europe of a few fake sticks. Typical, or so I think! What matters is how we think things are, not so much the truth of their reality. Wouldn't you say so, Edward? See too the serpent with the apple in its mouth, near the skull. The idea of the Fall lay deep in the late medieval mind: that crashing descent from innocence and bliss. Today we are less rooted in dogma, in belief. The other figures I must mention: the thieves on either side of Jesus, the repentant and the unrepentant; the Blessed Virgin to the right, her left hand up to her face in a pose of sadness going back to Hellenistic times; St John to the left. Then the sun and the moon, originally pagan symbols, assimilated into the Christian religion when Christmas superseded the feast of the sun. The Bible mentions a great darkness from midday until the mid-afternoon on the day of the crucifixion, an eclipse perhaps. Here it is said that the moon represents the Old Testament and the sun the New. As usual the sun is on Christ's right, the moon to his left. Sometimes they are carried aloft by angels but not here.' He turns quickly and sees Rose clutching Edward's arm. 'Do you think it beautiful?'

267

Edward stares at the thin figure of Christ bowed in wounded virtue, limp acceptance before victory, then the blurred, nameless thieves. 'Why do you come to this place, Alex?' he asks.

'Because I love it.' He raises his eyes slowly and stares straight into the Englishman's face.

'But the solitude –'

'It is not solitude.' He turns to Rose. 'I am sorry. I have talked for too long. Edward may be implying that this is one of the faults of a lonely old man.'

'That wasn't what I meant. I've often wondered whom you see.' Again that grammatical precison, the pomposity as a defence.

'I have told you.'

'Of course I don't know the people at the hotel, but Frau Schneider is hardly –'

'Hardly enough?'

'For you.'

At the door Alex waits. 'So you have nothing to say.'

'About what?'

'The picture.' The lights go out with a quick move of his hand. For a moment they are in darkness before he opens the door to the warm September evening. 'Perhaps you think yourselves ignorant about art.' Alex locks the door, then straightens, the slight stoop of age momentarily gone. 'One does not need knowledge. Appreciation of something that is beautiful should not depend upon knowledge. Even Frau Schneider is aware of that: Frau Hartmann also. I have discussed the picture with them often. Neither has any knowledge.'

Edward looks up briefly at the sky where a wind moves small pale clouds in the twilight. 'I came here to see you.'

'Yes. I know that.'

Rose watches the two old men. For her the picture had been a resurrection of primeval power, some myth buried long ago in the depths of her childhood. Here outside it begins slowly to vanish from her mind, wiped away by this new, fresh moment.

For Edward, Alex's unspoken thoughts seem tantalizingly close. Perhaps they are of his beloved painted death of Christ or those days in Washington or Africa, or the truth about Jane. It might be any of these, or earlier times in Berlin, at the eastern front, in the Plötzenzee Prison awaiting his death. Suffering has a perversity, a mystery of its own making. It becomes an entity in itself, set apart from the victim, an example to gaze upon and to fear.

This is the secret that he has come in search of: not the vague nightmare of betrayal to which Jane had every right to subject him. He could not offer the comfort she needed, the example perhaps of a different distinction: some moral worth outside ambition, lust, the old wish to climb away from a dull dead beginning towards a new life.

Jane might have wanted to find someone else; Alex surely would have had no part in it, not this tired old man who speaks gently about the sufferings of Christ. Edward feels ashamed of his doubt: that influence of jealousy and vanity on his reason. Now there is Rose, who knows only some of the mystery, the odd chinks of light. He remembers Alex's words: 'No one must be hurt.' Then he had agreed, Jane suddenly rising in his mind between the two of them, a victim also: one who had needed a better man. The business with Rose is incidental too, or should be, he thinks. This evening the view back is clear at last when he turns to consider its truth.

They have reached the main door of the Kloster. 'How did you come?' Alex asks. 'By car? Good. I walk here always, unless the weather is bad. Now, if you will forgive me. I should see poor Marietta.'

It is a dismissal. The promised dinner with Otto Friesen has been passed over as no longer appropriate, perhaps because of von Kierich's disappointment in his English visitors. They walk away slowly, looking back once to have a last sight of an old man framed by the great curved arch, apparently quite still for an instant before he turns to enter the darkness behind.

In the car they speak precisely about what they should do, seeking refuge in the plans for their journey home. Then they stop at a hotel some ten miles away from the town of the Kloster and Alex's retirement. It seems late, surely well into the night, when Edward comes to visit Rose and gets into her bed, hardly talking at all before they make love in a strange outpouring of relief and joy. Afterwards he murmurs about the past. 'Darling, I don't mind,' he says, realizing how hard it will be for her to understand. She is too young. He nods off soon, almost immediately, here in the narrow bed where there is barely enough room for them both, not hearing her other questions which come softly from beside him, a postscript to their love. 'I don't know,' he whispers in his sleep. 'I don't know.' She lies awake, sensing an end to the mystery of these old men. It is time for the balance of history and the next generation's cold, clear eye. The adventure is over. Now she sleeps as well, dreamless, oblivious to imagination or memory.

On the way home they talk, and Edward sees that Rose is as strong as he is in her wish to escape. It should be possible for them both to move on, to look back on this odd interlude as a brief settling of curiosity, a short break in their ordinary lives. Will she go back to Ben? he asks, secretly knowing the answer. No, she says: that would not be right. She hopes they will still see each other, she and Edward. This is what she would like, just as friends, for she is determined to be grown-up. Slowly they both start to realize that it is unsatisfactory after all, this odd affair. He must try to give a lead.

They drive to the village. Edward drops her off at the manor, avoiding Isabel and James. He knows what her parents must think: also that neither of them will mention their concern, showing it only by pushing him slightly to the edge of their lives. He may not to be invited to their house when Rose is there; at other times he will be welcomed in the same friendly way. He returns to his own home and enters the cold clean house alone.

'How did it go?'

So many of them want to know: Martin and Nancy Riley, the Finches, Mrs Gifford. From Martin he retreats, saying only that Alex is quite fit but aged of course. The old mysteries remain. Now these do not worry him, for there can never be a proper solution; this he sees. One must be tactful, reluctant to probe.

The General stares at him, then seems to take pity, saying, 'At least it wasn't painful.' They are alone in Church House; Nancy is doing flowers for the new vicar. 'Edward, you won't tell anyone what I told you the other night, will you?' Martin adds. This is what really worries him: that moment when he too had slipped. 'Is Rose well?' 'Yes, thank you,' Edward answers, as if he is responsible for her, 'very well.'

Rose is well. It has been an adventure. Ben Talbot rings her and she speaks to him, saying that she will not be alone in London before the beginning of term because she has so much preparation to do for her next year at the university. To put Ben in his place, she may tell him eventually what had happened. Then she thinks, No, that would be cruel and Alex had been right: one should be loyal to friends, especially to old friends.

So she greets Edward with a kiss when she sees him in the village, talks openly of their German trip, describes von Kierich to her father and mother as a hero who has been misunderstood, someone faced with possibilities neither she nor any of them here can understand. Such courage, then such degradation: these are not the stuff of their own calm lives. Isabel Finch listens in an apparently distracted way. The friendship with Edward still does not seem to worry her at all.

At first Rose is satisfied, not ashamed of her coldness. She remembers their vow to be grown-up, to leave things as they are. Surely this is better. Yet soon she begins to hate the charade, its hollow heart, not only for her but for Edward as well. She persuades her mother to ask him to supper one evening; his eyes scarcely meet hers whilst they discuss such matters as the saw mill or the problem of traffic in the village. But his farewell in the hall in front of her parents has a lingering regret: his rough cheek against hers, that slight delay, then the assumed cool kiss of friendship trembling surely for a moment on the edge of a great demonstrative embrace. This is the strength of self-denial, a heroism even here in these quiet lanes of a peaceful country.

She does not love him, or so she tells herself as she listens once more to the saga of the saw mill. They await the decision of the planners. Both James and Isabel have forgiven Martin Riley, who has written such a nice letter of apology about his unpleasant campaign. They respect his views of course, which he will continue to hold. How decent everyone is! But alone at night she remembers Cologne and their journey across Germany. She does want him, although she tries so hard to push herself away.

For Edward it must be easier. He is older, so much more measured in his approach, reflective in the way that those of his age are said to be. She envies him this; suddenly she wants to trade all the years to come for slow serenity among the roses and sunlight of a country garden, the friendly bickering with the Rileys. Martin and Edward will discuss Alex together, arguing endlessly about the man. They will never agree, but this is perhaps one of the charms of their friendship, or so she imagines. Edward may reveal to the General what had happened in Cologne and the other hotel. 'Never again? You never had her again?' Martin might say, slightly tipsy in the drawing-room of Church House. 'Good God, Edward!' Edward will reassure him: 'Oh no, of course not, you don't know these young girls of today, they are so free, as relaxed about that sort of thing as any man. She was quite happy to leave me and go back to the rest of her life.' What else could one expect? Martin and Edward have known each other for so long. Probably there is nothing barred when they talk, nothing at all.

This is not true. Edward West keeps to himself most of what happened over that weekend.

Martin tries to worm his way in. 'Did von Kierich mention Jane?' he asks, turning suddenly away from his own drinks tray, and Edward looks angry, erecting a sealed frontier.

He answers, 'I am satisfied. I trust Alex.'

To this the General makes no response, not even the usual snort of anger; that curious sensitivity wins a silence for them both. Then Martin asks again how von Kierich had seemed. He is interested in the Kloster and the great picture. Finally he blurts out, 'Will you see her again?'

'Who?' Edward asks.

'Rose.'

'Oh yes, of course, in the village and with her parents. It's not like that, Martin.'

'I see.' The General falls back, possibly to regroup rather than to retire.

But it does not end. Edward does some gardening. He goes to London for two meetings. His son Charles telephones and suggests himself for the weekend, but the father makes some excuse about a paper he must write for a conference. He thinks, Soon I will be calmer, the feelings will die. It is not Jane now who bothers him – her ghost seems to have gone at last – but thoughts of Rose and her strange silences that rush towards Alex and a dying past. He sleeps soon but wakes early, the long hours ahead filled with desperate visions of what he wants and needs. Then one morning a letter arrives with a German stamp. He makes some coffee, sits at his kitchen table before opening it, remembering with relief that this is not one of Mrs Gifford's days.

My dear Edward,

I have been thinking so much about you and the way you so bravely came across to see me, most probably for the last time. I could not ask you what brought this about really: no doubt it was a number of different things, perhaps some wish to settle matters before time took this opportunity away from us. I felt at the beginning you were awkward. That was why I was pleased to have Marietta Schneider there, because sometimes a strange person can help the talk along. I thought she did do this, although you and I may well have been able to manage on our own, not forgetting of course your friend Rose whom I liked. What intelligence!

I am sorry about Marietta's loss of temper. For a moment I feared you might leave then, before we could see the chapel, but this did not happen and we were able to go there together which was what I wanted so much to do. What upset Marietta, I think, was the way the girl seemed to doubt me. She may also have been annoyed at a young person's lack of respect, because she is quite old-fashioned. I felt I had to go to her at the end of our tour so was not able to dine with you. Will you forgive me?

Poor Marietta is rather fragile. Rose will pardon her, I am sure. Please also forgive me for saying that you should be careful with Rose as well. Remember what we used to say: the most important thing is not to hurt people. This lay at the back of our work together, I like to think: also a wish to protect others from those who would hurt them. We fought an honourable battle, even if we did not always win.

Please go forward now. I have my life, as you have seen: the visits to the Kloster, some friends to whom I can talk, a sense of completeness. For you there is more time. Use it well. Goodbye.

Yours
Alex

Edward reaches for the telephone. He knows the number of the manor.

Isabel answers. 'Oh, Edward.'

He does not waste time trying to deceive her. 'Is Rose there?'

There is a brief silence. 'No. She's gone back to Scotland. To university.' The words are strained. 'Term starts next week.' Isabel knows.

'I see.' She does not respond. Edward thinks, What the hell. 'Goodbye.'

He hangs up, then realizes that he should have asked for the Scottish address, but this does not matter because he knows the city and can find her for himself. It is time for a second journey.